G000088049

Sowing Promises

Anne E. Thompson

The Cobweb Press

Cover Design: M. Todd

Edited by P. Salmon
J. Todd

Published by The Cobweb Press
www.thecobwebpress.com
thecobwebpress@gmail.com

For Bob Beffins

Chapter One

Dot first saw the man on Wednesday. They were sitting in the Costa coffee shop in Marksbridge, which had been Elsie's idea, and Dot was unsure about the whole exercise.

"Oh do let's have coffee in Costa," Elsie had pleaded, staring through the window at the couples huddled over their lattes and iced drinks in fat plastic beakers. "We never do, and it's what all the young people do. We don't want to become old and boring do we Dot? Come on, let's, just this once..."

And so Dot had listened to her sister, allowed herself to be persuaded, even though it was clearly a waste of money, and the chairs would probably be uncomfortable.

They had stood in line, behind a mother coping with a fretful baby and a toddler, both strapped into a buggy that was too wide really for the narrow pavements of Marksbridge. Dot watched, as the mother ordered a coffee for herself, and a drink full of sugar and ice for her child, and she wondered why young people chose to buy their drinks, rather than save the money and make tea at home, like she had when her own children were young. She was still wondering this, and trying to calculate how much money could be saved, if a daily trip to a coffee shop was a regular thing, when the young man in the overly bright shirt smiled at her and asked what she would like to drink.

"Two lattes please," Dot heard Elsie order. Elsie turned to her, her face creased into happiness. "It's what Susan always orders," she whispered. "Large please," she added, rather daringly.

The two sisters watched in horror as the young man removed two soup bowls – they really could not be described as anything else – and placed them under the flow of coffee from the machine. Dot turned, and looked at Elsie, who started to giggle, her eyes wide. Dot wondered if there was a way to change their order, but the coffee was already flowing, and she felt sure they would be charged for the vats of coffee, even if they switched to a more sensible size. So, she simply stood there, watching as milk was steamed and whisked and added to the ocean of coffee.

The bowls of coffee were placed on a tray, but Dot didn't feel that either she or Elsie would be strong enough to carry it, so they left it sitting on the counter, two damp rings marking where the coffees had sat. They carried their drinks – two handed so they didn't spill – and found a table next to the window. When the giant cups were safely on the table, they lowered themselves onto the pastel-coloured chairs, pleased to find they were more comfortable than they appeared. Elsie was both giggling, and bemoaning the size of the cup in relation to the size of her bladder, and Dot was nodding in agreement, when she noticed the man.

He was leaning towards a taxi window, passing money to the driver, and as he glanced up, and stared down the High Street, Dot realised that she recognised him. Or at least, she half did, somewhere in her subconscious, she knew him.

"I know him..." she said.

Elsie stopped talking and stared past her, towards the man, who was now shouldering his bag and marching away, his back disappearing up the High Street.

"Old school friend perhaps?" she suggested.

Dot shook her head. "Much too young, his hair is grey, but his face is young, he's nearer to Susan's age.

"No, I know him, I know that I know him. But I can't think how..."

Elsie lifted her cup, and took a slurp of coffee. "Think what good arm exercise these cups are!" she said, lowering the cup back to her saucer. "We should have brought the thermos, there's enough coffee here for the whole week."

But Dot wasn't listening. She was staring after the man, frowning. There was something about the man, something which sent alarm bells ringing through her mind, sent jangles of worry through her stomach, but she couldn't quite remember why. She shook her head. Probably she was being silly.

"This coffee really is a ridiculous size," she said. "How did we manage to order such ginormous cups? There's enough to bath in here!"

***

At Netherley Farm, Susan dropped the knife in her hand and fumbled for the phone in her apron pocket. Snatching it, she glanced at the number, and relaxed slightly.

"Hello?" she said, her voice sharp.

It was her mobile network, and the voice droned on, keeping to script, not allowing her to interrupt, offering her an exciting new deal. Eventually, when the flow of words ended, Susan, who for some reason unknown to herself was unable to simply cut off an unwanted call, reminded them that she had opted out of all telephone marketing and ended the call.

She glanced across the kitchen to find her sons grinning at her. They were lounging at the kitchen table, their long limbs stretched out in front of them, coffee mugs in hand.

"Not Neil then Mum?" said Ben.

Susan shook her head, her frustration dissolving as the knot of excitement seeped back into her stomach. As she started to chop salad vegetables, she could hear Ed and Ben as they chatted at the table. She smiled to herself, thinking that she wasn't the only one living on tenterhooks – it was unusual for Edward to drop in at the farm unannounced.

"No," she thought, "we're all waiting for Neil to phone." She carried the lettuce to the sink, and started to rinse the leaves under the tap, droplets of water spraying across the work surface and splashing up to wet her cheeks.

"So, will you hold it? When it's born I mean, will you want to hold it?"

Susan turned to see Edward shrugging.

"I don't know," he said, sounding surprised, "haven't really thought about it. Why – will you?"

"No," said Ben, his voice definite. "I don't like new-born babies. They have that whole wobbly head thing going on and I'm worried that I might kill it by mistake. It's not the sort of thing you can recover from really, is it? There's no real comeback after you've done something like that. At family gatherings and stuff...I mean, everyone would always remember, wouldn't they? And Kylie would be unlikely to ever forgive me, if I killed her baby – even if it was a complete mistake."

"Yeah, I can see that," agreed Ed with a laugh. "It would put bit of a damper on future family events. Not sure you'd ever get past that one..."

Susan carried her chopping board to the table and sat between them while they finished their coffee. Water dripped from washed tomatoes, running in rivulets across the board and dripping onto the table.

"They're tougher than you think," she said, running a peeler along the length of a cucumber. A thin ribbon of green fell onto the table. "Babies I mean – not mothers – I think you're right that Kylie would never forgive you.

"But you wouldn't kill it, not really, it's surprising what they can survive. When you think about it, being born isn't exactly gentle, is it? And mostly they survive that. Think about when that bull was born last year – it was you who helped Dad wasn't it Ben? I bet that wasn't as smooth as you were expecting."

Ben wrinkled his nose. "Thanks Mum," he said, putting down his mug, "lovely image of Kylie giving birth in my mind now, which I really didn't want." He shuddered.

"You'll get over it," said Susan, laughing. "Anyway, my point is, babies are pretty tough. You fell off the bed once, you know, when you were a baby – and you survived."

"Ha!" exclaimed Edward, "That explains everything!"

"You all did, actually," said Susan, shaking her head, the memory flooding back. "You'd think by my fourth son I'd have learnt not to leave a baby on the bed, but I always did, it always took me by surprise. Not that it seems to have done you any harm, just gave you a shock at the time."

"Well," said Edward, "I'm not sure about that. Not in Ben's case...and on that note of confessions of child-abuse by my mother, I'd better get going. I have a whole lot of exciting tools to show to a builder's merchant. They'll never be able to resist my salesman's charm…"

Susan stood to hug him, reaching up to feel his solid shoulders, feeling the roughness of his cheek where he had neglected to shave properly.

"Thanks for calling in, it's lovely to see you."

"Yes, I know," said Edward, with a grin. "It must be disappointing for you, that out of all of your sons, you're left with only Jack and Ben living at home – the dregs…" He laughed, as a piece of cucumber, snatched by Ben and flung with exquisite aim, bounced off the top of his head.

"Let me know if you hear any news," called Edward, and disappeared into the boot-room.

Susan sat with Ben for a while, chopping vegetables. They heard the back door slam behind Edward, and the sound of his car as he drove from the yard. Noises from the farm drifted into the kitchen, the quiet sounds of the cows in the near field eclipsed by the sound of the tractor, returning to the yard. There was a bang, as the boot-room door was flung open, the thump of wellies being kicked onto the floor, the rustle of overalls being hastily discarded, and then Tom appeared in the doorway, snatching a hat from his head. Specks of cut grass rained down, and more was stuck to the sleeves of his tee-shirt where they had protruded from his overalls.

"Oi! Brush off some of that grass before you come in," said Susan, carrying the salad back to the work surface and dumping it all into a large china bowl.

Tom dipped back into the boot-room, then reappeared looking slightly less dusty.

"I need my tools," he said, "there's something wrong with one of the tedder blades. Any tea?"

Susan went to refill the kettle. "What's the trouble?" she asked, knowing that any delay would be a nuisance. June was late for the first cut of the grass, and Susan knew that Tom hoped to turn it all today, to dry it slightly, before taking it to the silage pit. The faded green grass would be covered with tarpaulin, secured with ugly tyres, and left to ferment, ready for the winter feed. Any delay could be costly, as if it rained, the cut grass would get wet. She glanced at Tom, who was looking tense and cross.

"Not sure what's wrong with it," said Tom, moving to sit next to Ben at the table. Susan noticed the back of Tom's neck was hairy with specks of grass, which dropped from his neck onto the floor. "One of the blades keeps jamming, and they're too sharp to move by hand, so I needed to bring it back. I don't expect it'll take long to fix, just a pain to have to stop half-way through. Oh, thanks."

Susan passed him a mug of tea and turned to slide the salad bowl into the fridge.

"No news then?" Tom asked.

***

Tom had returned to the hay field, when Susan heard a car draw into the yard. One of the collie dogs, Molly, was lying in her basket, and she lifted her head, ears upright, but didn't bark, so Susan remained in her chair, with her magazine, waiting for the knock at the boot-room door.

"Cooey!" Susan heard, as the door opened, "It's only us." Susan smiled, and got up to greet her mother and Aunty Elsie.

"Hello," said Dot, crossing the room to press a firm kiss on her daughter's cheek. "Hope we're not disturbing you. Oh, you're just reading, that's good, not busy then."

Susan nodded, feeling, irrationally, that she really ought to have been doing something that looked more productive, and that perhaps reading a magazine before lunch made her appear lazy.

"Have you heard any news?" asked Elsie, sounding excited. "It's any day now, isn't it? We brought a little something for you to take, when you hear..."

She handed Susan a mound of tissue paper. It was softened by many wrinkles where it had been reused many times, and a tiny slither of sticky tape was stuck, needlessly, to one side.

"You can look," said Elsie, "we made them ourselves. It's all so exciting, isn't it!"

Susan looked at her aunt. Her grey curls were bouncing, and her eyes sparkling.

"Shall we go into the sitting room?" said Dot, walking from the kitchen. "Do you have time to have a cup of tea while we're here? Though we're still fairly full of coffee. Elsie persuaded me to go to a coffee shop in Marksbridge earlier, and you should have *seen* the size of the cups!"

Susan nodded and forced herself to smile, going to refill the teapot. It hadn't yet fully cooled from when Tom had popped in, and Susan reflected that it was just as well that she hadn't needed to do anything important with her day, as so far she had mainly made cups of tea for people.

Susan left the kettle to boil and joined her aunt and mother in the little sitting room.

Dot marched across the puddle of sunlight that was seeping through the window, and lowered herself into an armchair with a groan. There was dust on the occasional table, and Susan saw her mother lean across, and wipe it away with her sleeve.

"That's the trouble with summer," thought Susan, carrying the tissue paper parcel to the sofa, "it shows up all the flaws." She thought about the grey streaks in her own hair, and the single wiry hair she had plucked from her chin that morning. "Goodness knows where that came from," she thought.

Susan unfolded the tissue paper and lifted soft woollen garments from the parcel. There were tiny booties, with white ribbons to fasten them; a miniature yellow cardigan, knitted with lacy stitches; and a small pink dress.

"The dress won't be any good, if it's a boy," said Elsie, watching her. "But I'm really hoping she'll have a girl, don't you? It would be so lovely to have a little girl in the family, after all these boys..."

"Elsie made the dress and the booties," said her mother. "I made the cardigan. You can dress a boy in anything really, but these days people like to keep to certain clothes and colours, even for new-borns, don't they? I keep reading things in the newspapers about making clothes gender-neutral, but that's rubbish really – that's nothing new. My father was one of the generation that was dressed in a dress until he was old enough to be 'breeched' and given his first pair of trousers. Boys and girls all wore dresses then, I've got photos of him, looks like a girl. Quite pretty dresses they were too, with embroidery and things on them. He must've been about five before he got his first pair of breeches.

"But young people, they like to think they've thought of new things, don't they? They like to think they're changing the world."

Susan nodded, and got up to make the tea. She didn't really want to start a long discussion with her mother about gender issues.

When Susan carried the tea back into the room, Aunty Elsie was elaborately refolding the clothes, her ancient fingers reverently stroking each item, as though they were something holy.

"Best to keep them wrapped," she said, glancing at Susan. "White shows the dirt."

Susan nodded, thinking that this made it a slightly bizarre colour for baby clothes.

"Really," she thought, pouring tea from the red pot, "really, grey would be a better colour. Especially when they start to crawl and all their clothes get covered in dirt from the floor." She passed a cup of tea to her mother, and poured a second cup for Elsie.

"Just half a cup for me, I can still feel that coffee sloshing around my insides!"

Susan smiled at the two elderly women. "Well, I think it's lovely of you both to knit things for the baby," she said. "I'm sure Kylie will love them." She went to the window, and looked outside.

The sitting room faced north, and Susan looked out, across the yard. In front of her was the big barn, and the outside enclosure – empty now as all the cows were in the fields. The sun was high, making the yard a bright pool of light, and casting the interior of the barn into a black shadow. It looked cold and forbidding, though she knew it was a place of vibrancy and life. To her left, the other side of a low stone wall, was the lane that went to Broom Hill Farm, where her third son, Jack, was working hard to save it from bankruptcy. Behind her, Susan could hear the two women talking while Elsie lifted the dress once more to admire it.

"That was a waste of several evenings, if Kylie has a boy," Susan heard her mother scold. "We're too old now to be wasting time on things like that – who knows how long we've got left? – I don't even fill the car with petrol any more...no sense in wasting money if it's not needed."

Susan snorted. "Mum! That's a terrible thing to say."

She heard her mother chuckling. "Yes well, my point still stands – Elsie shouldn't be wasting her time making things that might not be worn.

Susan stared out, over the yard, wondering how Tom was getting on.

"Oh," said Elsie, her voice wistful as she folded the garments again and wrapped them in the crumpled tissue paper. "I wonder *when* the baby will be born."

"Yes, well, the due date is only a guide," said her sister, sounding cross. "The actual birth might be up to three weeks either side of that day, and still be considered a 'normal' birth."

"I do know that," said Elsie.

There was something in her voice, something indefinable, that made Susan turn in surprise and look at her aunt. As she gazed at Elsie's face, there was hardly a hint of anything untoward, simply a spark of something in her eye that Susan had never noticed before – but even as she watched, her aunt's expression softened to the folds that were normally there, and she returned Susan's look with a smile, then busied herself with placing the parcel of clothes on the table, and returning her teacup to the tray.

"Well," said Susan, deciding to move the conversation on, "I don't know when the baby will be born, but they usually arrive when it's most inconvenient. We've got the church group coming here Monday evening, so I'm sort of hoping nothing happens before then."

"Oh?" said her mother, "What church group?"

Susan grinned and went to join her aunt on the sofa. "Our pastor, Rob–"

"Black Rob?" interrupted Dot.

"Yes Mum, but really you should just call him *Rob*," said Susan. "Anyway, Rob has decided that rather than have weekly Bible studies at the church, we'll only meet as a big group once a month, and the other weeks we'll meet in smaller groups, in people's homes. We did it last summer, and it worked okay. So I said I didn't mind people coming to the farm."

"And Tom doesn't mind?" asked Dot.

Susan shrugged. "Tom wasn't ecstatic, but he'll cope. Anyway, the first one is Monday night, and we're starting with a 'social' – whatever that means." She glanced out of the window and frowned.

"It's an annoying time of year for doing things in the evenings, because the chickens don't want to roost until it's dark, so I either have to leave the coop door open until late – which risks the fox getting in, or else I have to decide to not let them out in the morning, and leave them shut inside all day."

"I should just leave them shut inside," said Dot. "They're only birds."

"Yes, but they're meant to be 'free range' birds," said Susan. "Besides, when they're inside they seem to produce even more poop than usual, so I have to do an extra clean-out the next day, which feels like a waste of time." She sighed, and shook her head, reminding herself that it didn't really matter. "But really, in the grand scheme of things, it's not a big problem to have, is it? We're lucky really, we're not having to cope with anything major in the family, are we?"

***

When Dot and Elsie arrived home, and Dot was thinking about what to have for tea, she saw the man again. He was standing, opposite the house, staring at the front door as if trying to decide whether or not to cross the street and knock on the door. Dot watched him from the safety of an upstairs window, peering around the curtain so she couldn't be seen.

There was definitely something very familiar about him, the way that he stood, holding himself very upright, his head held high. And his face, under the thick grey hair, the set of his eyes, the curve of his nose, that mouth...Dot knew that she had met him somewhere, knew him well, in fact. But where and when? Who was he? She tried to imagine the face a few decade ago, to see beyond the few wrinkles, to see him with hair before it was grey. Could he have been an old boyfriend of one of her daughters? Was he an old neighbour?

Dot shook her head. Trying to remember was simply muddling her. She would probably remember in the middle of the night, when it would be no longer relevant.

The man pulled back his jacket sleeve and checked his watch, then began to move away. Dot watched him go, recognising the way he walked, remembering the angle of his head, the swing of his shoulders. There was something faintly alarming in the recognition, something which made her want to lock the door and close the curtains. But she didn't. Instead, she went downstairs, and boiled some eggs to make sandwiches.

***

They were sitting in a circle, chairs moved from the kitchen table to fill the gaps, Rob perched, somewhat precariously, on a bean-bag, his long legs stretched out in front of him. It was he who suggested the game, obviously thinking it might be an icebreaker, something to make them all speak and to provide a few laughs, possibly even a few gasps of surprise. But it had all gone horribly wrong, and no one was making eye-contact; no one even knew what to say.

It had started well, Rob proposing the idea while Susan poured glasses of wine – though most people wanted tea – and offered cake. They were in the parlour, as that was the largest room in the farmhouse, occasional tables were moved to convenient places and people were fiddling with paper napkins and pieces of cake. Outside, the sun was sending crimson rays across the sky, and the window was pink-tinged. It was still light, though Susan thought the shadows would soon fill the parlour, and she ought to switch on some lamps before it became gloomy.

"I've got a game," Rob had announced. "It's very easy, everyone can play."

They all smiled, and Susan could tell they were pleased someone had suggested something, no one wanting to spend the whole evening in meaningless chat, especially those unfortunately sitting next to a person they didn't particularly like.

"It's called 'True or False' and it's very easy," Rob explained. "All you have to do is think of two facts, about yourself, one being true, the other being false. You then tell the group, and we have to guess which is which. The true one can be anything you feel comfortable sharing – that your best friend at school was called Billy, or you once wore your brother's coat to a party. Something like that."

People were nodding, smiling, beginning to decide what they might say. Susan passed the last glass of wine and turned on a couple of lamps, then settled back on the chair next to Tom. He glanced at her, letting her know that although he had agreed for the church group to meet at the farm, he was not especially enjoying the evening. She pretended to not notice, and smiled back.

"I've got one," said John, "I'll start.

"Number One: When I was at school, I used to have one of those old wooden desks with a lift-up lid. I used to spend every evening finding snails in the garden, and I kept them in my desk at school, and sold them to my friends at playtime, so we could have snail races. All my books were covered in snail slime, but the teachers never found out why."

People smiled, sure this was the true event.

"Number Two: When I was sixteen, my brother had a motorbike, and one evening when he was out, I decided to take it for a spin. I found his keys, and helmet, and drove the bike round the block. I'd never driven before, so it was a bit dodgy, and I nearly came off at one corner, but I made it safely back, and he never found out."

He grinned round at everyone.

"Which one is true, which one is false?"

Susan had no idea, both seemed plausible. She turned to Tom, and they began to discuss which might be the correct answer.

Rob called time, and they all offered their answers, the group being split as to which was the correct answer. Susan thought the snail story was probably true.

"Snail story is true," said John. "Right, who's next?"

"How about you Eileen?" said Rob, turning to the nervous woman on his right. Eileen had never attended a home-group before, and was relatively new to the church. It would be good for her to speak, for people to notice her, get to know her a little. He smiled, encouraging her to speak.

Eileen nodded, and surprised everyone by standing up.

"Yes," she said, "I can tell you something."

"It can be anything," said Rob, clearly wanting to reassure her, reminding her that she could choose some meaningless event from her school days.

Susan looked at Eileen. She guessed she was about sixty, short grey hair and a large nose. She was twisting her hands together, staring at the clock on the wall, swallowing repeatedly; Susan wanted to tell her not to worry, someone else could have a turn.

Eileen cleared her throat, and stared straight ahead.

"When I was six, my father came home drunk, and he ran over the cat, and killed it. He was drunk a lot, and when my mum found out, she said he couldn't keep coming home in that state, and he had to find somewhere else to live. So he took a suitcase from the loft, and packed his things, and left. And I went outside, to say goodbye like, and there was the cat, squashed, on the road. So me and my brother got the garden spade, and shovelled it up, but we didn't know where to put it, so my brother – who was older than me, threw it, off the end of the spade. And it went right over the fence, into Mrs Craddock's garden, who lived next door to us. And it was my cat, and I've never got over it, seeing it all squashed flat like that."

Eileen stopped speaking; she stood for a moment, staring ahead, and then sat down.

There was silence.

"And number two?" said Rob, as if hoping desperately that this story was the false one and some insignificant event would now be described.

"No," said Eileen, "I can't think of a false one." She began to scrabble in her bag, looking for a tissue.

Susan felt an overwhelming desire to giggle.

Tom frowned at her, which made it worse. She knew she *mustn't* laugh, the rational part of her brain actually felt very sorry for the woman, for Eileen. But the tension of the moment, the way that everyone was avoiding eye-contact, no one could think of anything to say, made the tension in her stomach bubble up, and she worried she might burst with giggles.

She leant forward, picked up a couple of dirty plates, and took them to the kitchen.

In the kitchen, Susan leant against the sink for a moment, trying to control her giggles.

"That poor woman," she thought, trying to be stern with herself. "Eileen obviously didn't understand that it was just a game – was meant to be fun – not a time for confessions. I shouldn't laugh, it's completely inappropriate." Susan stacked the plates in the dishwasher and refilled the kettle. "It's only because of the tension," she thought, "all this waiting for Neil to phone. I'm sure I'm not usually so heartless..."

She collected the teapot from the parlour – avoiding Tom's eyes for fear he would make her giggle again – and refilled it from the kettle. As she replaced the lid, her phone buzzed in her pocket. Susan snatched it up, and read the message on the screen, a huge grin appearing on her face. The bubble of tension in her stomach swelled to fill her whole being with excitement, and she carried the teapot back to the parlour.

"Neil texted," Susan told Tom, in a voice designed for the whole room to hear. "He's just popped out from the delivery room in the hospital. They've been there since three this afternoon, and all is going well. We should hear in a couple of hours."

Susan began to hand round the plates of cake again, her face beaming. Above the buzz of her happiness, she could hear murmurings from the group of people around her: "Oh, how lovely," "Ooh, that's very exciting, do let us know when you hear," "It might still be days yet, these things are never quick, as you know," "Do you know if it's a boy or a girl?"

The door opened, and Ben put his head round the door. "Hi Mum," he said, "I'm back."

Susan smiled at him. "Neil texted. They're in hospital," she said.

"That's exciting!" said Ben, returning her smile and coming fully into the room.

"Hello Ben," said Mrs Simpson, helping herself to cake from the plate Susan was offering. "How does it feel to be nearly an uncle?"

"Good...I think," said Ben.

"Do you want cake?" asked Susan. "No? Okay, well you can join us if you want, we're nearly finished..." She knew that he would be tired from his commute home from work, and sitting with a group of people from the church was probably not what he felt like doing, even though he had known most of them since childhood.

Before Ben could answer, John Carey spoke, his voice loud and teasing: "What about you then Ben? Are you going to be bringing a young lady for us to meet soon?"

Ben grinned at him. "Nope," he said, "I'm gay." He turned to Susan, who had taken a slice of chocolate cake and was sitting back beside Tom. "I think I'll just go and check my emails thanks Mum, so I'll say goodnight."

He turned, and left.

The room was silent.

Susan stared after him, her bubble of happiness burst into a thousand shards of ice. "I never told him that I wasn't telling the church people," she thought. "He's hardly ever here at weekends because he's usually with Kevin, so there seemed no point in mentioning it. I'm not ready yet, for other people to know – not outside of the family – I'm not ready..."

As Susan stared at the empty doorway, she could feel other people staring at her, almost as if their gaze was hot, searing into her. Next to her, Tom was shuffling.

Someone coughed.

"Oh..." began John Carey, "Oh. I thought Ben was a Christian..."

Eileen leaned closer to Susan. "Did you always know that he was gay?" she whispered, "Can you tell things like that when they're little?"

"I didn't know," Susan wanted to say, "it never occurred to me that he felt like that. It was a shock when he first told me."

But she stopped before the words were spoken, tested them for a moment in her mind. "No," she decided, "I can't say that, I might cry." And she was very keen to not cry, to not display any emotion, but to appear accepting, as casual as her children had been when they heard the news. She didn't want to give any reason to be discussed later, any clues that might lead to the conclusion that she was finding this difficult. "Because people love that," she thought, "they love to be able to say that someone isn't coping very well, that they might be having problems. And I want this to simply be normal, an everyday occurrence which doesn't need to be discussed. Something boring to other people." So she said nothing, and instead lowered her head and cut her cake into tiny pieces, waiting for the moment to pass.

Of course, the moment didn't pass, not immediately. After those first few minutes of silence, of knowing that she was being stared at, assessed for her reaction; those few seconds while people processed the information and decided on their response, there was then a quiet mumble, as people began to speak. Susan was aware that a few people were muttering to each other in the corner, that someone had turned to Rob and asked him for his views, and that next to her, Tom was telling June Brown that Ben was an adult, and could make his own decisions in life.

Then John Carey suggested that perhaps they should have a time of prayer, and pray that Ben might repent of this terrible sin, and someone told him that perhaps it wasn't such a terrible sin after all, and perhaps they should all pray for some temptation that John Carey was currently struggling with. Susan felt that the meeting was sliding into chaos, and looked to Rob, who was looking at Tom, but who noticed her expression and nodded.

"I think," said Rob, raising his voice so that everyone fell silent and listened. "I think that perhaps it's time to close the meeting now, and leave Susan and Tom in peace. Thank you both, very much, for hosting this evening, and we'll meet again next week, at the same time.

"Now, let's pray."

Rob bowed his head, and everyone looked down while he prayed aloud, saying things about all being in God's family, and getting to know and love each other. But Susan was hardly listening, and she felt that probably no one else in the room was listening either. They were all thinking about Ben being gay, and what that meant, and how it must feel to be his parents.

Much later, as Susan lay in bed listening to the regular grunts of Tom snoring, she considered how things might change now that her church friends knew about Ben. It was something she hadn't wanted to discuss, not sure herself what she felt about the situation. His *friend* – she couldn't quite bring herself to say 'boyfriend' – had regularly visited the farm since last year, and, she had to admit, she liked him. He was a nice boy – well, young man really, she supposed – and most importantly, he made Ben happy. But as to the morals of the situation, the right and wrongs, there she was muddled. It was something she had stopped thinking about, deciding that her role was to be welcoming, and that she would leave the theology to other people.

But now, she thought, turning on to her side, now those 'other people' might become rather vocal. Now she might have to start listening to them, possibly defending her son's position, and it was a situation she had hoped to avoid. Up until now, if people had asked whether Ben had a girlfriend – which in a small church people tended to – she had simply avoided the question, smiled and said no. Which had felt, at times, like lying, but she decided it was kinder than blasting them – as Ben had now blasted them – with the truth.

"It's all so complicated," she thought, rolling on to her back and staring through the blackness towards the ceiling. "I still don't really know what God thinks about it all," she thought, pulling the cover up to her chin. "I only know that I don't want anyone to criticise my boy."

Suddenly, the room filled with blue light, and Susan sat up, reaching for the phone next to the bed before it could ring.

"Yes? Neil?" she said. "She has? Oh, that's wonderful. Oh how lovely. How big? And Kylie – she's alright? Oh lovely darling, that's so lovely. Yes, I'll tell Dad," she said. "Do you want me to tell the others? Okay, okay, you take care now. Lots of love. Bye..."

Chapter Two

The following Saturday, as Jack entered the yard on his way to the kitchen, he heard cries for help. There were sounds of a commotion coming from the corner behind the big barn, so Jack detoured that way. He could hear yells, and lots of squawking, and he grinned, guessing what he would find.

As he turned the corner, the scene was pretty much as he had imagined. Kevin was standing in the corner, his arms raised to shoulder height, his back pressed into the wall of the barn. By his feet were two cockerels, and they were moving in for the kill. Their necks were outstretched, the feathers standing on end, and their wings were fluffed up, making them look much bigger than they were. Their legs were dancing, strutting backwards and forwards, as they surrounded Kevin, swaying as they planned their attack.

"Get back! Get back! You nasty creatures! Help me someone...Ben! Ben! I need help..."

The birds continued their dance, and Jack watched as Kevin raised a boot and kicked out at one. This acted as a catalyst, the cockerel moved back, took aim, then leaped forwards, both feet raised, spurs ready to wound.

"Hey! Don't kick them," shouted Jack. He was running forwards now, "It'll make them worse. You need to pick them up."

"*Pick them up?*" squealed Kevin, "*Pick them up? They want to kill me!*"

"Yes," said Jack, arriving to where they were, "they do..." He reached down towards a cockerel. It tried to dart away, his fingers made contact with a wing, and he pulled it towards him, then in one movement, he lurched forwards, enclosed both wings in his hands, and lifted it up. Without pausing, he immediately tucked it under his arm, ensuring the wings were clamped tightly between his arm and side, and used his free hand to clasp the neck, so the bird couldn't peck him.

The other cockerel was hopping between the two men, as if unsure which to attack first. Its neck was elongated, the yellow skin showing between the raised feathers, the beak sharp, the eyes cruel. It skittered backwards, preparing to attack.

"Here, you need to take this one," said Jack, moving towards Kevin, "then I can catch the other one."

"Me? I'm not holding it! It wants to kill me!" protested Kevin, his eyes wide with alarm.

"It's easy," said Jack, laughing. "They're birds – light as a feather – you just need to keep the wings tucked in or you'll be in trouble."

Jack repositioned the bird under his arm, so that his hands were over the wings, keeping them firmly against the bird's body. Then he passed it to Kevin, not letting go until the other man had clamped his arm over the wings.

"Now hold the neck – no, not tightly, you don't want to kill it..."

Kevin glanced at him, and Jack realised that he probably *did* want to kill it.

"Just make a sort of ring with your fingers," said Jack, "so he can't reach round to peck you, but you're not squeezing it...that's right. There's no strength to them, you don't need to use any pressure, just keep the head secure. Now, hold on for a minute..."

He reached down, but the other cockerel darted away. It was still dancing, almost on tiptoe, the wings raised, the head high, backwards and forwards, side to side. At last, before the bird could launch another attack, Jack managed to grab it. He tucked it under his arm and stood, facing Kevin, and laughing.

"You shouldn't have kicked it," said Jack, "it makes them worse. When they start to dance around like that, they're sort of challenging you to a fight. If you kick them or hit out, they take that as an acceptance of the challenge, and the fight begins."

"Yes, well, I don't think I like chickens much," said Kevin. His voice sounded shaky, and Jack realised the other man had been genuinely frightened by the attack.

"They're annoying," agreed Jack, "but I guess it's humans' fault that they've got like this. I think too much breeding of fighting birds in the olden days has made them vicious sometimes. Once they start fighting each other, they won't stop until one of them is dead – even if it's their own father or son or brother – they just keep at it.

"Mind the spurs," he added, seeing Kevin begin to alter his position. "They're really sharp, like knives grown on the back of their legs, they'll cut you if you're not careful."

Jack watched, as Kevin moved his hand away from the spikes on the chicken's leg. The spurs curled, like fat, long nails on the back of the mottled yellow legs, waiting to be used as a weapon.

"So, now what?" asked Kevin, staring down at the bird under his arm. "If we put them down, won't they just start to attack us again?" His eyes were worried, and he looked at Jack, clearly uneasy. The cockerel, now it was contained, seemed contented and was simply sitting under Kevin's arm, small round eyes looking around, as though all the fight had gone out of it, though there was, thought Jack, something evil lurking behind the surface of that apparently benign gaze.

"Well," said Jack, "they're pretty stupid birds, and sort of pre-programmed to fight. But they have no concept of us being bigger than them. If we carry them round for a bit, they'll learn that we're bigger than them, and when they see us getting food, and not attacking the females, and stuff, they learn that we don't want to fight them – we're not a threat. So they stop attacking...mostly. Sometimes they don't," he admitted. "Sometimes you get a bird that's just plain vicious. Then it has to go."

"Go?" said Kevin.

"We wring its neck," said Jack.

"Oh," said Kevin, and Jack could see that although he had claimed to have murderous thoughts towards the bird, the actual killing of it, now the warm body was securely tucked under his arm, was not something he would relish.

"Where's Ben, anyway?" said Jack.

Jack knew that his parents had gone to see Neil and the new baby. Leaving the farm for a day was never easy, and even though Jack was there, Ben had said that as it was a Saturday, he and Kevin could also spend the day at the farm, to help with the jobs that Susan would normally have done. Jack was dividing his time between the farm and helping Josie, with the land that adjoined their own, so the extra help was needed.

As if on cue, Ben rounded the corner, saw his brother with Kevin, and stopped.

"What happened?" he asked.

"Your boyfriend was being attacked by the cockerels," said Jack, *thinking: "Now there's a sentence I never thought I'd have to say!"*

He looked at Ben, adding: "And I saved him, so you owe me."

Ben grinned at Kevin. "Nasty things, aren't they?" he said. He turned back to Jack. "Are you here now – for the rest of the day? Have you finished helping at Josie's farm?"

"Yeah, for now," said Jack. "I'll go back later, to check the cows for the night, but they're all sorted for the day. Thought I'd have a cuppa before I started here, but I heard Kevin screaming, so went to save him first."

"I'm not sure I was screaming," said Kevin, looking perturbed. "I think I was just calling for help. Before I was eaten. Or slashed to bits," he added, staring at the spurs on the cockerel he was holding. "Can't you cut them off? Or trim them or something?"

"You can do most things," said Jack, walking towards the house, the cockerel still under his arm, "but mostly we try not to be cruel to the animals we look after – and if a bird is vicious it's really better to get rid of it. It's not wasted, we eat it."

"Even boys?" said Kevin, sounding surprised, "I thought only females were eaten. Because they have more meat?"

"Well, they do, generally," said Jack, "but some of the birds you buy, even in the supermarket, are males. You can see – if you know where to look…"

"Oh," said Kevin. "Oh. Are you going to take that bird into the kitchen?"

They had reached the boot-room door, and both men were still carrying the birds.

"Well, he needs to be held for a bit longer, so he gets the idea who's boss," said Jack, reaching for the door handle. "And Mum's not home, is she? She'll never know…"

He opened the door and went inside, kicking off his boots in the narrow boot-room, and going through to the kitchen. Kevin followed, looking uncertain. The bird under his arm squirmed, and was staring around the house with wild eyes.

"Won't they poop?" Kevin whispered to Ben.

Ben shrugged. "They might," he said, following Jack and going to fill the kettle. "We'll just clean it up if they do. Tea?"

Jack pulled out a chair and sat at the kitchen table, the bird comfortably tucked under his arm. He could see it, looking around with its round eyes, unsure in this new environment. There was no weight to it, he could hardly feel it there, but every so often it gave a slight twitch, as if testing its captor's hold. He glanced across at Kevin.

Kevin was standing in the middle of the room, appearing as uneasy as the bird he held.

"I'm not sure about this," he was saying, "I mean, won't your mother mind, having animals in the kitchen? Not the dogs, obviously," he said, glancing towards where Rex and Molly were sitting, attentively watching everyone. "I mean, obviously dogs go in kitchens. But birds? I mean, alive ones – I know they come in when they're dead, ready for a nice roast dinner, with some stuffing and sausages – one of my favourite dinners that is… Oh! Should I say that in front of them?" He peered down at the bird under his arm. "Sorry!" he whispered.

Jack grinned. He knew Kevin was always like this, always used about fifty words when two would do just as well.

"It's like listening to a radio," he thought, "a radio that's being tuned and so is bouncing around from topic to topic." He looked back at his cockerel, which was turning its head. He stroked the copper neck-feathers, feeling their silky softness. It was, he thought, a lot like cuddling a pillow.

"I reckon these birds have a lot of Rhode Island Red in them," he told Kevin, "and probably some Maran...they're hybrids you see – a mix of breeds – so we can't be sure." Jack pointed to the bird's neck. "These copper feathers, look, they appear in both breeds – and Marans were bred initially for fighting; cockfighting was popular in France at the time, so they bred them with feral birds, to make them more aggressive." He glanced up at Kevin, who was nodding whilst staring down at the bird under his arm, as if absorbing information might somehow make him better equipped to handle it. "That's probably why they can turn nasty, even now, after generations when they haven't been bred for anything other than eggs and meat."

Jack stared into the distance, thinking about chickens, and all he had learnt about their ancestry. He smoothed the cockerel's feathers, his hand sweeping across the brown back and along to the very tip of the long black tail. The bird seemed to be enjoying the attention, it certainly didn't seem frightened.

"Do brown birds lay brown eggs, and white birds lay white eggs?" asked Kevin, "I've always wondered about that. I mean, you don't see many white eggs now, but when I was little, I remember we always had white eggs. I think my Mum bought them from the butcher's..."

"Not really," said Jack, interrupting before Kevin moved on to a description of the butcher. "I mean, some white hens lay white eggs, but some lay blue eggs. And we had a very light brown hen once, almost yellow she was, but she laid brown eggs. And some black hens lay white eggs – like the Minorca – though I think that's rare."

"When did you become an expert?" said Ben, dumping mugs of tea on the table. He turned to Kevin. "Are you going to sit down?"

"I'm not sure I can with this..." Kevin moved across to a chair, and perched on the edge, the cockerel in his arms.

Ben laughed and went to take the bird from him. There was a slight flutter, as the bird managed to get one wing free and tried to flap before Ben managed to fold it back in place. Jack saw Ben shut his eyes so they were protected, and grab the loose wing. He felt the wind from the flapping wing on his face. A small parcel fell to the floor, the smell strong and pungent, filling the room.

"Eugh, that's foul," said Jack, his face wrinkling.

"Fowl, even..." said Ben.

"Right, they've been held for long enough," said Jack, moving to the door. He placed the cockerel on the ground outside, and watched it run across the yard, looking like a pantomime dame holding her skirts high as she ran. Then he tore some sheets of kitchen paper from the roll and wiped the floor.

"I can still smell it," said Ben, between slurps of tea.

Jack went to the sink and took the blue cloth that was next to it. He ran warm water over it, then used it to wipe the floor, throwing it back towards the sink when he'd finished. It landed inside the sink, and he nodded, satisfied.

"Come on you," said Jack, taking the bird from Ben. "Time for you to go back to the flock too." He released it outside. For a moment the cockerel stood, looking at him, as if considering whether to resume the fight. Then it turned, fluffed up its feathers – almost like a shrug of the shoulders – and started to run across the yard, to where it would find the other chickens.

"I feel quite fond of it now," said Kevin, watching the cockerel running over the yard. It stopped half way across, raising its head to crow to the flock, before disappearing behind the barn where the coop was. "I feel we bonded." He giggled, a short loud noise that made Jack smile. "I think I'll call him Henry."

"I've been thinking about getting a flock, for Broom Hill Farm," said Jack, sitting back at the table, and taking another swig of tea. "That's why I've been learning about the different breeds – it's interesting when you start looking. Chicken breeds are as diverse as dog breeds – you wouldn't get a Labrador as a guard dog, yet people get all sorts of breeds of chicken, and then wonder why some lay better than others...But to be honest, I don't think it'll be worth it for us...I wondered if it might be a way to make some money, but I doubt we'd even cover our costs."

"Because the eggs are expensive to buy?" asked Kevin.

"No," said Jack, looking at Kevin and shaking his head, "it's easy enough to get hatching eggs from other farms. It's the amount it costs to feed them – you'd never make it back by selling the eggs...or the meat really, not with the cut that the butcher wants – no pun intended. Not unless you keep them in cages and feed them rubbish, and I wouldn't want to do that.

"No..." he said, as if thinking aloud, "the only way would be to sell direct to the customer..."

"Right you two," Jack said, downing the rest of his tea and scraping back his chair. "How about you come and help me move the cows to the corner field?"

Kevin looked worried.

"They're easier than cockerels," said Jack. "In fact, this will be very easy, because the two fields connect, so we're not taking them along the lane, we just need to herd them through the gate. I could manage with the dogs, but it'll be easier if you help – are you up for it? Bit of standing where I tell you with your arms outstretched?

"We need to move them," he continued, explaining to Kevin, "because they've eaten most of the grass where they are, and it can recover while they're in the small field. We're all hoping this summer won't be as dry as last year, when we ended up having to use some of the winter feed to supplement the grass, because it never regrew."

He shook his head, remembering how tough the long dry summer had been, wondering if that was what had tipped Josie's dad over the edge, made him decide he couldn't cope any more.

"Do they bite?" asked Kevin, still unsure after his experience with the chickens.

Jack laughed. "No, cows don't bite. They can kick – but only forwards, so don't stand to the side of a cow. They're not like horses, they don't kick out from behind, but their back legs can move forwards and out quite fast – but you're not going to be standing that close. Come on, it won't take long."

"You sound just like Dad," muttered Ben, following his brother from the kitchen.

***

Jack drove the tractor to the field, Kevin and Ben followed on foot. They passed a field of wheat, almost full-grown, but still green. It swayed in the breeze as they passed, hissing at them. It was a bright, clear day, a good temperature for walking. Crows were wheeling over the fields, and the air felt clean. As they walked, Kevin asked Ben about Jack, and why he was spending so much time at Broom Hill, the neighbouring farm.

"I mean, I know about Josie's dad dying and everything, obviously," said Kevin. "But that was months ago – why is Jack always there? Is it just because he's in love?"

Ben shook his head. "Partly the love thing, obviously," he said. "But it's more complicated than that. You know about leases?" he said, wanting to explain. "You know that my parents lease Netherley Farm, and Josie's family lease Broom Hill? They don't actually own the land – only the business, the farming business."

Kevin nodded.

"Well," said Ben, "both the farms are owned by the same landowner, and the two farms have been run by the same two families for generations – both being tenants under the old 1948 Agricultural Act, which allowed tenants to continue farming 'in perpetuity' unless there's a problem. So, although – almost a year ago actually, not a few months – Josie's father nearly bankrupted the farm, they managed to continue paying the rent, and her mother has agreed to not give notice. Which means Josie is now running the farm, with help from Jack. But, they need to make it pay, they have to sort out her dad's debts, and turn it all round. Otherwise they won't earn enough to pay the rent, and they'll have to give up the farm.

"Jack is helping Josie to keep on top of everything, plus..." Ben paused. "My *guess* is that looking ahead, Jack plans to become a partner, and go on the lease."

"Can he do that?" asked Kevin.

"If they marry, he can..." said Ben. He looked up. They were nearing the field now, and he could see Jack waiting for them. "But don't ever mention that I said that!" he added.

***

They arrived at the field, and stood for a moment, watching the cows. When the herd saw Jack, they came to the gate, looking for food. Their black faces watched the men through a cloud of flies that buzzed around their eyes. Jack waved the flies away, and the sudden movement caused the cows to step back in panic. Then they crowded forward again, keen to see what was happening, like, thought Jack, a group of nosey children.

Kevin stepped back as the big heads loomed over the gate, and Jack laughed.

"Honestly, they won't hurt you," he said, "not unless you get too close and one steps on you." He reached out a hand, and scratched a rough cheek. The cow put out a long grey tongue, wetting his cuff.

Kevin stepped forward, and put out his own hand, as if to stroke one. Jack watched as the young man reached for the top of a black head.

"Don't try and stroke the top of the head," he said, watching the cow shaking its head, "they're born with a 'butting instinct', and anything that touches the top of the head makes them want to shake it off."

"And these are boys and girls?" said Kevin. "All in the same field."

"Heifers and steers," corrected Jack. "You can tell the difference if you look." Jack pointed to a cow standing a small distance away, in profile to them. "Look," he said, "the heifers have udders, but because they've never bred, the udders are tiny. The easiest way to tell is to look for that tuft of hair, hanging about half way along the underside...can you see it?" He pointed towards a steer. "That shows that they're male. They're called 'steers' or 'bullocks' or a variety of other names, because they've been castrated." He glanced at Kevin, who was looking shocked.

"It doesn't hurt them," laughed Jack. "When they're very young, we put a rubber band round the testicles, so the blood flow doesn't reach them, and it makes them infertile. Stops all those hormones that create a rampant bull."

Kevin looked even more alarmed.

"Come on," Jack said, shaking his head and opening the gate, "we need to move them through that far gate. I'll go first, and most of them will follow me, knowing that they're going to be fed. You stay and shut the gate after me, and stand here for a bit. If any wander off, head towards them, and drive them over to where I am."

He opened the gate, and drove the tractor into the field. He was pulling a small trailer, and the cows recognised the bale on the back, and began to lumber after it. Jack drove slowly, feeling the bumps of the field, moving across the dry grass to a wooden gate in the far corner. He glanced behind, and saw that Kevin and Ben had followed him into the field, and shut the gate behind them. Kevin was hanging back, near the gate, and Jack grinned, knowing the man was feeling nervous. Ben, who'd been called upon to help move cattle numerous times during his life, was directing Kevin across the field, and they followed the cows at a distance, ensuring that they all followed the trailer, into the smaller field.

When the last cow was in the new field, Ben closed the gate behind them.

"That was easy," he said.

"Yep," said Jack, climbing down, "they all know me, so I thought they'd follow. But you never can tell with animals, so it helps having someone else there." He frowned. "I had a bad experience last autumn, when Dad's back was bad. I needed to move them down the lane, and I just had one of the dogs – Rex – to help. We were all right for most of the way, but then we got to the corner, near the stream, and there's the cottage which doesn't have a gate..."

Ben nodded, knowing which house his brother meant.

"Well," continued Jack, "when we got there, the lead steer decided he'd veer off, and the whole herd followed him. I had thirty cows packed into a cottage garden! Of course, when they realised, they all went into panic, and me and Rex had a right job turning them again, trying to get them back into the lane. They did loads of damage, completely wrecked the flower beds. I thought we'd be in trouble, but the owner was very good about it, seemed to think it was funny. I did go back, helped him repair the beds a bit later in the day. And he got a whole lot of free fertiliser for his lawn!"

"Ha!" snorted Ben.

While he was talking, Jack pulled out his phone. It was new, his brothers had given it to him last month for his birthday. They had clubbed together, though Jack guessed that Neil had been the main instigator – partly because as the eldest, Neil tended to be the main organiser in the family, but also Jack knew that Neil understood how much he wanted a decent phone and couldn't afford one. He looked at it now, clicking on to the 'find-a-friend' app. He wanted to see where Josie was.

There was a pause, while the phone searched for signal, the screen blank. Then gradually the pattern of the fields appeared on the screen, small green boxes with grey roads dividing them, dark green lumps indicating where the wooded areas were. Jack waited. The map whizzed to one side, and a blue blob with Josie's photograph could be seen. Jack smiled, recognising the field that was indicated, knowing that she must be checking the cows.

"Josie's still with her herd," he said, looking up at Ben. "I think I'll scoot over there, give her a hand for a bit. You don't need me now do you?"

Ben frowned, and Jack knew he wasn't happy to be left again. But Jack was keen to get back to Josie, to help her with her herd, and he figured Ben and Kevin would be fine on their own. Kevin had been visiting the farm for over a year now, it was time he learnt more about the workings of it.

When Jack arrived at the field where Josie was working, he stood for a moment, watching her. Josie's back was towards him, and from behind, in overalls which were almost as large as his own, she could have been a man. Tall and heavily built, her frizzy hair was hidden under a cap, and her strong arms had been painted brown by the constant exposure to sunshine. She took long strides in her wellies, and Jack watched as she tugged a bale of hay from the back of a trailer and started to scatter it in the corner of the field. The cows were watching, waiting for her to move back so they could start to eat.

Jack whistled, and Josie looked up, using a hand to shield her eyes from the sunlight. Her face was in shadow, but he knew she'd be smiling, and he found he was smiling back. Then he climbed over the stile, and went to join her.

***

Dot and Elsie had finished their dinner, and Dot was upstairs, when she saw the man again. Elsie was washing up, singing an old pop song in the slightly too sharp key that she tended to sing everything in, and Dot was thinking that it was lucky her sister had never wanted to sing in a choir, and had gone to the window to close the curtains, when she saw him.

The man was standing, opposite the house again, staring at the front door, just like before, as if trying to decide whether or not to knock. Dot took a step backwards, so she could observe him from her position, hidden behind the curtain, looking down at him as he considered. He sucked in his lips, and then seemed to sigh, before moving his hand to brush away his fringe from where it had fallen over one eye, and it was that motion, that casual gesture, which struck a chord deep inside Dot.

"I know him," she murmured again, searching her memory for where she knew him from. Her heart was beating, and when she swallowed, Dot found her mouth was dry, as if she was frightened. Was he an old boyfriend of Susan's? Someone who had broken her daughter's heart? But no, Dot was fairly sure that wasn't who he was.

She couldn't quite place him, but there was something about the set of his eyes, the slant of those broad shoulders, the *casualness* of his demeanour, which Dot recognised and knew, remembered, meant trouble. Why was he here, staring at her house? Was he *looking* for her? The thought made her feel slightly sick, and Dot took another step back.

The man turned, and began to walk away, shouldering his bag as he marched along the road. Again, that gesture, that hefting of a heavy bag, was mirrored by one in Dot's mind, one which lurked just beyond the memories she could retrieve. She watched him, until he was quite hidden from sight by the trees that lined the road, and then she crossed the room and sank onto the corner of the bed. Her heart was racing, and she felt slightly dizzy.

"I don't think I'd better mention it to Elsie," Dot decided. "I don't want to worry her."

Chapter Three

When Susan returned to the farm, she was tired. After she had thanked Ben and Kevin for their help, she went out, to check on the chickens. It was late, nearly 10pm, and they had all wandered back to the coop for the night.

The chickens were free-range, more of a hobby than a serious source of income, though the farm did sell the eggs through a local butcher. Each morning, Susan let them out, into a tiny fenced field attached to the coop, where they could run freely. But although fenced, there was no roof, and when the chicken's flight feathers grew, they could easily flutter over the barrier, and into the rest of the farm. Susan didn't mind, she rather enjoyed seeing them wandering round the yard, and certainly she felt that not clipping the cockerel's wings was a good idea, as it enabled them to have more space to roam, and they were able to keep several males in the flock.

As soon as the light started to fade, the chickens would wander back to the coop, wanting to roost inside for the night; however, sometimes, in the summer months when the days were long, the birds were loath to return. Susan stood, waiting for the last few to go inside.

"Hurry up, silly birds, I'm tired," she said, watching while a pair paused to peck at something in the mud. "If you don't hurry up, I'll shut the door before you're in," she threatened, "then you'll have to take your chances with the fox tonight."

The birds took no notice, and one veered away from the coop, to investigate a bush. Susan moved closer, but it dodged away, under the bush and even further from the coop. She sighed. She knew that there was no way to hurry the birds inside, they had their own clearly defined order, and if she tried to herd the flock inside, there would be fights and upsets, and it would all take much longer than if she simply waited, and watched them saunter inside in their own time. But when she was tired, it was frustrating, and she didn't want to go indoors and start relaxing and then have to come outside again later to shut the door.

Eventually, the last bird came to the door of the coop. Susan came behind it, and tapped the tail feathers with her foot, so it squawked and puffed up its wings in alarm, but also ran a couple of steps forwards, which was all she needed to shut the door.

Inside the coop, the birds were sorting themselves for the night. Some were taking a last drink from the drinker, raising their heads to swallow the water. Others were scratching the soil floor, searching for bugs and lost grain. Most were beginning to fly up to the perch where they would sleep, careful to preserve the order, with the dominant birds perched first, at one end, and the others flying up in turn, roosting in their allotted position for the night. The pecking order changed regularly, decided by small but fierce skirmishes during the day, but they all observed the order in the evening, it was an unwritten but closely observed law of chickens.

When the door was shut, Susan returned to the kitchen and made tea. She was sitting at the table, drinking it, when Jack returned from Josie's farm.

"Hello," said Susan, glancing up. "The kettle's hot."

"Thanks Mum," said Jack, sitting next to her. "How was he then? Has he grown much in the last week?"

Susan smiled, her face beaming her delight as she thought of her grandson.

"Oh Jack, he's gorgeous," she said, "I do wish they were nearer so I could see him every day."

Something in Jack's face told Susan that he thought it was probably just as well that she didn't live near enough to see the baby every day, but he only said: "Glad you had a good time. Was Kylie okay? And Neil?"

Susan's face clouded. "Yes – they're both tired of course, because that's just how life is with a new baby. But

Kylie fed him while we were there...and...well." She stopped, debating with herself how much she should reveal to Jack. Her relationship with Kylie was much improved, "I'm very fond of her," she reminded herself. But this – the way she was feeding her son, *"my grandson,"* thought Susan. Well...

Jack was staring at her. "Go on?" he said.

Susan was battling with herself. She knew that Kylie was Noah's mother, and that it was completely right that a mother should make decisions regarding their child, and that Susan – as a mere grandmother – should simply watch, only offering advice when it was sought. But she was also worried. Noah was her grandson, and she cared about him, and was sure that in this instance she was correct. Susan took a breath, deciding all at once that she would share her worries with Jack. After all, he was the baby's uncle, and perhaps he would have more sway with Neil than she had.

"Well," began Susan, "Kylie fed Noah while we were there, and well..." she paused, all the frustration flooding through her again, at not being able to suggest how this tiny baby might be cared for, her frustration that she knew best – which she clearly did, she had raised four healthy sons – and yet she had to watch, impotent, while Kylie risked the health of her grandson...

"Kylie isn't feeding him herself," she said at last. "She gives him a bottle."

Susan thought about the defensive way her daughter-in-law had explained that, "breast feeding isn't for me," and how she had casually moved the conversation on, not asking Susan for her views, not seeking her advice.

"She didn't even explain," thought Susan, "whether she used bottles by choice or because she had tried and failed at feeding herself. And there was no opportunity to ask, when I started to speak, Tom just gave me that warning look, so I knew I wasn't to say anything."

"Also," said Susan, leaning closer to Jack, hoping for an ally, "because Kylie's a vegan, she doesn't want to feed that poor little mite proper milk. He's drinking some soya rubbish, which I'm sure is giving him tummy ache."

Susan thought about when she'd held Noah, trying to rock him while he cried, and how he had pulled up his knees, obviously distressed.

"His tummy hurts," Susan had told Kylie, recognising the symptom of pain in the new-born.

"Yeah, the midwife said he gets wind," said Kylie, leaning forwards and taking the baby back from Susan.

"Not that he settled," thought Susan, remembering those thin screams. "He wasn't any happier with his mummy…"

Now, in the kitchen, Jack sighed, and shook his head.

"You have to let Kylie do what she thinks is best Mum," he said. "You know you do."

"Yes, well, it's all very well for you to say," snapped Susan, "you weren't there listening to him cry."

"I'll see them on Saturday," said Jack. "Are they still coming down, so we can all meet him?"

"Yes," said Susan, summoning the memory, the wonderful memory, of holding that tiny warm bundle, and knowing that he was part of the family. She smiled again. "He was terribly sweet, Jack, and I think he has Neil's eyes. It was hard to tell when we first saw him, babies are so squashed when they arrive, they all look like rotten beetroot. But this time, he had plumped up a bit, and you could see more of his features, he looked more human."

"Being 'plumped up a bit' sounds like he's gaining weight then," said Jack, thinking of how carefully they monitored the weight of the new calves when they arrived. "He must be getting enough to eat."

"Perhaps," said Susan, reaching for a piece of paper and a pen from her bag. "It's a shame none of you managed to pop in and see them when he was first born, apart from Edward."

"I couldn't leave the farm," said Jack, sounding, thought Susan, exactly like his father. "Anyway, Saturday will be nice, won't it? Having them here for the day, and all of us meeting him at once. I know Josie wants to see him, she's gone all girly on me." He smiled, and Susan grinned back.

"What colour is he?" asked Jack, looking unsure. "Is that an okay thing to ask?"

"No idea," said Susan, "– about whether that's an okay thing to ask, I mean – though I don't think it matters in the family. I wasn't sure what to expect myself, when we first saw him – I think it can vary depending on the genes that are passed on. He isn't as dark as Kylie, but he definitely looks sort of tanned. I think people will see that his parents aren't both white, but I don't know if that changes, as people grow older..." She thought for a moment, thinking of her friend Esther's children, and their father Rob. Both their boys were obviously not 'white' but only the eldest was properly dark, more like his father than his mother.

Susan shook her head, not particularly interested in the skin tone of her grandson, more concerned with his health. She began to write names on the paper.

"Neil asked me about the family tree," she explained, drawing lines between the names, "and I said I'd try and write it out for him..." Susan wrote: 'Noah Compton' at the bottom of the page, her face beaming proudly. Above she wrote 'Neil, Edward, Jack, Ben,' then added her name and her sister's, Cassie. On the line above she wrote 'George, Elsie, Dot.'

She stopped. "I have no idea of dates," she said. "When did my parents get married? And what was my grandmother's maiden name?" She frowned, staring into space.

"I'll have to ask my mother to help," she said, "I don't remember. And I'm not sure if some of the names I know are the real names, or just what we called people."

Jack peered over her shoulder. "It's quite a narrow family tree," he said. "Neither your aunt nor uncle had children, and nor did Aunty Cassie. And your dad was an only child...We're not a very fertile breed, are we?"

Susan stopped writing, and lifted her head, frowning. "Does it smell funny to you in here?" she asked. "I noticed it when we got back, and I can still smell something. Smells like the chickens."

Jack shook his head. "I can't smell anything," he said.

"Oh. Well, I think I'll wash the floor tomorrow," said Susan. She stood, leaving her scribbled family tree on the table. "I think I'll go to bed now though," she said. She kissed the top of Jack's head, and left him at the table, looking at the spider's web of family names that she had scribbled on the paper.

***

The following Monday the church group was due to arrive for another session. Susan had washed the kitchen floor, and the smell of chickens had disappeared.

It had been another warm day, and after sorting the animals, Susan decided to bake a chocolate cake for when the church people arrived, but as it was so hot, she decided she would leave the door to the yard open. It was always difficult, in the summer, because the kitchen got very hot when she cooked, but opening doors and windows let in the flies. There was no way to stop the flies, which fed on the muck and silage in the barns, and crowded around the cow's eyes when they were out in the fields.

"Really," she thought, as she sieved flour into her mixture, "we need insect nets for the house, like they have in hot countries." When she had first moved to the farm, there had been coloured strips of plastic that dangled from above the boot-room door, allowing a slight breeze into the room but keeping out most of the flies. But the constant stream of muddy dogs and damp farmers, meant that the plastic ribbons, whilst once bright, had become grey and splattered, and Susan had felt sure they were a breeding ground for germs. Plus, if she was honest, she equated them with cheap shops and council houses in the sixties. So she had removed them – which had caused her mother-in-law some consternation.

"That's the trouble with farms," thought Susan, reaching for a metal tablespoon and folding the flour into the mixture. "Each generation has their own way of doing things, and sometimes change can feel like an insult. I think Tom's mother assumed everything we did would be exactly the same as they did things, and any change we made was noticed and frowned upon."

She paused, licking a dollop of cake mixture from her thumb. Through the open doorway, she could see a head. One of the cockerels had crossed the yard, and was now peering round the boot-room door, and across to the kitchen. His long neck was stretched out, as if he was trying to look in without being seen. Then, as Susan watched, his body moved forwards and one yellow foot was placed inside the room. He stared at her, poised.

"Oi!" she shouted, moving towards the doorway, "What do you think you're doing?"

The bird stared at her with round eyes, then fluffed his feathers in alarm, and disappeared from view. When Susan looked out of the window, she could see him, charging across the yard, the red crown on his head wobbling, his wings held high.

"Cheeky thing!" thought Susan, spooning the cake into a tin. "I wonder why he thought coming inside would be an okay thing to do!" She placed the cake in the oven, and wiped her hands, before going to the boot-room and closing the door. "Flies are bad enough," she thought, "I'm not having chickens inside too."

***

At eight o'clock, the first car drew into the yard, and Susan turned on the kettle. As people arrived, she offered them tea and warm cake, and showed them into the parlour, wondering when Tom would appear.

At nine o'clock, Tom joined the group for the Bible study, sidling into a seat near the door and avoiding Susan's eye. Rob was teaching, explaining what the passage meant, and trying to involve everyone in a discussion, but only Eileen was answering. Eileen had obviously recovered from her nerves of the previous week, and was now answering every question, as soon as it was asked, at great length. Susan found her voice rather irritating, and had stopped listening.

It wasn't until the end of the evening, when people were beginning to gather their bags and put on jackets, remarking that summer evenings were often colder than you'd expect, that someone raised again the subject of Ben, and being gay. Susan, who had sort of hoped that people might have forgotten, even though the rational part of her brain knew that was impossible, stopped helping Eileen with her jacket, and stared across the room. John Carey was addressing Rob, his voice loud, too loud, thought Susan, *as if he wants us all to hear.*

"Now, that news that young Ben told us last week, about being gay – are we going to address that at all Rob? Not something we should really sweep under the carpet, is it? Are we going to hear some teaching from you, about the Bible saying it's wrong? Seems very relevant, doesn't it?"

Before Rob could answer, a man called Dean spoke up. "Hang on a minute John, you're assuming we all feel the same way as you. But some of us see the issue differently." He turned to Rob, "As it's the summer, and a bit different, could we plan a debate? A proper, church debate, where we can hear both sides, and then maybe you could do a sort of summing up at the end? Not that I don't feel you would represent both viewpoints fairly, of course," he added, as if worried he may have sounded rude. "But it's such a tricky subject, isn't it? And hard – I'd have thought – to represent both sides properly if you hold a particular view. So why not have two speakers, both explaining exactly what they believe and why? So that both sides are fairly represented. Because," he turned back to John Carey, "there are plenty of Christians who don't feel the Bible condemns homosexuality. Not in the way I think you're insinuating, anyway."

John Carey was frowning, clearly affronted.

Rob held up his hands, as if trying to calm the atmosphere in the room.

"This is a tricky topic," Rob said, "and I'm very keen that we examine it properly, and in the right way. Other churches have been torn apart by this issue, and I don't want that to happen here."

He paused, as if considering.

"I need to discuss this with the leadership team, but my feeling is that perhaps we could have a debate. If there are two people willing to speak, who will respectfully explain their viewpoint – respectfully towards those who hold a different view, I mean. It mustn't descend into slanging matches or nastiness, that won't help anyone...

"But yes, I can see that a healthy debate might be good, might let everyone examine the issue properly. We will make some ground rules, ensure that both sides base their arguments on what the Bible says, that nothing personal is mentioned because that would be inappropriate...but yes, it might work."

Susan listened, her heart sinking. Although Rob was saying that the debate would be tactful, not personal, she knew very well that everyone would have her family in mind as the topic was discussed. At least it wouldn't be held at the farm, she could hear them planning to advertise the event, and hold it in the church. She looked up, to find Tom watching her. He gave the slightest shake of his head, warning her to not say anything, not to speak before she had thought about her response. She lowered her head, and went to gather dirty plates and screwed up napkins, wishing she was invisible.

"The trouble is," she thought, as she threw away the dirty napkins, "it's harder for me. Everyone else is struggling to work out what, exactly, the Bible means when it mentions gay sex. But whatever it means, right or wrong, I simply want to protect my son. It isn't an intellectual debate for me, or even a religious one, it's a deeply personal issue. And I do *not*," she thought, slamming down the lid of the bin, "wish to hear it debated by other people."

Chapter Four

Jack was in one of the disused sheds when Josie found him. Broom Hill Farm was immediately next to Netherley Farm, but it was, thought Jack, much more run-down.

"Hi," said Josie, peering round the shed doorway. "What are you doing in here?"

Jack looked up, and shook his head. "Searching for inspiration," he said. He went to join her, kissing her cheek before moving back into the yard. It was dusk, the last light of the day fading away. The yard was surrounded on all sides by barns and sheds, and their long shadows reached across the yard, so it felt even darker. Something, probably a mouse, was investigating some empty food sacks, and Jack could hear them rustling in the corner.

"We need to change something," said Jack, "but I still don't know what." He stared round the yard, looking at buildings which had been left to go to ruin. At one time, the farm had been a thriving business, diversifying into different areas, keeping pace with the change in markets. It was actually a bigger farm than Netherley, but for years now many of the buildings had been empty, the fields left fallow. Jack turned back to Josie. "I keep hoping something will occur to me, that one of us will have a good idea, but the last of the money is almost gone, and we can't keep going."

"How long do we have?" asked Josie.

Jack noticed she said "we" and smiled, glad she was including him. He had started to help her from the moment, last September, that her father had died, but he realised he had no 'rights'. The Broom Hill tenancy belonged to Josie and her mother, and although Jack considered himself a permanent fixture, it was nice to hear her assume it too.

"I'm not entirely sure how long the money will last," he said, "but I think not much longer. I was wondering about sorting out some of these defunct barns, getting stuff working again that your dad left to rot..." He stopped. He didn't usually say anything negative about Josie's father, it was too soon, and her pain was still very raw. He saw Josie's eyes fill with tears, and went to her, angry with himself for causing her pain, but also knowing that he needed to broach the subject.

"Hey kiddo," he said, putting an arm around her shoulders. "This isn't a criticism of your dad. I know he tried, everything was against him..."

Josie sniffed. "It's okay," she said, wiping a hand over her face and turning to look at him. "Really Jack, it's okay. It's time I faced this. I know Dad...let things slide. I know he made some bad decisions..." she paused, and Jack knew she was struggling to get past the hurdle of those words, and all that they meant.

Josie continued, her voice husky, "I know that we can't just keep on doing things the way Dad was, because the farm is leaking money. But I haven't felt up to thinking about it – I haven't felt *ready*." She glanced up at Jack, meeting his eye. "But I know I've got to, and I can't leave it all to you. I want to, I want to be sensible, and think about it, and face the problem and find a solution. It's...time, isn't it? I have to do it now, don't I? Before it's too late."

Jack nodded, grateful that she had put into words what he'd been worrying about and felt unable to say. He took hold of her hand, and led her across the yard, to where one of the disused buildings stood. He flung open the double doors, and led her inside.

"Look," he said, "look at this."

They were standing in a disused milking shed. The processing plant was all there, laced with cobwebs, the once-sterile fixtures heavy with dust. Pipes hung from above them, some were cracked, one tube lay, broken, on the floor. Milking claws lay on the floor, their teat-cups dirty from disuse. Food troughs hung from the wall, some at jaunty angles where screws had fallen out. There was an air of decay, of hopelessness.

"Hard to imagine this was ever used, isn't it?" said Jack, jumping down into the central channel and peering up at the array of tubes and pipes above him.

"Yes," said Josie, sounding uncertain. "What were you thinking? Surely no one would want to buy all this stuff..."

"Nope," said Jack, climbing up and picking up one half of a rotted milking pipe. "But I've been checking it all, and some of the equipment is sound. The vacuum trap and the milk tank are both solid, the motor works...I reckon, if we buy some parts from dairy farms that are going out of business, I think, with a bit of luck, we could get it going again."

Josie stared at him. "You're kidding, right?" she said. "All our herd is beef cattle. We haven't had any dairy cows for ages. I know Dad was trying to start again, had decided to breed a dairy herd when...when..."

Josie's voice tailed away, and Jack saw her duck her chin, hiding her face. He moved to her and put a hand on her shoulder, waiting until she was composed again. They needed to have this conversation, however difficult it was for her.

"I know," said Jack, his voice gentle. "I know. I'm guessing your dad originally stopped milking when the EU milk quotas got too expensive – lots of dairy herds did, it was a stupid system – having to pay thousands of pounds upfront, and then trying to produce a set quantity of milk. The only people who got rich were the people who were trading the quotas, the farmers got hit on all sides, and were then left owning worthless quotas when the system died. But that's finished now.

"I think, if we keep a mixed herd, if we start to breed from some of the heifers, with good dairy cattle, then maybe it will be enough to keep going. The trouble with keeping all beef cattle, is if the price of beef keeps falling – and with our generation shouting about methane and global warming, plus all the people who are deciding to be vegetarian – then I think the market is only going to shrink. Especially for non-organic meat.

"But if we can afford to get this going again, if we could sell some milk, and sell off the males for beef, then it gives us two chances, doesn't it? I wonder if perhaps, this was your dad's plan, all along. We never got to ask him, did we? And he wasn't one for sharing his ideas, so it's just a guess, but I think he may have been planning this – he just never managed to see it through..."

Jack paused. He knew he was on dangerous ground, and he didn't want to rush Josie into a decision which would, at the end of the day, either make or break the farm. But he was sure that he was right, so he plunged on, trying to persuade her.

"Eventually, I reckon that we need to be organic, because the prices are better, but I don't think we can afford that, not yet."

Josie was frowning. "How can we afford any of it? This looks like it's for the scrapheap..."

"Yeah, well, I haven't finished looking yet," said Jack, "so you still might be right. But I've been phoning round, and I think I can get the parts I need fairly cheaply. I could fix most of it myself, we'd have to pay for an engineer for some of it...but it might be affordable. I still need to phone round the dairies, negotiate a contract that would work... and we'd have to fork out for artificial insemination, and wait while the heifers calved, obviously...so there's more to think about...nothings certain yet..."

He went and stood next to Josie, lifted his hands and placed them on her shoulders. They were almost the same height, so he was standing, looking straight into her eyes, trying to read her expression through the gloom of the barn.

"What do you think?" he asked. "Is it worth me doing some sums, working the money out properly? Are you up for trying it?"

He waited. There was much he wasn't saying, he had more plans, for the future, which would mean even bigger changes. "But I won't mention them yet," he thought, "better to go slowly, one step at a time..."

Under the weight of his hands, Josie shrugged. "Okay," she said. "Though this all seems a bit new and scary – we still don't know how the 'Maize Maze' is going to go, and changing so much, all at once..."

Jack leant forwards and kissed her nose. It was cold.

"We need to keep moving forwards Kiddo, so we can make the farm viable. I'll do some sums tomorrow," promised Jack, "after we've been to Mum's, to see the baby."

"Oh yes," said Josie, frowning. "Who will be there? Do I have to dress up?"

Jack smiled, knowing how much Josie agonised over choosing what to wear. "It's only the family," he said, "it doesn't matter what you wear." He looked at her dirty overalls and dusty hair. "As long as it's clean," he added with a grin, "I don't think Kylie will like it if we introduce Noah to cow dung too soon..."

Chapter Five

Susan was filling the teapot when Jack and Josie arrived. Sometimes, she felt it was her default position, and if she were to come back as a ghost, her spirit would be found hovering over a kettle.

"Hello," she smiled in welcome, as Jack and Josie came into the kitchen. "Go on through to the parlour, everyone's in there." She picked up the teapot and followed them.

The hallway connecting the kitchen and parlour was always dark, lit only by whatever daylight managed to filter through the little window next to the front door. In comparison, the parlour was warm and welcoming, sunlight flooding through the bay window. The family was seated on the sofas and chairs, some near the now-empty fireplace, others on the long sofas under the window. Opposite the door, Kylie had her back to the window, and was using a cushion to support her arm, as she held her baby. At her feet were two large bags, and Kylie leant down and pulled a square of white muslin from one, which she used to wipe the baby's chin.

Susan crossed the room, passing Jack, who had stopped, staring, as he entered the parlour.

"Oh golly, he's *tiny*!" she heard him say, his voice sounding slightly shocked.

Kylie laughed. "What were you expecting?" she asked.

Ben was agreeing with Jack. "Yeah, I know, but really, he's so small. And a person...who would've thought a person could be so small?"

Susan looked at her sons, seeing awe in their faces. They were all staring at the baby, each one taking in his tiny features – and when an arm and tiny fist emerged from the bundle of shawls, each man's face reflected the same delighted grin. Susan felt suddenly emotional, and blinked away tears. Jack was still standing, not moving, staring at his nephew. Josie had moved closer, and was peering down.

"Do you want to hold him?" asked Kylie.

"Oh," said Josie, sounding unsure. "I mean, yes, yes, if you don't mind?"

Kylie shook her head. "Why don't you go and wash your hands – I'm still a bit paranoid about germs – and then if you sit next to me, I'll pass him to you. Move up a bit Neil," she said, turning to her husband.

Susan began to pour tea, thinking that baby Noah would develop a much healthier immune system if he was introduced to a few germs, and that *if* Kylie was feeding him herself, then she wouldn't have to worry so much because the baby would absorb his mother's immunities with the milk.

"But it's not my place to say," she reminded herself, passing a mug of tea to Jack.

"I'll leave your tea here, Josie," said Susan, as Josie came back into the room, with washed hands, and sat next to Kylie. Susan thought she looked rather nervous.

Josie sat on the sofa next to Kylie. Behind her, the sun streamed through the window, and Susan noticed the flowers she had put on the windowsill were drooping, the water in the glass vase evaporated. The sun lit the back of Josie's hair, lending it highlights of gold. Beside her, Kylie's hair seemed blacker than ever, and the sun glinted from the clip fastening her fringe to the side.

Kylie shifted in her seat, and placed the baby in Josie's arms. "Just mind his head," said Kylie, easing her hands away. "Make sure his neck is always supported."

In the corner of her eye, Susan saw Ben glance at Edward.

"He's really light, isn't he?" said Edward, letting his brothers know that he had, of course, already held the baby when he had visited earlier in the week.

Susan thought that neither Ben nor Jack looked as if they especially wanted to hold the baby. They seemed fascinated simply by watching him. Jack was watching Josie, his expression soft as she took the baby, adjusting her position so that Noah's head rested in the crook of her arm. Her shadow fell across the baby, and she rested her elbow on a blue velvet cushion that crumpled beneath the weight.

Josie's face was beaming, as she looked down at baby Noah. The baby started to whimper, and Susan watched as Josie began to rock him. It was more of a bounce than a rock, and although the baby was at first shocked into silence, he soon decided that he didn't like it, and began to yell. Josie looked dismayed.

"What am I doing wrong?" asked Josie, looking up.

"Probably nothing," said Neil, taking his son from her arms. "He can make that noise for hours. Especially at night. Honestly, he might be tiny, but he certainly isn't quiet. And the smells he can produce! I mean, you should see the nappy I had to deal with yesterday..." He began to describe, in great detail, his exploits with his son's nappy. He stood as he talked, swaying backwards and forwards, while the baby's yells quietened to a whimper.

The other men were laughing, and Kylie shook her head. Josie took her tea, and began to sip it. Susan heard the kitchen door open, and got up to welcome her mother and aunt.

"Where is he? Where is he?" said Aunty Elsie, hurrying past Susan and into the parlour.

Dot kissed Susan, and let Elsie go ahead.

"There's something I want to tell you at some point," Dot said. Susan looked at her mother, surprised by her tone. "It's probably nothing," continued Dot, "but there's a man I keep seeing. And I can't remember where I know him from."

"Have you asked him?" said Susan, wondering if her mother was building up to announcing she had a man-friend, and wondering how she would feel if her mother was, in fact, romantically attached to someone again.

"Oh no, I haven't actually spoken to him," said Dot, her tone lightening. "I just keep seeing him. But he bothers me, and I don't remember why."

"Oh," said Susan, not really sure what, exactly, her mother was trying to tell her.

"Never mind," said Dot, sounding decisive, "it can wait." She went to join her sister, just as keen to see the baby. Susan refilled the kettle, and followed them.

Neil was standing, still swaying back and forth, the baby in his arms. Elsie peered at the baby, and stretched out a finger, tracing his forehead, his cheek, his chin. Her grey curls brushed against Neil's arm as she stood, stretching to see.

"Oh," she sighed, "he's so beautiful..."

"He's got your eyes Neil," said Dot, looking over her sister's shoulder. "Can I have a little cuddle?"

Susan watched as Neil passed the baby to his grandmother. Beside her, Susan was aware of Kylie moving, as if about to say something, and then sitting back in her chair. Susan turned to look at her. The young woman held herself stiffly, as if both tense and extremely tired. Her eyes were red-rimmed and puffy from lack of sleep. She sat awkwardly in the chair, and Susan remembered that the birth had not been entirely smooth.

Dot stood, rocking the baby with the same motion that Neil had used. Elsie stood next to her, peering at the baby and smiling.

"Yes," said Elsie, nodding her head. "I think he looks just like Neil. His eyes are the same shape, and he's got the little Compton chin, and his nose is just the same...I remember you at that age," she said, looking up at Neil, "and you looked just the same...identical. You could be twins!"

"Noah's black," said Dot, frowning at her sister, "so not 'exactly' the same!"

"Well, no..." said Elsie, "not his colour perhaps, but everything else I think." She crooked her little finger, and held it near the baby, who reached out a fist and clenched hold. "He's got a good grip," reported Elsie. "That's a good sign."

"I've read somewhere," said Edward, "that new-born babies can support their own weight with their hands. Shall we hang him up somewhere, and test it?"

"Like Tarzan?" asked Ben. "Shall we try it?"

"No!" said Susan and Neil simultaneously.

"He's not a toy," said Neil. "Have your own baby if you want to start experimenting."

Susan shook her head, thinking that her sons might be bigger, but their humour hadn't changed much since they were children. She passed her aunt a cup of tea, and went to sit on the arm of Kylie's chair.

"How are you?" she asked in a low voice. "Are you beginning to recover a bit? The first few weeks are a bit unreal, aren't they?"

Kylie nodded, and Susan saw tears glistening. "I'm just so tired," she said.

Susan reached out, and put an arm around her shoulders, giving her a quick hug. She remembered that tiredness, those days and nights that seemed to merge into one long grey sentence of wakefulness, remembered how obsessed she had become with sleep, how angry she had felt during a trip to the shops when her new-born baby had fallen asleep in the shopping aisle, and Susan had thought, with desperation: "Don't sleep now, I have to be *awake* now, sleep later, when I can nap..."

"It's very tough," said Susan, nodding.

"But you're doing so well," she forced herself to add, knowing that her daughter-in-law needed some encouragement.

Kylie glanced up, looking surprised, and grateful.

Susan continued: "And Noah is so gorgeous. It will get easier, honestly," she said. Though as she looked around the room, at Neil who was hovering over his grandmother, at Ben who was keeping his distance, at Edward and Jack who seemed mesmerised by the baby; Susan wondered at the truth of her words. Was it easier, she wondered, or was it just different?

"Let me get you another drink," she said to Kylie, "while you've got two hands free. And will you eat something? Chocolate cake?" Then, remembering, she said, "Oh no, the flapjack I bought – that's vegan. Will you have another piece?"

Kylie nodded. "Yes, thanks."

Susan poured the tea, taking care to use the milk from the pink jug, as that was soya milk. It had a grey tinge, and looked artificial, but when mixed with tea it looked the same. She placed two pieces of flapjack on Kylie's plate, thinking that if you didn't know, you would think they contained butter, but that when you tasted them – as she had when opening the packet – you would find them rather insubstantial and overly sweet. She wished that her daughter-in-law would eat 'proper' food, that she would allow Susan to cook her a decent meal, full of nutrients that grew naturally in the meat they raised. "But it's not my place to say," she reminded herself, again.

"Is Kevin coming?" asked Neil, turning to Ben.

Ben shook his head. "Not today," he said, "he had to work."

"That's a shame," said Neil, sounding relieved.

"Hello everyone," Susan heard Tom say, and looked up to find him standing in the doorway. He had come straight from the fields, and although he had kicked off his boots in the boot-room, he still wore his overalls.

He grinned at Kylie. "Don't worry," he said, "I won't hold the nipper until I'm a bit cleaner. I just thought I'd pop in and say hello before I start the next feed...got a new lot of babies myself to get sorted."

Tom turned to Ben. "Did you hear about the debate?" he asked. "The one the church are organising? Twelfth of September, if you want to come. They're debating what the Bible says about homosexuality. Had you heard?"

Ben shook his head. "No, I hadn't. Is that because of me?" he asked.

"Not officially," said Tom, "but I suspect that's what instigated the idea. Will you go? They've got a couple of people talking – one giving the traditional view, one of them disputing whether that's right. No idea who, or what they'll say, but might be interesting."

Susan frowned, wishing Tom hadn't raised this, not today, when everyone had come to see the baby. It removed the glow from her day, reminding her of feelings that were muddled and worried.

"I'm not entirely sure I'm going to go myself..." she began to say. "I mean, it's fine for everyone else to discuss what they believe, obviously, but I'm not sure if I want to hear it."

"Well I do!" said Ben, sounding buoyant. "It will be interesting. Besides, if I'm there, it will ensure that I won't become the topic of conversation, people will have to behave if I'm in the room."

"I think perhaps we should all go," said Neil, slowly. He glanced at Kylie. "Not you Kylie, you shouldn't use up energy on something like a church debate. But the rest of us should go, especially if they might start to discuss Ben."

"Won't you agree with them?" said Edward, his voice teasing. "Don't you agree with the traditionalists?"

"I might agree with their views of the Bible," said Neil, moving to take his son from Dot and going to sit back on the sofa. "But if there's any danger that this might become about Ben, I think we should all be there, to keep some order."

"Perhaps I'll bring Emily," muttered Edward, "she's certainly scary enough..."

Susan noticed that Josie blushed at the mention of Emily, her head dropping so her hair covered her face. She glanced up, and saw that Jack had noticed too, and was frowning. "Oh dear," thought Susan, "this is all going badly wrong. The last thing I need is all my sons at the debate, spoiling for a reason to defend Ben. They're so big, just their presence will dominate the room, and I don't want this to be about us. It's not my family the church is discussing, it's the gay issue." But inside, she knew that this was naive, and it was very much her family who would be in everyone's minds during the debate, whether they were physically present or not.

Neil had passed the baby to Kylie, who was feeding Noah, holding a bottle while chatting to Josie. Susan could hear him feeding, listened to him making contented grunts as he fed. She smiled, remembering that Neil had made the same noises. It feels like yesterday, she thought, and now they're all grown up. Wherever did the time go? She sat, enjoying having the family with her, listening to them all.

Edward and Jack were discussing the debate at the church, planning to attend. Edward was checking the date on his phone, and saying that he could be there, perhaps they should make placards. Jack was laughing, saying that he would get some tee-shirts printed. Neil was joining in, saying he thought they should take it more seriously, and Ben was saying that he didn't care, he'd heard it all before and nothing they said would be new.

Kylie put down the bottle, and moved Noah to her shoulder. She started to rub his back.

"He gets terrible wind," she told Josie. "Sometimes I dread feeding him, because I know it will give him pain." Noah started to cry – a thin wail that grew in volume.

"He sounds like a sheep," said Jack.

Elsie was sitting in one of the chairs by the fireplace, and Ben moved to the chair opposite her.

"So, Aunty Elsie," he said, "how are you?"

Elsie smiled up at him, and Susan thought how pleased she looked to be noticed.

"I am very well, thank you Ben," said Elsie, sipping her tea, then moving to get up.

"Shall I help you?" asked Ben, moving to take the tea from her.

"It needs a little more sugar," said Elsie, handing him the cup. "Two spoonfuls, and a good stir." She watched while Ben went to the table and stirred in more sugar, then passed her back the cup. "Thank you dear, you're very kind," she said. She took a sip and sat back in her chair. "Ooh, that's perfect, a lovely cup of tea."

Ben returned to his seat, and Elsie stared at him.

"Are you going to get an earring?" she asked.

Ben looked shocked. "Er, no. Why do you ask?"

"Well," said Elsie, "I thought that's what you people do – get an earring, just one – doesn't it mean something?"

Susan noticed that Edward was also listening to the conversation, and he came and sat on the arm of Ben's chair.

"Excellent idea, Aunty Elsie," said Edward. "Left for love, isn't it?"

Ben ignored his brother and shook his head. "No Aunty, I don't think it's really me – do you?"

"No, not really," said Elsie, before adding: "You're still my Ben, aren't you...I forget that sometimes, I think you must be different."

Noah's wails grew louder, and they all turned to look at him.

Neil stood, and took his son again. "Come on son," he said, rocking him.

"He'll be sick," warned Kylie, "he's just been fed."

"He'll be fine," said Neil, then moved backwards as a stream of regurgitated milk flowed from the baby's mouth. The white liquid splashed onto the floor, drips landing on Neil's leg.

Edward laughed.

"Now I'll have to feed him again," said Kylie, sounding defeated.

"He'll be all right, for a little while," said Susan, wanting to reassure her. "Babies always look like they've sicked up a whole feed, but they haven't really. Some will be left in his tummy. Why don't you let him have a rest, and feed him some more in a little while?"

Kylie delved into a large bag that rested by her feet, and passed Neil a cloth; Susan went to fetch a damp kitchen cloth, so she could wipe the carpet.

Noah was still crying, a nerve-jarring, high pitched sound that dominated the room.

"Let me have a try," said Dot, taking the baby from her grandson.

Noah screamed louder.

Susan finished cleaning the floor. She went to her mother. "My turn," she said, taking the baby.

Noah's face was purple, and he was bringing his knees up to his tummy, screaming. Susan recognised the signs of tummy-ache, and flipped him over, so his stomach was against the heel of her palm, pressing into where he hurt. She rubbed his back, feeling the ridges beneath his vest where his nappy started, the bones of his ribcage either side of his spine. As she rubbed his back, she rocked, a gentle rhythmical movement, to and fro. She could smell his uniquely baby smell, and feel the warmth of him seeping into her arm as his body moulded against her. Gradually his screaming subsided, and became a thin wail, then a quiet hiccup. His dark eyes scanned the room with a glazed expression, and he began to blink, very slowly, his eyes closing for longer and longer, until he was, quite suddenly, asleep.

"Gosh," said Edward, sounding impressed, "I didn't know you could do that Mum."

"She's hypnotised him," muttered Jack, "that's probably what she used to do to us."

Susan smiled at them, supremely content. "I have raised a few babies myself," she said, feeling smug. "There're some things you never forget."

Kylie was holding her plate, nibbling flapjacks, so Susan took the sleeping bundle over to where Aunty Elsie was sitting.

"Would you like a cuddle Aunty Elsie?" said Susan. "Actually, you're *Great, Great,* Aunty Elsie now."

"Oh, yes please," said Elsie, hurrying to put her cup on the side table, and smoothing the flowery skirt of her dress. She shuffled in the seat, sitting up very straight.

Neil moved nearer, looking concerned.

"Aunty Elsie held all of you, when you were small," said Susan, guessing his thoughts and giving him a look that told him he was being over-protective.

Very slowly, Susan moved her arms, folding one over the other, so that Noah was turned onto his back. He stirred, flinging out both his arms in the reflex common to new babies, snuffling back to sleep. Susan gently edged him nearer to Elsie, lowering him onto her lap, waiting for her to move an arm to support his neck before inching her own arms away.

The baby lay, breathing evenly, safe in the elderly woman's arms. Elsie looked down at him, and Susan noticed that flicker of something indefinable in her aunt's eyes – something that looked close to agony – clouded by a rush of tears that sparkled for a moment before Elsie blinked them away. Elsie took a breath, and smiled, her face settling into the same lines and expressions that Susan was used to seeing. She showed her long crooked teeth, the lines from her eyes reaching down to join those around her mouth as she smiled.

"How precious," breathed Elsie. "He is completely perfect."

Susan looked across the room, to where Tom was talking to Jack. She hoped they wouldn't start to argue – Jack was experimenting with some new ideas at Broom Hill Farm, and Tom wasn't very keen on new ideas.

"That maize is growing well Dad," she heard Jack say. "I reckon drilling at fifty-centimetre spacing will make quite a difference."

"What's all this?" asked Neil, going to join them – as if, thought Susan, he was keen to show that he was interested in things beyond his baby, though she knew that he had never really been interested in the farm, and she didn't feel his feigned interest now was very convincing.

"We're going to try having a maize maze, over at Broom Hill," Jack was explaining. "I heard that if you drill the seed closer, at fifty centimetres rather than seventy-five, then the new plants will compete for the light, and will grow taller much faster. So far, it seems to be working."

"I'm assuming a 'maize maze' is what it sounds like?" said Neil.

"Yep," said Jack, "there's a clue in the name. I cut pathways through the young plants – miles of them, because they twist and turn so much. As the plants get tall, it becomes a maze. As soon as the plants are about six foot, we'll open to the public, and charge an entry fee.

"It's already pretty tall," said Jack, sounding pleased. "You have to check the soil temperature, before you plant – make sure it's at least 10°C for a week before – I had to take readings at nine o'clock every morning; but I got it drilled in nice and early, pretty much dot-on 15th of April, which is the earliest they say you should drill."

Susan watched Jack's face while he spoke. His hair was beginning to recede at the front, and she wondered if he would one day be as bald as his father. He was standing as he spoke, and kept glancing back to where Elsie was holding the baby, as if drawn by a magnet, even his enthusiasm for the farm couldn't quite detract from the wonder of seeing his baby nephew. Neil was also regularly checking the baby, his eyes darting from Noah and back to Jack. He was half-standing, leaning back against Kylie's chair, looking relaxed. Susan thought he seemed older suddenly, as if fatherhood had aged him, made him mature.

Jack was still explaining his farming techniques: "I got a good lot of potash in before I drilled, and I deflated the tyres on my machines, because maize has lazy roots, you know – if it meets compacted soil, it won't push through, and you end up with stunted plants. Short plants would rather defeat the point of the maze." Jack laughed. "I wouldn't be able to charge much, if people could see over the top of the plants!"

Susan could see Neil was beginning to look around, as if wanting to escape. He had never wanted to be involved with the farm, and Jack, now he was in his stride, was obviously enthusiastic about sharing his new-found knowledge. "You have to drill maize slowly," he was saying, "otherwise the drilling fluctuates too much, and you don't get the right depth and spacing. Once the plants are up, you have to get rid of the weeds – there's a lot of nightshade and fat-hen on Broom Hill, so I gave them a good spraying, before they could get established."

"I hope you've renewed your national sprayer testing scheme certificate," Tom interjected. "Grandfather rights don't make you exempt anymore."

"Of course," said Jack, sounding, Susan thought, irritated with his father.

"I think it might be good," he said, turning back to Neil, "we need to find ways to make more money."

Jack lowered his voice, glancing across at Josie, who was still chatting to Kylie.

"If it works, I'm thinking we could do even more next year, maybe have a kiddie's playground, a petting barn, things like that. It depends how much red tape there is. At the moment we'll just have the maze, and a picnic area – I don't have to be hygiene inspected if people are eating their own food."

"Wouldn't fancy it myself," said Tom, and Susan could hear the disapproval in his voice. "All those strangers traipsing over the farm."

"Well, it'll only be open for August, maybe a couple of weekends in July and the last week – I need to find out when the schools are on holiday," said Jack. "We don't have to do it again if it doesn't work. I'm hoping the weather isn't as warm as last year, because an early harvest will mean it's only open for a couple of weeks. But last year was exceptional, wasn't it? Unlikely to be another scorcher this year…"

"You never can tell with the weather," said Tom. "That's why it's best to stick with what you know. And how much animal feed did you lose, cutting those pathways? Young plants won't ferment down for silage like maize left to dry out properly, so that's all wasted money. Doubt you'll get enough visitors to recoup what you've lost. But there you go, it's your and Josie's decision…"

Susan watched as Tom walked away, disapproval evident in the straight back and grumpy expression. She saw Neil grin at his brother, before turning to her.

"Ooh Mum," said Neil, as if suddenly remembering, "did you ever write the family tree? And I have a gift for you."

Susan stood up, frowning. "Well, I started," she said, "but I didn't get very far. It's in the kitchen drawer." She looked across at her mother, and asked, "Do you know any dates? And the proper names of people? I've been trying to write the family tree for Neil, but I'm not sure of people's maiden names."

"Let's have a look," said Dot, following Susan and Neil into the kitchen.

Susan found the piece of paper and put it on the table.

"Ah. You really didn't get very far did you?!" said Neil, looking at the few names scribbled down.

Dot took the paper and frowned. "Have you got a pencil?" she asked. She sat at the table, and began to add names, scribbling a line through the ones that Susan had written wrongly. "Aunty Minnie was really called Celeste," she mumbled, "and my mother's maiden name was

'Brown'...but I'm not sure of the year they got married..."
She passed the paper back to Neil. "That's all I can
remember," she said.

"Not many relatives on your side Mum," said Neil.

"There might be more cousins," said Dot, "if you go far
enough back. But we never kept in touch with my mother's
family – well, it was harder in those days, no email or texts
or anything, and postage was expensive and took forever,
so when people moved away, they tended to lose touch."
She placed the pencil back on the table.

"It's a shame," said Neil.

"Yes," said Susan, taking the paper from him and
staring at the names, "it is a shame. I'd really like to know."
She screwed up her eyes, trying to remember names that
she may have heard as a child, long since forgotten. "I don't
know, something about having a new baby in the family,
and realising how quickly time passes – all those distant
aunts and uncles don't feel quite so distant now. I'd quite
like to do it properly, do some research and look at old
documents and things. I think I'd find that rather
interesting."

Neil was smiling, looking smug.

"Well," he said, going to another of the large bags that
Kylie had brought with her, and abandoned in the kitchen.
"I have something for you that might help..." He pulled out
a white package and passed it to Susan. "I thought perhaps
you should join one of those online things," said Neil,
leaning back against the sink and folding his arms. "You
know – 'family-tree-dot-com' or whatever they're called.
Would you like to?" he asked, sounding enthusiastic. "I
sent off, as an early birthday present, if you'd like it? They
check your DNA, and show you who you're related to, and
you can research the family tree online, so you don't have
to go to registry offices and things, you can do all the
research from home.

"If you don't want to, I can use it myself. Kylie did one,
and I thought you might enjoy it too."

"Oh," said Susan, considering. She looked at the
package, reading the instructions on the back. "I've never
really thought about it. But yes, I think I would probably

enjoy that. It would be like detective work, looking for old documents and things. Yes, yes, I think I would like it. Thank you, that's a lovely thought.

"Thank you," said Susan again, going to kiss his cheek. "Would you like more tea?"

"Yes, please," said Neil, "and perhaps I'll rescue Aunty Elsie," he added, as a rather angry baby began to yell in the parlour.

Chapter Six

By the middle of July, the barley was mostly golden, only the barley growing under the shade of the trees still had a tinge of green. It had dried out from the top down, so golden heads stood on green stalks for a while. After a week of sunshine, it smelt warm and malty, rattling when blown by the breeze, the scratchy seed heads rubbing against each other.

In the farm kitchen, Susan turned on her laptop, and checked her emails. There was another one from the family tree website – they seemed to contact her fairly regularly – not that they told her anything other than that her DNA was being processed and the results should arrive in a couple of weeks. After Neil had given her the gift, she had sat in her bedroom, spitting into the slim vial, then followed the instructions on the pack and posted it in the small white box provided. She wasn't expecting the results to be terribly interesting, as she knew that her family had originated from Scotland and had lived in England for many generations. Susan frowned, wishing the results were already available. She wasn't hatching any birds this year, as she'd managed to avoid foxes and diseases this year, so the flocks were still large enough.

"But," she thought, "you never know on a farm when something will happen and absorb all your time. If one of the cows falls sick or gets injured, I might find I have no time for playing detective and researching my ancestors. I'd like to be doing it now, really, while I seem to have some time."

The website also promised to link her to people who shared her DNA – though as her family was relatively small, she suspected that only very distant cousins would be linked, and she wasn't terribly interested in finding them, even though Tom had suggested that maybe one of them might be a millionaire, and perhaps she could inherit some money.

"Money would be nice," thought Susan, flicking onto a site where she could order animal feed. She typed her credit card number and checked the amount. "I wish we could help Jack and Josie a bit," she thought. But as she looked at the price for protein pellets to supplement the silage and grass the cows would eat, paying out several thousands of pounds for a few weeks' worth of feed, she knew that offering financial help to anyone else was beyond them.

Beside her, Molly barked, making her jump. A car had drawn into the yard, and Susan got up to look out of the window. Her mother and Aunty Elsie were climbing from the small white Ford.

"Cooey! It's only us," said Dot, walking into the kitchen and kissing her daughter. "We're off to Broom Hill, to help Jack."

"Yes," said Aunty Elsie, sounding excited, "we can't stop, we're workers today."

Susan smiled back at her mother and aunt, pleased to see them so happy. They both wore trousers and tee-shirts with hand-knitted jumpers. Aunty Elsie was wearing a large sunhat, and Dot had a baseball cap balanced precariously on the back of her head. Their faces were dominated by huge grins, their eyes sparkling. Susan realised that helping Jack, feeling useful, was a rare treat for them.

"Jack asked us last week," said Elsie, "do you remember us telling you? He wants to open his maize maze, and him and Josie are busy, so he asked us to help. He needs someone to take the money, when people come to visit the maze."

"*IF* people come," said Dot, though she sounded as excited as her sister. "I said I didn't mind, as long as there were chairs – we can't stand up all morning, not at our age."

"And toilets," said Elsie.

"Oh," said Susan, frowning. "Will people have to go to the house if they need the toilet? I can't imagine Josie's mother will like that..." She thought of Claire, and her interior design business, which had resulted in a carefully manicured house. The last time she had visited Broom Hill, she had felt strangely uncomfortable amongst all the cleverly designed features, and she really could not imagine a bunch of mothers marching their weak-bladdered children across that white tiled hallway to use the flower-strewn washroom.

"No," said Elsie, shaking her head so violently that she had to put up a hand to secure her hat. It slipped to one side, giving her a rather lopsided appearance. "Jack has arranged for there to be Portaloos – you know, those temporary toilets. Like camping toilets, I suppose. He needed to get two, because someone told him that he has to provide disabled ones as well as normal ones. But men and women can use the same one." She frowned. "I shall use the disabled one," she announced. "I expect there will be more room in there."

"Let's hope we don't get any disabled visitors then," muttered Dot, "because their toilet is likely to be fully occupied..."

Elsie ignored her. "We've popped in because we forgot milk, for our tea," she said to Susan. "Could we steal some of yours? We've got a picnic for lunch time, so I hope it doesn't rain."

"Yes, of course," said Susan, moving to the fridge. She poured some milk into a plastic cup and pulled open the drawer where she kept all the lids. She stared at the lids, all different colours and sizes, the older ones beginning to smell of old plastic, the new ones still shiny. "Why can you never find the lid you're looking for?" she muttered, stirring them as she looked.

"For the same reason socks never come out of the wash in pairs," said Dot.

Susan found the lid and snapped it onto the beaker of milk, before passing it to Elsie.

"Thank you dear," said Elsie, "now we can have a nice cup of tea."

"As well as a lot of rubbish," said Dot. She turned to Susan. "Elsie's diet has got very bad you know," she said. "Tell her she needs to eat some vegetables, and less sugar and salt. She'll get fat. She never walks you know, just sits and reads silly novels all day."

"I like reading," said Elsie.

"I've a good mind to send you into that maze," said Dot. "You'd be sure to get lost, that'd be good exercise for you."

Elsie raised her eyes to the ceiling, and shook her head. "Shall we go?" she said, catching her hat as it fell off. She jammed the hat back over her grey curls, and moved to the door.

Susan thought that Elsie had become rather accustomed to her sister's complaints, and was unlikely to change. "Does it really matter at their age anyway?" she thought. "A little bit of extra weight is hardly going to make any difference, not now." She waved goodbye, as the two women went back to their car.

***

At Broom Hill Farm, Jack was waiting. He watched as his aunt and grandmother parked the car against the stone wall. It slowed to almost a stop, then bounced back as the bumper made contact with the wall. He watched his grandmother reverse slightly, then, even slower, repeat the same action, edging forwards then bouncing back from the wall. He heard the grate of the handbrake being applied, and the engine died. Both women opened their doors and smiled up at him. Jack guessed that this was perhaps the normal method for parking.

"Hello Jack, we're all ready," called Aunty Elsie, scurrying across the yard to where the Portaloos stood. She stood for a moment, as if deciding which one to enter, then disappeared behind the grey door.

Jack looked around, hoping he had planned everything properly. When customers arrived – he sorely hoped there would be customers – they could park against the wall. He had set up a table and chairs to one side, with a large sign saying the maze cost £3 for children, and £5 for adults. He and Josie had argued about the price for hours, and eventually had agreed they would begin with these prices, but adjust them if necessary. The entrance to the maze was through a wooden gate, and another sign hung there, painted yellow with red writing, telling visitors they must keep to the pathways, and dogs were not allowed, and they were welcome to use the small paddock for picnics. In the paddock, opposite the maize field, there were four picnic tables. Jack very much hoped he would recoup the price of the wood he had bought to make them.

"Right," said Dot, "where do you want us?"

Jack nodded towards the table. "If you sit there," he said, "then you'll be able to see everyone when they arrive."

Dot carried two large bags and put them under the table, then sat down. Jack showed her the tin where they were to put the money, and said he would come regularly throughout the morning to empty it, so they would never have too much, and he could give them more change if they needed it.

"I'm not sure whether people will come," he admitted. "But I've advertised it around Marksbridge and Jameston, and put a notice in the Parish magazine, and put posters up in shops and pubs." He sat down next to his grandmother, stretching his legs straight out and crossing his ankles. "I'm only a few minutes away, if you need me. And I'll keep coming back to check on you, and you can phone if there's a problem – you did remember to bring your phone, didn't you?"

Dot delved into one of the bags, and put her mobile phone on the table.

"Do you want to have a little practise?" said Jack, "Just to check you know my number?"

Dot sighed, picked up the phone and found Jack's number in her contacts, then depressed the call button.

"I do know how to use it," she said, sounding defensive. "I might need it one day, if that man should come back..."

Jack looked at her, surprised. "What man?"

"I want to talk to you later," Dot said, her voice determined, as if she had decided something.

Jack nodded and glanced at the time. "Okay, we can chat later," he said, keen to explain everything before he went to join Josie.

There was a basket of whistles on the table, and a stack of papers, weighed down by a large stone.

"Give every family a whistle," said Jack, "and tell them to blow it if they get into trouble. Then we can go in and rescue them. But give it to an adult, because the kids will just blow it for no reason, and we'll waste time going to get them when we don't need to.

"And those are maps," he said, pointing to the papers. "Just give one to each party. They shouldn't need them, but you know...just in case."

Dot reached out and took a map. It was hand-drawn, and showed various markers along the route, showing when to turn right or left inside the maze. She placed it back under the stone, and looked up as the door to the Portaloo banged shut behind Elsie.

"There's not much room in there," called Elsie, walking towards them. Her hat was in her hand, and she was smiling.

Jack stood as Elsie approached, and she took her place at the table. He went over their instructions once more, thanked them both for helping, then left them.

"I do hope they'll be okay," he thought, climbing into the tractor. He pulled out his phone, and used the app to see where Josie was. He could see the small circle that represented her phone on the map, where she was waiting with the heifers. He glanced once more towards his grandmother and great-aunt as he started the engine.

"It's quite a responsibility for them," he thought. Then reminding himself that he would be checking with them frequently, he drove to the cowshed.

***

Back at Netherley Farm, Susan was still working at the computer, when Molly barked again, and came to find her. The dog whirled around the kitchen, running from Susan to the door and back again. Her black and white fur was a blur, as she turned in circles, letting Susan know that she needed to get up and answer the door. The dog ran to the door, then back to the table, did a loop of the room, returned to the door, then back to Susan.

"Stop it!" said Susan, sighing. They needed collies, as reliable workers, but they had a very stressy gene, which she sometimes found irritating.

The dog's barks changed from warning to happy, and the turning became more of a wiggle of joy than an instruction to Susan. Susan looked up as Edward poked his head round the door. She smiled, thinking that she hadn't yet managed to order the animal feed this morning.

"Hi Mum," said Edward, coming into the kitchen.

Susan stood to greet him and offered him tea. She wondered why he had come – Edward didn't usually visit the farm unannounced. She looked at him, and noticed grey shadows under his eyes.

"Everything okay?" she asked, putting tea bags into two mugs.

"Not really," said Edward. "Emily and I have split up."

"Oh," said Susan, not sure what else to say. She had never felt that Edward was particularly committed to Emily, or any of his girlfriends when she thought about it. She was surprised he looked so sad.

"Yeah," said Edward, sitting in Susan's chair and stroking Molly's head when she rested it on his knee. "It didn't work out after all – seems she was seeing someone else, and decided that he was 'the one' – and that I wasn't. So she gave me my marching orders. Can I stay here for a few days? Just 'til I've sorted somewhere else? It'll only be for a couple of nights, I've already got somewhere lined up with a friend in Clapham."

"Goodness," said Susan, pouring boiling water into the mugs and going to the fridge for milk. Inside, her thoughts were as much a whirl as Molly had been. She had thought Edward had left home for good, it would be strange having him back here, even temporarily.

"Yeah," said Edward, staring out of the window. "I really..." he paused, as if choosing words suitable for his mother, "...mucked up, didn't I?"

"I wasn't sure how much you really liked Emily," said Susan, passing him a mug of tea.

"No," said Edward, "nor did I. Not until she gave me my marching orders..."

His voice broke, and he turned sharply away.

Susan thought she glimpsed moisture in his eye before he turned, and something clenched her heart. It was rare for Edward to show feelings, he was a master of disguising his emotions, playing the clown, appearing to not care. Susan detected something vulnerable in him, and wasn't sure how to react. He was a man, but he was also her son. She put out a hand, and covered his.

"I am sorry," she said. "And yes, of course you can stay here. For as long as you need to."

"Thanks Mum. It'll only be a couple of days," he said, moving his hand from under hers. "I asked for some leave from work, to sort everything and move my stuff. I thought I needed some time, you know, to get used to the idea and everything..." His voice tailed away again.

He drank his tea, and they sat in silence for a while. Susan didn't like to ask too many questions, to probe into his private life. He was too old for that, too far removed from the little boy who had climbed onto her lap with scratched knees and whispered jokes into her ear.

Susan sipped her tea, thinking that Edward had always hidden his feelings; he'd always been more angry than upset when he was small and a hurt had caused him to cry. She remembered the time when he fell from the apple tree in the orchard, breaking his wrist – how when she found him, a ten-year-old boy in pain, it had been anger rather than tears that had flowed from him. Neil had run to the house to fetch her, and she had found Edward still in the orchard, kicking the tree and swearing, his arm limp by his side, tears of fury running down his cheeks. As he grew older, he had always played the fool rather than admit something was difficult; he would opt out rather than risk failure. Edward was the son who would cry into his pillow not onto her shoulder, would go into the barn and break things when life was difficult, would never ask for help.

"How do I help him now?" wondered Susan, watching as Edward stood and walked, restless, across the kitchen. She felt, as she often did, that parenting adults was so much more difficult than parenting children. More sleep, but less certainty, she thought.

"Where's Jack?" asked Edward, putting his empty cup in the sink.

"Over at Broom Hill," said Susan. "They've opened his 'maize maze' and Gran and Elsie have gone over to help. I think they were quite excited to be involved."

Edward forced a smile, obviously pleased by the diversion. "That sounds like a recipe for disaster," he said. "I think I'll go over there, see how they're getting on."

Susan frowned. "Well, I'm sure they'll be pleased to see you," she said, "but don't do anything...funny...will you? This matters to Jack, he needs to try and make it pay. And he's had enough negative feedback from your father already. You won't joke about it, will you? Don't do anything that will embarrass him?"

"Hey, Mum, trust me," said Edward, as he left.

**

Josie was waiting with the heifers when Jack arrived. They had decided to breed all the full-grown heifers, in the hope of starting a dairy herd the following year. It was a risk, because the buildings were still in a state of near-ruin, and new ventures were always a risk.

"But we need to do *something*," Josie had said, "and at least this is a plan. At least, if it fails, I'll know I tried everything I could to save the farm."

They had made a plan, and created a schedule of work. Together, they were repairing the disused sheds, replacing broken equipment, improving the facilities. Josie had contacted a dairy farm that was closing, and had managed to negotiate a good price for some of the machines – those that were beyond repair in Broom Hill's dilapidated milking shed. She had borrowed some money from the bank, which they both found scary, but decided was worth the risk.

"It has to be in your name," Jack had explained, "because my credit rating is shot to pieces."

Josie had nodded, not asking for details.

"Which was kind of her," thought Jack, driving along the lane, "but also makes me wonder whether she sees me as a permanent fixture..." He frowned, glaring at the young herd that pushed their faces over the hedge top to watch him pass. Jack told himself that it was silly to feel insecure, that he had no reason to worry about Josie absorbing all his time and energy whilst he had absolutely no claim to the farm.

"If the relationship ends, if she dumps me, then I've wasted an awful lot of time," he thought. "But I can't think like that, I mustn't keep assessing how much I am giving, and evaluating the risks. Either I trust that this relationship is permanent, or I don't. And I do," Jack told himself, parking the tractor and climbing down.

"I do." He said again, ignoring that voice, which refused to be silent, the voice that whispered inside that Josie had never actually said those words. Josie had not, actually, ever agreed to anything permanent, because he had never asked her.

"But it's too soon," thought Jack, walking towards the barn. "I can't exactly propose marriage or anything when we've been together less than a year, can I? She'd probably run a mile, think I was off my head, or something.

"No," he decided. "Let's just see how things turn out. It's sure to be fine. I'm overthinking this." He saw Josie, waiting, and grinned at her. She was wearing her normal attire of dirty green overalls and muddy wellies. There was hay in her hair, and a dirty smudge on one cheek.

Josie was standing next to the crush, where the cows stood when they needed to be kept still. Jack always thought it sounded like a torture device, but the cows seemed quite happy to go into it, and it held them securely while they were being clipped or examined. He had heard – he couldn't remember where – that someone had used the same idea with children who were very autistic, and found that they felt secure when firmly held, in a similar way to cattle.

Jack removed some vials of semen from where they were stored in liquid nitrogen, and placed them in his back pocket, so they could start to warm up a little. He looked around the shed while he waited for Josie to direct the first heifer into the crush.

They had started to rebuild some of the barriers in the shed, and the smell of freshly planed wood mingled with the sweet smell of hay. The cowshed was large, and was now divided into three sections. He glanced across, to where they would keep their 'wet cows'. They had decided to keep them on sand, and they were building small booths – almost like cells, he thought – where the cows could lie down. Each bedding area, or cell, would have sand to lie on, which would be comfortable for the cows and easily (and cheaply) replaced when it was dirty. They would avoid using bedding with gypsum, as this could cause a build-up of slurry gas. The cows would lie with their rears overhanging a central gulley, ensuring that all their excrement was expelled into this ditch, and their udders would remain clean and dry.

"They're not really like cells," thought Jack, as he looked at the few small spaces they had already completed, "because they can stand up, and walk out of them, whenever they want to. They're more like beds in a dormitory...or seating on an aeroplane."

Most of the section was still unbuilt, with wood stacked in the corner, waiting for Jack to continue. He felt the tension in his stomach when he looked at it, knowing that by inseminating the heifers today, he was setting himself a time-limit.

"It'll be fine," he told himself, "we'll be ready long before the heifers are ready to be milked, it's months and months away yet..."

The central gulley would be swept straight into their slurry pit. They were using the old slurry pit, though they knew it would need to be replaced in time, when the lining gave way. Jack shivered, not liking to think about the slurry pit.

His father had told the four boys gruesome stories of farmers dying in the slurry pit, and Jack had often had nightmares. He understood, now he was an adult, how important it was for children to understand the dangers, and that for his parents, brutal stories about people being overcome with fumes and sinking into the evil slurry was essential. Although now Jack could name the toxic concoction of gases – ammonia, carbon monoxide, hydrogen sulphide – as a child they were nameless evil clouds, green and yellow and purple, that swirled malevolently above the earth, waiting to drag children down into a pit of death. In his dreams, if anyone walked too near the slurry pit, the gases would seep towards them, engulfing them, until they fell unconscious; before dragging them into the depths of the slurry, never to be seen again.

Looking now, at that central gulley, Jack shivered, remembering his old fears. Then he looked up as Josie arrived with the first heifer, and the memory of old nightmares dispersed as easily as those evil gases. He helped her to secure the cow into the crush.

"For the rest of the world," he said, pulling a capsule from his back pocket, "*A.I.* means '*artificial intelligence.*' But from now on," he said, gently feeling his way into the heifer with the capsule of seamen, "I will only ever be able to associate it with artificial insemination."

Josie looked up from where she was recording the number from the heifer's ear-tag and matching it with the number on the vial. She grinned at him.

"Farmers have different brains to other people," she said.

"Do you miss the tech stuff?" she asked, setting the heifer free and watching as it lurched away, into the middle section of the barn.

"Not really," said Jack, thinking of his life before he moved back to his parents' farm. He watched the heifer as she went to the food trough and started to pull mouthfuls of hay between her teeth, the grey tongue long and wet.

The heifer was now in the section of the barn where they would eventually be keeping their 'dry cows' – those who were pregnant, and unable to be milked. When they knew for sure that the insemination had taken, and they were pregnant, they would be let out into the fields. Jack and Josie had decided to use one of the far fields, where few dog-walkers went, as the best place for the heifers to live. They would hopefully – and there was, thought Jack, a lot they were being 'hopeful' about – avoid the diseases carried by dog-mess that caused cows to miscarry. They would *hopefully* carry the calves to term, and start a whole new dairy herd.

The third section of the barn would be where they kept the heifers while they were waiting to calf. Heifers and cows, Jack corrected himself, because after an animal had managed to birth two calves, it would be called a 'cow.'

"Did you sort the contract with that dairy?" asked Josie, arriving with the next heifer.

"Yep," said Jack, guiding the cow into place. "It seems daft that we'll be sending the milk all the way to Southampton, but they were offering the best contract. Mind you," he said, pulling another vial from his back pocket, and checking the temperature against his wrist, "the dairy will only give us 27p a litre. If," he continued, from the depths of the heifer's bottom, "we go organic, we can get more." He gently extracted his arm, and patted the heifer's rump. "Good girl," he said, moving backwards so Josie could release the cow.

"We could get as much as 40p a litre," said Jack, "if we get organic status."

"But that takes two years?" said Josie.

"Yes," said Jack. "Two years of paying out for organic protein pellets, and only using organic sprays on the crops. And we'll only be able to charge non-organic prices during those two years, so I can't see how we can manage it."

"How much more would the organic pellets be?" asked Josie, entering the next number on her record.

"For 90 cows, for one month, I reckon we'd pay £14,000. Or thereabouts," said Jack.

"I'd better marry a millionaire then," said Josie over her shoulder, as she set off to collect the next heifer.

***

Back at Netherley Farm, Susan was frowning at the computer.

"That cannot be right," she thought, staring at the screen. "They must've made a mistake…"

The animal feed had finally been ordered, and Susan had switched once more to the family tree website. She read that her results were available, and had clicked to see what her DNA revealed – more from curiosity than anything, as she was certain that she knew the result. The company had given her a breakdown of her ethnic roots, showing on a map where her ancestors had originated from, and telling her which percentage of her DNA came from various places. It also connected her to other members of the site who shared parts of her DNA.

Susan stared at the long list of names, which were grouped according to relationship. There were, she saw, lots of very distant cousins. But she ignored those, and was staring at the name at the top of the screen: William Evans.

William Evans was listed as a first cousin.

"But I don't have any first cousins," thought Susan, clicking through the site to find the definition, thinking that perhaps 'first cousin' meant something other than she thought it did. But no, the definition was clear. 'First cousin,' as defined by the website, meant the child of one of her parents' siblings. They both shared the same grandparents. However, Susan knew for a fact that none of her parents' siblings – well, none of her mother's siblings as her father was an only child – had ever had children. Neither Uncle George nor Aunty Elsie had even married.

Susan pushed back her chair, and folded her arms, considering possibilities. Perhaps there had been another child, one who had never been acknowledged. Maybe one of her grandparents had produced an illegitimate child, and never told the rest of the family. There were no ages on the website, this 'cousin,' this William Evans, might be a lot older than Susan, might be the son of a child born before either of her grandparents were married. If her grandparents, who Susan dimly remembered as shadowy figures in her childhood, if they had produced a child before they were married, they may well have given the child away. People in those days wouldn't have advertised the fact, and the child – a brother or sister to one of Susan's parents – may have grown up never knowing they were adopted. They had now produced a child of their own, this William, who was genetically Susan's cousin. It was possible.

"Or," thought Susan, moving to shut down the computer, "perhaps the website is wrong. Maybe they muddled up my DNA with someone else's. I guess I'll never know." She closed the computer and went to put it back in the parlour before returning to the kitchen. If Edward was going to stay for a few days, she had better check she had enough food for dinner.

***

When Jack returned to the maize maze, he found his grandmother looking worried, Aunty Elsie was in the Portaloo, and Edward was leaning against the table.

"Hello," said Jack, surprised. "I didn't realise news of the exciting new maize maze had reached the far suburbs of London!"

Edward grinned back at him, the breeze ruffling his blond hair, the too-long fringe covering one eye. He pushed his hair back with a hand, and propelled himself forwards from the table.

"Nope, unexpected treat for you," he said, adding: "Lucky I came though, Gran's got bit of a disaster brewing."

There was a crash, and Elsie emerged from the Portaloo, waving her hands to dry them.

"We need more toilet paper in there," she said to Jack.

"Never mind toilet paper," said Dot. "Jack, we've got a problem."

"But only a little one," said Elsie, as if keen to show that they had, mostly coped very well with the morning. "We've had lots of visitors, look." She passed him the money box, and Jack took it, surprised by the weight.

Most of the weight was due to a large rock, which almost filled the space.

"The stone is to stop the notes blowing away, when we open it," explained Elsie.

Jack was pleased to see that below the stone, were several notes – some of them twenties – and a handful of change.

"We've been very busy," said Elsie, beaming at him. "We've had lots of families, haven't we Dot?"

"A few," agreed his grandmother, frowning. "But that's not the problem. The problem," she said, looking at Jack sternly, "is the people we've lost."

"Lost?" said Jack, confused. The maze wasn't really big enough to lose people in, and besides, he had provided maps. "Did you give everyone a map?"

"Yes, of course," said his grandmother, sounding cross. "We did everything you told us to. And for everyone else it was fine..."

"Apart from the fat family," said Elsie.

"You shouldn't call them fat," said Dot, turning to her sister. "Though they were," she admitted to Jack, "and very badly behaved."

"They peed," whispered Elsie, looking shocked, "against the maize."

"Yes," said Dot, her voice full of disapproval. "We saw them, two little boys—"

"Two fat little boys," said Elsie, as if that made a difference, "wearing vests, and shorts and those trainer-shoes that flash when they walk..."

"The clothes don't matter either," said Dot. "But they peed, and it was right near the entrance, so they could have used the Portaloos. But their mother, I heard her, they said they needed to wee, and she said – in a very loud voice – 'Oh don't use those, they'll be dirty, just pee in the maze, no one will see you'!"

"But we did!" said Elsie, sounding shocked.

Jack looked at his aunt and grandmother. Both women's eyes were sparkling, their grey hair wild around their faces as the wind tugged at it, their faces animated. He smiled.

"Did you say anything?" he asked.

"Of course," said Dot, sounding indignant. "I shouted at them, and told them they weren't to use the maze as a toilet. But they just laughed at me, and ran back to their parents."

"And we didn't like to say anything to the parents," explained Elsie, "in case they shouted at us. They looked the sort."

"But that's not the problem," said Dot, reminding Jack, "the problem is the people we've lost."

"Lost?" said Jack again.

"Yeah," said Edward from where he was leaning against the fence post, "Gran was just telling me. A couple went into the maze at 12 o'clock, and they haven't come out yet."

Jack glanced at his watch. It was almost 1:55. He frowned, thinking that the maze would, at most, take people half an hour to negotiate. He looked towards the maze. The tall stalks of maize rustled in the breeze, the leaves beginning to dry, the cobs nestling in their paper-like sheaves, brown wisps of hair-like strands tangled at each end. From his position next to the table, he could see the entrance, the flattened soil where people had walked, the pathway disappearing behind a wall of corn as it turned a corner.

"Two people," said Elsie, trying to be helpful, "a man with a bald head, and a woman wearing very high heels.

"I worried about those heels," she added, shaking her head. "I told you, Dot, didn't I?"

"Yes," said Dot. "They weren't very suitable shoes for a field. Perhaps she's twisted her ankle and they're waiting for help."

"But they had a whistle?" said Jack.

Both women nodded. "Everyone had a whistle and a map. We were careful," said Dot.

"I did that," Elsie told him. "I gave out the equipment while Dot took the money."

They all stood still for a moment, looking towards the tall maize, listening for the sound of a whistle. But all they heard was the wind, rattling the leaves, and crows wheeling in the distance, and a car, as it sped along the lane.

"Could they have come out without you seeing?" Jack asked, thinking that perhaps both women had used the Portaloos at the same time.

Dot was shaking her head. "No," she said, sounding definite. "We were very careful about that, weren't we

Elsie? If I needed the ladies' room, I waited until Elsie was here, and she waited for me. We didn't want to miss any customers. And they couldn't have got past us, not while we were sitting here, we'd have noticed. Besides, their car is still here." Dot pointed to a shiny blue sports car, parked next to the wall, near the lane so it hadn't needed to drive across the dried ruts of mud.

"Nice car," said Edward.

"They must be around somewhere then," said Jack. "I wonder if they decided to break through the walls, take their own route out.

"I hope not," he said, more to himself than the others, "they'll have caused some damage."

"Would it be possible?" said Edward, looking at the thick stalks, growing so closely together that they looked almost like a solid barrier. "Could they have snapped a new path to the edge? Or uprooted some of the maize?"

Jack shook his head. "They couldn't have uprooted it," he said, "the roots go as deep as the plant is high. But they might have snapped some, if they were strong enough and were prepared to risk a few cuts and bruises." He sighed. "I suppose I'd better walk the perimeter, look for signs of breakage."

"Wait," said Edward, "I've got an idea. I've got my drone, in the boot of my car. We can use that, send it over the maze, see where they are." He lifted his head, his face to the sky. "Yep," he said, "I don't think it's too windy."

"Why have you got your drone?" asked Jack.

"Got lots of stuff," said Edward, walking towards his car. "I'm moving back for a bit – keep you and Ben company."

Edward turned away before Jack could ask anything more. He opened his boot, and pulled out a large box, which he carried to the table.

"What's a drone?" asked Elsie, looking excited. "It sounds like something from outer space!"

"It's like a tiny aeroplane," Edward said, lifting the drone from the box and turning it on.

The two elderly women leant over, staring at the drone. Two green lights, like eyes, stared back at them.

"It looks like an alien, with television buttons on top," said Elsie.

Edward grinned. "It does look a bit like a tv-remote," he agreed. "It's much lighter though."

The drone was fairly small, much smaller than the box that kept it secure. It had tiny propellers, with plastic guards at each corner to protect them. Edward attached a small cylindrical object to the top. "That's the camera," he said. He put the drone on the table. Elsie reached out her hand.

"Don't touch it," said Edward, "it's more fragile than it looks."

He reached into his pocket and pulled out his phone, then shook his head.

"Battery's dead," he said to Jack. "Have you got the mobile with you that we used before?"

Jack nodded. "Edward brought the drone to the farm," he explained to his grandmother, "and we were using it in the yard. I downloaded the app, so I could use it with my phone." Jack was staring at his phone while he spoke, using the app to connect with the drone. He looked up.

"All set," he said.

"Edward lifted the drone and held it on the flat of his hand. Jack used his phone to turn on the tiny propellers, and it began to whir, a high-pitched fizzing noise, sounding like a grass strimmer. Rocking from side to side, the drone rose from Edward's hand, hovered for a moment, then drifted towards the maze.

Jack used his phone to guide the drone over the maize. He could see, on the screen of his phone, everything the eye of the camera picked up. He saw the tops of leaves, the pathways below, as he sent the drone across the field.

"I think I'll record this," he said, "in case there's trouble. Then I'll have evidence, for the insurance or whatever."

The drone was crossing the field. Every so often the breeze caught it, and it drifted away from where Jack was directing it, but mostly it stayed on course. He was following the route of the pathways, checking for damage, searching for people.

Elsie and Dot were standing next to him, straining to see the screen. Edward was behind him, looking over Jack's shoulder, offering the occasional advice when the wind pushed the drone to the wrong place.

"Right a bit more, hover, yes, go forward..."

There was a flash of something in the screen, and Jack paused the drone.

"What was that?" said Dot, sounding excited, clutching at his arm. "I saw something."

"Try not to jiggle," said Jack, moving the drone back on course. He could feel his family around him, almost holding their breath, waiting to see what would appear on the screen.

Concentrating, Jack moved the drone in a circle, hovering over the area where the image had flashed onto the screen.

"I can see someone," said Elsie, "is it them? There's a face. Oh...oh! Goodness!"

Jack laughed, as both elderly women stepped away from him, shocked.

"Should've guessed really," said Edward, laughing.

"So not what I was hoping people would do in there..." mumbled Jack, shaking his head.

Jack directed the drone back to where they were, and Edward reached up to take it. He turned it off and placed it back in the box.

Elsie was sitting at the table, shaking her head, her eyes wide.

"Goodness," she was saying, over and over again. "Goodness!".

Dot was chuckling.

"So now what do I do?" asked Jack, exasperated. "Could the drone throw a bucket of cold water over them?"

Edward grinned. "Not strong enough for that," he said. "I guess you'll have to just wait until they come out."

"And then throw a bucket of cold water over them?" asked Elsie, sounding hopeful.

"Not much point in that," said Jack, shaking his head. He watched as Edward took the drone back to his car, wondering why he had come to visit. Perhaps his work wasn't going as well as he'd hoped – or maybe he just needed a break. You never really knew with Ed.

Edward slammed the boot of his car and looked at Jack. "Where's Josie?" he said, "I thought I might pop over and say hello on my way back to the farm."

Something inside of Jack contracted, but he couldn't quite define what the feeling was – a sort of sinking of his stomach, a squeezing of his heart. He shook his head, telling himself he was being silly. Josie's crush on Ed had finished ages ago, and Ed was with Emily; he was just being friendly, meeting up with an old friend.

Jack used his phone to see where Josie was, the tiny dot that represented her position flashing onto the map.

"Over by the old milking sheds," said Jack. "You can tell her I'll see her after dinner, I'm staying here now, until those lovers emerge, and then it'll be time to go home. I've got some stuff to do for Dad. I'll see you at dinner?"

Edward was already getting into his car. He waved an arm through the window, and Jack watched as his brother drove away.

"Now," said Dot, leaning close and laying a wrinkled hand on Jack's arm, as if to compel him to give her his attention, to take her words seriously. "I want to ask your advice, about a man. I think I've got a stalker..."

Jack turned to his grandmother, and forced himself to listen.

Chapter Seven

By the time Jack arrived back at home, Susan was putting the dinner on the table. She looked tired, and he washed his hands and went to join her as she pulled a chicken from the oven. He took a knife, and began to carve it into chunks. Ben was watching him.

"Not exactly thin slices," said Ben, as a fat lump of meat was prised from the carcass.

"No point," said Jack, "it all gets chewed up anyway."

"I'm just glad someone is helping," said Susan, as if making a point.

Ben looked at Edward, who raised his eyebrows.

"We've been invited to Noah's christening," said Tom, as though wanting to change the subject before Susan could tell them that she didn't intend to start cooking for four other adults every day, and if her sons wished to stay at the farm for the time-being, that was fine, but expecting meals to appear without helping to prepare them, was not.

Jack paused from hacking the chicken into pieces, and looked across the kitchen at the card his father was holding up. He could see a photograph of Noah, and white words inviting them to attend the christening, which was in November. Across the top was written: *Dad, Mum, Ben, Jack* in black pen, and Jack recognised his brother's scrawled writing.

"You get one too Ed?" he asked, turning to his brother.

"Assume mine's at—" Edward paused. "At Emily's flat," he said. "Guess she'll post it on, if she's in the mood..." he added.

Jack nodded, thinking that the break-up, which his mother had told him about when he'd arrived home, seemed to have happened very suddenly. He had the impression that there had been time for Edward to collect his few possessions and leave – there had been no time to think about forwarding mail or changing his address details. Almost as if Edward had not been warned, as if the break-up was unexpected.

"Which is kinda scary," thought Jack, pulling the last of the meat from the bone and carrying the plate of warm chicken to the table. "It shows that you never know what's coming, and even people you rely on, people you love, might prove fickle when it comes to the crunch."

He sat at the table, thinking of Josie, with her tangled hair and ready grin, remembering the feel of her when he held her, the way that she gazed at him – her grey eyes intent with concentration – when they discussed the farm. He considered how he would feel if Josie left him, told him that the relationship was over. It made him feel cold inside, and a little bit frightened.

"Potatoes?" said Susan, breaking into Jack's thoughts.

Jack nodded, and began to fill his plate. There was a bowl of roast potatoes, and one of carrots. A Pyrex dish held stuffing – crusty around the top where it had been cooked for too long; another dish held peas. There was gravy, with lumps of fat floating in it, made in the meat tin when the chicken was removed, the stock from the vegetables used to thin it. Jack wished there were sausages, but there was only chicken. He spooned peas onto his plate and passed the bowl to Ben. Around him, his family were laughing and eating, and discussing the christening.

"Isn't it a bit late?" said Ben, his mouth full of meat while he added more peas to his plate. "I mean, don't you usually have a baby christened when it's tiny? Noah's going to be really old by November."

"I don't think it matters," said Susan, getting up to refill the jug of gravy from the tin on the hob. "I think Neil and Kylie have been arguing about it actually," she said over her shoulder, "because Neil didn't want to have a christening at all, seeing as they don't attend an Anglican church; but Kylie's mother got very upset, and said they should do it for the baby, not for themselves. In the end, I think they decided to compromise. Neil said they've agreed with the vicar to say different words, or something, but it's still being called a christening."

"What's to disagree with?" asked Edward. "I'll be there, anyway, giving my support to the Compton Clan. And at that debate," he said, turning to Ben.

"Isn't your church having their 'let's debate Ben' session soon?" Edward reached across the table for the jug of gravy.

"It isn't about Ben," said Tom, and Jack saw his father glance at Susan. "But it would be nice if you boys were all there, to lend support to the family. Make people less likely to wander from the point, as it were..."

Jack noticed that his mother had stopped eating, her face strained. She was cutting a potato into tiny pieces, and using her fork to mash it into the peas, almost as if her thoughts and actions had become momentarily disconnected.

"I'm really dreading it," said Susan, her voice quiet. "I wish they weren't holding the debate, and they're making such a big thing of it, advertising in town and everything. I'm dreading it."

"Don't worry Mum," said Edward, tipping extra gravy over his meal. "We'll all be there."

Jack glanced at his brother. He thought Edward looked thinner, and he was pale. Jack wondered if perhaps Edward hadn't been sleeping very well lately. "I wonder if he knew," Jack thought, "if inside he kind of knew that it wasn't working out with Emily, but he was ignoring it." As he looked at his brother, Jack felt that Edward was trying a little too hard to be part of the conversation, to be part of what everyone else was doing. As if reassuring himself that he belonged here, even if he didn't belong with Emily any more.

Susan shook her head, as if trying to shake the thoughts away, and Jack watched while she took another mouthful, drank some water, her focus back on the meal. He decided that she would be all right, the debate was a worry for her, but nothing too major. He reached for the bowl of stuffing, and began to scrape away the crunchy almost-burnt crumbs that had stuck to the sides. They were, he thought, the best bit...

"Oh!" said Susan. "Changing the subject entirely, my DNA results came through – at last."

"What DNA results?" asked Edward, looking confused. "Did you think Gran might not be your real mother or something?"

"Neil gave her a DNA kit as part of that 'find-your-family-tree' website thing," said Ben between mouthfuls of peas and potato. He was, thought Jack, a disgusting eater.

"Ah," said Edward, "I see. And what was the result? Are you half monkey?"

"Thank you, Edward," said Susan. "No, I'm mostly English with a little bit of Irish and a tiny bit of Spanish."

"That explains the temper," said Tom.

"But, more interesting," said Susan, ignoring him, "is that it links you with people who share your DNA. I seem to have about 200 cousins – but most of them are very remote, we share a great, great, great, grandparent, or something similar. Except for one..." Susan frowned.

"I have one DNA match who looks really close – a first cousin. Which must be wrong. So it makes you rather doubt the whole test, doesn't it? I'm wondering if they muddled up my DNA with someone else's, or if the whole thing is rubbish."

"Probably not the Spanish bit," said Tom under his breath.

"Yeah," said Edward. "Now we know it was you, sneaking off to the bull field with your red tea-towel..."

"I have real trouble keeping her off the table at night," said Tom, giggling. "She likes to climb up there and dance, stamping her heels and shouting '*Olay!*' and waving her skirt about."

"Didn't know Mum owned any skirts," said Ben.

"Thank you, everyone," said Susan, grinning. "I knew I could rely on you all for some helpful input.

"Ben, if you've finished chewing that bone, can you stack the dirty plates?

"And Ed, I haven't had time to make up your bed – you can grab some clean linen from the laundry cupboard can't you?

"Does anyone want plum crumble?" She started to gather dirty crockery.

"Plums already?" said Edward.

"Last year's," said Susan, carrying the dishes to the sink. "They're from the freezer."

Jack glanced at his phone. He decided he had enough time for pudding before he went back to Broom Hill, Josie wasn't expecting him for a bit. "I'll have some," he said, passing his empty plate to Ben.

As he ate, his face blank, Jack allowed a myriad of thoughts to chase themselves around his brain, dancing in time to his jaw as he chewed. Did Edward have any inkling that Emily was moving on, and would he, Jack, notice if Josie should ever have similar thoughts? And would the church debate be a veiled attack on his brother, and if so, should they all stay and argue – or walk out in protest? And then there was his grandmother, who seemed sure she was being followed but was probably imagining it...Round and round went the tangle of thoughts as his spoon scraped the bowl, and his mouth ate the food, and around him, his family chatted and laughed and existed as a sort of solid foundation that would never change.

Chapter Eight

Susan saw her mother and Aunty Elsie a couple of days before the debate. Dot had phoned, asking her daughter 'how she was fixed' for driving them to the supermarket, because their car 'had a low battery' and kept refusing to start in random places, so they were trying to not use it. But they needed to do a 'big shop' to buy their food for the next two weeks. Susan agreed to drive them, saying she had some cheques to pay in at the bank. She went to pick them up after she had fed the poultry.

"We're all ready," said Dot, answering the door. She left the door open while she pulled on her coat. "It's muggy for September," she said, "but I still need my coat...Elsie! Are you ready?"

"Just popping to the little girl's room," said Elsie, waving at Susan.

Dot raised her eye-brows, but didn't say anything.

Susan drove to Marksbridge, and parked in the supermarket car park. "I'll come in with you," she said, "because I need to buy some bread – I've got Ed coming for dinner again, before the debate." She frowned, a familiar feeling of dread twisting in her stomach whenever she thought about the church debate. She sighed, forcing herself to think about the matter in hand. "Then I'll pop to the bank, and sit in the car until you're ready," she told her mother.

Elsie and Dot went to collect a shopping trolley, wheeling it together as they crossed the car park. The trolley's wheels rattled across the tarmac, swinging to left and right as the women fought to control it. Cars paused to let them pass, the women crossing the road seemingly unaware of the traffic inching between the spaces. Both women had an array of shopping bags hanging from their elbows, and Susan wondered how much shopping they intended to do.

"We thought we'd buy enough for two weeks," said Dot. "Cassie said she'll come and sort out the car battery for us, but if we buy lots of food now, it won't matter if something comes up and she can't come."

"It's been very difficult," explained Elsie, letting Dot take control of the trolley as they moved into the shop. It veered off to one side, narrowly missing a lady who was struggling with a baby and a toddler – both of whom were screaming. Elsie raised her voice so Susan could hear her above the angry yells of the baby: "The first time it broke, Dot was at the doctors. And it all seemed fine, but then, when she came to drive home, it wouldn't start. We thought it was broken, but Jack came, and when he tried, it started straight away."

Susan nodded, having heard the story from Jack the previous day. She took a paper bag, and began to fill it with apples. After three apples, the bag split, the apples rolled around her wire basket. Susan sighed, knowing that the supermarket only supplied biodegradable bags, but they weren't really strong enough for the weight of apples. She added a few more apples to her basket, wondering how she could manage to stop them being bruised.

Elsie had moved to the next cabinet, and Susan could see her collecting bananas. She watched as her aunt pulled two bananas from a green bunch, then moved to some that were beginning to yellow, and pulled off two more. Elsie continued moving amongst the bunches of bananas, removing two from several different bunches – she looked across to Susan, and grinned.

"Well, there's only two of us, and we like a banana every day at bedtime. So I need some that are ready to eat now, and some that will be ripe next week. Otherwise they go bad."

"Yes," added Dot, from where she was inspecting the oranges, "we don't want them to go bad, do we?"

When Elsie changed her mind, and replaced two of the bananas in favour of some that were a preferred colour, Susan decided she would go and do her own shopping. She didn't really want to be with her relatives when an assistant came to tell them off. She noticed her mother, putting several empty bags into her trolley, and went to the bread aisle.

The supermarket was busy, full of mothers on their way home from the school run. Susan waited while two young women finished chatting long enough to notice she was waiting, moving reluctantly to one side so she could squeeze past. Her path was then blocked by an elderly man who was selecting yogurts, his trolley lengthways across the aisle. Susan pushed his trolley to one side. The man didn't seem to notice. She wove her way to the bakery section, and selected a couple of loaves, before meandering up to where the tills were. Every till had a queue, but the self-service tills were less busy, so Susan went and stood in line.

While she waited, Susan looked around. Mothers were struggling with cantankerous toddlers, people were trying to squeeze past each other, assistants were blocking aisles with trolleys heaped high with the fresh produce they were adding to the shelves. The lighting was severe, and one bulb was flickering, giving a migraine-inducing fuzz to the shop. The person in front moved away, and Susan shuffled forwards, noticing that there was music playing on the tannoy, but the general noise of tills beeping, and trolleys rattling, and people talking, made it almost completely undetectable.

"Invisible music," thought Susan, straining to try and recognise the song as she began to feed her purchases across the laser scanner of the checkout.

When Susan had paid, she took her bag and went in search of her mother and aunt. A man balancing several boxes, a bottle of wine and a multi-pack of crisps was in her way, so she waited for him to move, wondering why males seemed so incapable of carrying shopping bags. A toddler pushed past her, knocking into the man, who lost his fight with the crisps and the bag fell to the floor, in front of a passing trolley which careered over them. Susan walked past as the man struggled to pick them up, and she noticed him go to the customer-service kiosk – presumably for a refund.

"Though it was his own fault really," thought Susan, scanning the shop for her relatives. She could see several heads of grey curls, but none belonged to Elsie and Dot, so she moved to the next aisle. She was now in the pasta section, which was directly underneath the flickering light. Still no sign of them.

The next aisle was stacked high with toilet rolls and fabric conditioners and a tangle of synthetic scents wafted towards her. She saw a woman remove a sponge from a multi-pack, and a mother reaching for antibacterial spray while her toddler strained to reach the mops that were standing next to their trolley. But no sign of Dot or Elsie.

The music, barely heard, changed to a Scottish jig, and Susan turned in time to spy Dot moving away, down towards the alcohol section. There were two women chatting – a different pair to previously – and Susan pushed past them, avoided the small boy racing to find his mother, and the man with a walking stick carrying a single bottle of whiskey.

"Mum!" Susan called as she saw her mother add a bottle of gin to their trolley.

Elsie waved from the end of the aisle, looking up with a smile.

Then, as Susan watched, Elsie's face sort of crumpled, her shoulders hunched, and she clutched her head as if stung.

"Aunty? Are you all right?" said Susan, hurrying towards her.

Dot too was turning, noticing, moving towards Elsie, who gave a high-pitched cry and staggered backwards into a young man in an orange football shirt who was carrying cans of beer. The man half-turned, his frown turning to surprise as he saw Elsie, and he reached out a hand and caught her elbow. A bottle of Cherryade fell to the ground, smashing at their feet, red liquid spurting onto bottles and legs and trolley wheels; someone screamed – Susan was aware only of a blur of people, as she rushed forwards. The cans of beer joined the Cherryade, one bursting in a leisurely fountain of frothy brown that wet their legs and shoes, as the man caught Elsie in both hands to stop her falling. Dot reached Elsie.

Elsie was standing, propped up by the orange-shirted man, her face blank. Her mouth twisted up, in a half smile, as if the right-hand side couldn't quite keep up, and then she said something, but the words were lost en route, never made it past her lips, and she closed her mouth again, looking confused. As Susan watched, a tear slid from one eye, making a silver line along her cheek, to drip from her chin.

"Elsie, what's going on?" Susan heard her mother demand.

Elsie shook her head, opened her mouth, made a sound, but nothing discernible, nothing Susan could understand.

"Aunty?" said Susan, reaching them now, nodding her thanks at the orange-shirted man, taking her aunt's other elbow, together guiding her to the front of the shop where she knew there were chairs. "Aunty? What's the matter?"

People were staring, moving aside so they could pass, a woman in a green overall arriving with a mop, someone else asking if they needed help, Dot muttering that Elsie had always been clumsy and what did they need Cherryade for anyway, and would they have to pay for all the things Elsie had broken?

Together, they lowered Elsie onto a bench near the tills. She sat, her head lowered, then lifted a hand, pressed it against her left temple. When she looked up, Susan saw that her expression was puzzled, but her eyes were clear.

"What happened?" asked Elsie, looking at her sister.

"You made a right mess, that's what happened," said Dot, pushing the trolley to one side and sitting next to her on the bench. Susan heard the quiver in her voice, and noticed hands that were trembling as she smoothed her hair.

"Are you all right?" said Susan again. She stared hard at her aunt, noting that – unlike Dot who was very pale –

Elsie's colour was good, her eyes seemed clear, she seemed to have no problem with coordination. "Does anything hurt?" Susan asked.

Elsie shook her head slowly, as if considering. "Not now," she said. "But my head did. Very suddenly. Like a needle going through my eye." She shook her head. "It's fine now," she announced. "Shall we finish shopping?"

Susan looked up at the man, who was hovering above her. "Thank you," she said. "I'm not quite sure what happened, but my aunt seems to be okay now."

"Probably these lights made her a bit dizzy," said the man, nodding towards the flickering bulb. "They should get them fixed. You should complain."

He moved away, and Susan noticed the lower part of his jeans were wet, and he made beery footprints as he walked. She turned back to her aunt.

"I think you should sit here for a bit," she said. "Me and Mum can finish the shopping, then I'll take you home."

The shop assistant with the mop came over, carrying a bucket and a glass of water. She passed the water to Elsie and put the bucket next to them on the floor."

"Do we need to call an ambulance?" she asked.

Susan shook her head.

"No," said Dot, "she's all right now. Those lights made her dizzy. Do we have to pay for all that drink?"

"I don't think so," said the assistant, sounding uncertain. "Were you hurt? Do I need to fill in an accident form?"

"No," said Elsie, "I'm fine now. The headache has gone. It wasn't anything serious, probably a sudden migraine or something." She passed the empty glass back to the woman in green. "Thank you," she said.

Susan and Dot left her on the bench, telling her not to wander away, and began to push the trolley back through the shop. Susan's shoes were sticky, each step pulling at her shoe, squeaking, accompanied by the acidic scent of cherries. She glanced at her mother, who was still very pale, and decided that it was time to take her home.

"Mum, why don't you sit down and I'll pay for this, then we can go home."

"We never got the milk," said Dot, sounding half-hearted.

"I can get the milk. You go and sit down..."

Susan saw her mother open her mouth to object: "I'm all right, there's nothing wrong with me."

"No, I know Mum. But I'm not sure that Elsie should be left – don't you think it would be better if you sat with her? I'll get milk and pay for this, you go and...look after Elsie."

Dot nodded, and went back to her sister. Susan watched as Dot lowered herself onto the seat, as if she was very tired; watched as her mother leaned back, and shut her eyes for a moment, before turning and saying something to Elsie.

Susan pushed the trolley through the shop, heading for the milk. She was less patient now, letting her trolley push against those that were in her way, asking people to move, reaching in front of people if they were too slow. The drinks aisle was closed now, yellow tape strewn across one end, a cone with 'cleaning in progress' emblazoned on the side. Some people were ignoring the sign, squeezing past to reach their wine or beer or bottles of fizzy drinks, and the floor was sticky with a thousand pink footprints.

As soon as the shopping was paid for and thrust into bags, Susan wheeled the trolley back to the car, and drove her mother and aunt home.

***

When Susan arrived back at Netherley Farm, she went out to find Tom. He and Jack were busy filling the silage pit behind the big barn. Susan stood for a moment and watched them, breathing in the sweet smell of cut grass, absorbing the deep green. In an adjacent pit, the older silage was brown and dry, fermenting, lending a beery scent. The fourth pit was empty – last year had been a tough one, and they had used all their reserves when the fields turned brown through lack of rain, the cows unable to eat fresh grass. Susan shook her head, remembering. At least this year had been better.

Jack was tipping another load of cut grass into the silage pit. Susan looked up to where he was, watched the trailer tip, the grass falling as Jack drove slowly forwards, leaving a thick layer of grass behind him, a carpet of moist green velvet. As the trailer arrived at the end, Tom drove forwards, the tractor fitted with the snow plough, which pushed against the wall of grass, compressing it. Susan sneezed, and Tom looked up from the tractor, backed away from the silage and turned off the engine.

"Hello," said Tom, sounding surprised to see her. "Everything okay?"

"Yes, I think so," said Susan nodding uncertainly. "We had bit of an episode in the supermarket, Elsie had a dizzy spell and knocked over half the drinks aisle."

Jack too had noticed Susan, and was jumping down to listen. The grass clung to his boots and legs, making his ankles appear furry.

"She all right?" he asked.

"Yes, I think it was probably the heat in the shop," said Susan, "and it was very busy. Plus there was a bulb flashing, and that always makes you feel a bit weird, doesn't it? I think she just had a funny turn and lost her balance. Made quite a mess though, there was beer all over the floor. I took them both home, they were drinking tea when I left – and Aunty Elsie was eating half a chocolate cake, so I don't think there can have been much wrong!"

"Ooh, I could just eat a piece of cake," said Jack over his shoulder, climbing back to the top of the pit.

"Are you nearly finished?" said Susan, looking at the walls of the pit, seeing that the silage reached almost the top.

"Just need to finish compressing this last load," said Tom, starting the engine again. The rumble filled the space, and he shouted over the noise, down to where Susan stood. "Could you get the new cover I bought for this year? There's two left, but I'll only need one." Tom glanced towards the empty pit. "No silage left over from last year, so I've already used some of the first cut. Won't manage to fill the fourth pit...not this year." He looked back at Susan. "I left the cover in the corner of the shed – will you get it? Save me a trip."

Susan nodded at his back as Tom drove forward again, squeezing the layers of grass, pushing out the air, ensuring it was tightly compacted, eliminating the risk of mould growing.

She found the black plastic in the shed, where Tom had left it, next to the tubs of calf milk. The new-plastic smell filled the little shed, and as she lifted it, the layers slid unhelpfully across each other, threatening to slip apart into a single giant layer. It reminded Susan of dustbin sacks, and felt dirty, even though the thick plastic was new and shiny. It was heavy, so Susan heaved it into a wheelbarrow, and pushed it across the yard towards the silage pit. She left the final sheet where it was, knowing that the second layer could be an old cover, and Tom wouldn't want to waste a new one, not when he could use it the following year and save the money.

As the wheelbarrow careered over stones and ruts, lurching to the side, it reminded her of the shopping trolley, and how Dot and Elsie had fought to control it. Susan concentrated on keeping to the designated walkways, not wanting to meet a speeding tractor when she turned the corner. The wheelbarrow handles were rough, rubbing sore spots into her palms.

Back at the pit, Tom and Jack were rolling old tyres into position, ready to weigh-down the plastic sheets; the old ones were folded ready to go on top, their ragged sides flapping in the breeze.

"I've got the new cover," called Susan, pushing against the handles. The load was too heavy for her to get up the ramp, so she abandoned it at the edge of the pit. "I'm going to put the kettle on now," she called.

Tom lifted a hand in reply, and Susan left him there, spreading the sheets over the grass. She guessed it would take them about half an hour to cover it all with black plastic and then secure with tyres and sandbags. She decided she would have her tea first, and eat the chocolate biscuits she had bought. She felt that she rather deserved a treat after her morning.

Chapter Nine

The following day, Susan was in the kitchen when Neil phoned. She had just finished a phone call from Tom, who was spreading the old straw and muck from the cowsheds over the fields. As they chatted, she could hear the roar of the tractor in the background, and could picture the field, as Tom tipped out all the dry muck across the field. It would be ploughed the next day, back into the earth. By the time he left, the field would be covered in lumps of mud, and Tom would be covered in dust, which would cling to his collar and drop from his clothes as he walked. He would smell of cow dung too, thought Susan, the odour clinging to his clothes and hair until he had showered and all the clothes had been washed.

Susan and Tom had been chatting about nothing, planning what to give Noah for a christening gift, whether Tom could wear the same suit he always wore. Aunty Elsie and her mother had both bounced back from the escapade in the supermarket, though her mother's frailty had shocked Susan, so she told Tom she thought they should offer to transport the women to the christening, to save Dot driving.

It was nice, thought Susan, to think about something other than the church debate tomorrow. So when Susan finished the call, and almost immediately her phone rang again, she settled back into her chair and gazed out of the kitchen window. She could see Jack, moving the protein pellets that had been delivered, using the forklift truck to lift the pallets.

They had used a new supplier, and the 25kg bags had arrived, on one-ton pallets, and dumped unhelpfully in the middle of the yard. The driver had unloaded before Susan could tell him where to put the shrink-wrapped heaps, and refused to move the load when Susan noticed, and went to speak to him; telling her that his docket hadn't said to knock, and he was behind schedule. Now the pellets needed to be moved so that other vehicles could access the yard. In the kitchen, Susan frowned, deciding they wouldn't use that supplier again.

"I was hoping to save some money," thought Susan, frowning. "The older calves are eating about 3kg each every day, now we're weaning them from milk, so they're getting through them pretty fast. But Jack's going to tell me it's a false economy if we can't trust this new firm..."

"Hello Neil," said Susan into her phone, as Jack's back disappeared with another load into the barn.

"Hi, Mum," said Neil, "How's things?"

"Yes, all fine, I think," said Susan, holding the phone with one hand and reaching for the dog bowls with the other. Molly and Rex began to dance around her heels. "It's lovely to hear from you. How is my grandson today?"

"Noah's fine. Thanks. But Mum, I'm phoning about that message you sent last night, about the cousin who had contacted you on the family-tree website?"

Susan carried the bowls into the boot-room and began to scoop dog food into them. In the yard, she could hear as the truck returned from the barn for another load. The engine was revving, and she knew Jack would be lurching forwards and backwards, trying to stop the old engine from stalling as he picked up the pallets and took them to a dry corner.

The dog kibble rattled into the bowls, and both dogs were pressing their noses against her legs, reminding her that they were waiting.

"Yes," Susan replied, "but as I said, I think he's got the wrong person. He seemed to think he was a first cousin – well, the DNA result looked as if we were first cousins – but that can't be right because–"

"Mum, it is right," said Neil, interrupting. "That's why I'm phoning – I would have driven over, but I just haven't got time – but it is right. He *is* your cousin, this William

Whoever, it's not a mistake. But I'm not sure what we should do...I wasn't expecting this, when I gave you the kit, I'd sort of forgotten, to be honest, it never crossed my mind..."

"Neil?" said Susan, bending to place the first bowl on the floor. Rex pushed forwards, and Molly nudged Susan's leg again, trying to hurry her. Susan placed the second bowl on the floor, and went back into the kitchen. "You're not making much sense," she told Neil. "What didn't you expect? And how could I have a cousin, a *first* cousin, when Aunty Elsie never had..."

Susan stopped.

She sat on a chair and frowned. In her mind, she was remembering some of those strange expressions she had seen on her aunt's face, recalling sentences that had never been finished, unexplained tensions she sometimes noticed between her aunt and her mother.

"Mum?" said Neil, as if checking she was still there.

Susan looked out of the window. The protein pellets had all been moved now, the yard was empty. She watched as Jack walked towards the tractor, and guessed he was going out to check one of the herds.

"Tell me what you know," said Susan, her voice quiet.

"Aunty Elsie did have a child," said Neil. "It was a long time ago, I think before Gran was even married, and they went away together, while she had the baby, so no one would know. The baby – a boy – was adopted. I don't know who took him, or who arranged it, or anything. But Aunty Elsie told me about it, ages ago, when I was worrying about Ben and Kevin and everything. She didn't want me to interfere, and she told me her story. I don't know who else knows, apart from Gran of course. I think everyone else is dead."

"Well, I certainly didn't know," said Susan. There was a dirty mark on the table, and she began to scratch at it with her nail, watching as the dried sauce began to flake off.

"I suppose it must be him," she said at last, rubbing at the sauce flakes and making them into a tiny pile. She could hear the tractor as Jack started the engine, heard it die away as he drove down the lane. In the boot-room, the dogs were eating, bolting down their food as they always did, one choking, sounding as if it would be sick, followed by more chomping.

"It must be him, I suppose," said Susan, wondering how she couldn't have known this, couldn't have been aware of something so momentous. "It must be him," she said again.

"Yes," said Neil. "Yes."

Susan swept her pile of chipped sauce flakes into a tiny heap, and then drew her nail through them, scattering them, then drawing them together again.

"I'm not sure what I should do," she said, her voice slow, her mind considering. "Do you think Aunty Elsie will want to meet him? After all this time? Do you think, now she's put it behind her, she wouldn't want to know about him, wouldn't want to meet him..."

"She hasn't put it behind her," said Neil, sounding definite. "She has never forgotten him, of course she hasn't. You know that. Parents don't ever forget – do they?"

Susan shook her head, though Neil couldn't see her.

"Of course she'll want to see him," said Neil. "But I'm not sure when you should tell her – or if we should meet him first – you know, to check he isn't a weirdo or something. How sure are you that he's who he says he is?"

"Well," said Susan, thinking, "his DNA matches mine – which is how he managed to contact me, through the website. So, he has to be related, it has to be him. It's not like he tracked me down on Facebook or something.

"Okay," she said, making a decision, "I will let him know that I am in contact with Elsie, and I'll ask Aunty Elsie whether she would like to see him. Or maybe I'll ask Mum...she might be a better judge of how Aunty Elsie will take the news."

"No Mum," said Neil, "I really think you should ask Aunty Elsie herself about this. When she told me, she was... I don't know, sort of *resentful*. As if she blamed Gran for making decisions on her behalf. I think she needs to be allowed to decide this one for herself. William is her son, after all, it's up to her whether or not she meets him."

"Right," said Susan, feeling unsure.

"Do you have an email address for him, for this William?" said Neil. "I tell you what – how about if I email him, and arrange to met him, check him out a bit? You can tell Aunty Elsie that he exists, and we've found him. Whether she meets him or not is up to her, but if she does want to, I will have made contact first."

Susan gave the email address to Neil, thanked him for telling her and ended the call; then she sat there, not moving, trying to get used to the idea that Aunty Elsie had a son. *A son!* She wondered how it was possible to know someone so well, to have lived close to them her whole life, and yet not to really know them at all. Susan shook her head, feeling slightly disorientated, as if this one piece of knowledge somehow undermined everything she had thought she knew. All the things she had been so certain of before, seemed less certain now.

"I'll tell her on Tuesday, after the debate," thought Susan. "I can only worry about one thing at a time, and I'll feel better when that particular hurdle is crossed. It has waited over fifty years, it can wait two more days, can't it?"

Decision made, Susan went to get a cloth, and wiped the table, before calling the dogs and taking them for a walk.

Chapter Ten

Tom finished work slightly earlier on the day of the debate. He had spent another day turning the soil in the fields, ploughing the weeds and grass that had sprouted since the wheat was cut. The lumps of muck and old straw strewn across the fields the day before were now all buried, the field resembling the top of a cake that had been rough-iced, the lumpy furrows waiting to be smoothed down. The weather was still very sunny – unusually so, the air muggy, though heavy rain was forecast for the end of the week. Susan started to cook while Tom showered.

Supper was a hurried affair, with part-baked bread cooked quickly in the oven. Susan was trying to reduce the amount of time the oven needed to be on, to avoid over-heating the kitchen, but it was still very warm when they sat at the table. She fried some slices of steak, and placed large bowls of salad on the table. Tom asked if there were any chips or potatoes, and Susan told him that no, there weren't, it was too hot for cooking.

Edward arrived in time for supper, and took his place between Ben and Tom, his chair scraping the tiles as he reached forwards and hooked a piece of steak with his fork, the juices dripping as it was carried to his plate.

"When's Neil coming?" asked Edward, his mouth full of bread.

"He said he'd go straight to the church," said Susan, spreading a layer of mayonnaise across her baguette. "I did offer him a bed for the night, but he wants to get back home to Kylie, and she didn't feel up to a night here with the baby. Jack and Josie will meet us at the church too."

Her voice was tight, and a flutter of nerves swept through her whenever she mentioned the debate.

Susan added salad to her bread, and started to slice a tomato, forcing herself to focus on the present, on physical things, on family news. "I expect Kylie's right, actually," she said. "New babies tend to be unsettled in new places – Noah would probably just scream all night." She added some slices of warm steak, and took a bite. Crumbs rained down as she bit into the crust, and she brushed them from her tee-shirt.

"How's the new digs?" she asked Edward.

"Okay," said Edward, sounding depressed. "Not sure I would've chosen to lodge with them, if I'd had more time, but it's okay. Somewhere to sleep..."

It was seven o'clock before they were ready to leave. Susan was still feeling nervous, her dinner a hard lump in her gut, she would have loved an excuse to stay at home. She detoured via the chicken coop as she walked to the car, but the birds were all outside still, and she knew she would have to shut the coop door later, when it was properly dark. She looked up at the sky. The light felt unnatural, overly bright, and indigo clouds were looming over the hills. It felt ominous, and Susan shivered despite the heat.

"Don't let me forget the chickens," she said to Tom, as she climbed into the Land Rover, trying to avoid her trousers brushing the mud that clung to the sides.

Tom nodded, and drove to Marksbridge Baptist Church, in the nearby town.

They parked in the road, because the car park was full. As Susan walked to the door, she spotted Josie's car – and Neil's – parked close to the hedge. Her heart was beating very fast, and her throat was dry, so that she had to cough and clear her throat in order to say hello to Audrey Black, who was welcoming people at the door. Tom glanced at her.

"You all right?" he whispered, as they went into the main church hall.

Susan nodded. "Not looking forward to this," she said.

Tom put out a hand and squeezed her shoulder, leaving his arm draped around her. "It'll be okay," he said. "Just remember, it's not about Ben. Try to keep it a bit distant."

Susan nodded, knowing that this was impossible advice. Of course it was about Ben – how could it not be? What if she agreed with the arguments against being gay? What if she found that everything she heard convinced her that being gay was wrong? How could she live with the agony of knowing that one of her sons was living an immoral life, cut off from God, destined for destruction? Even if the arguments were flimsy, and she disagreed with them, hearing them was unavoidable, and Susan braced herself to hear friends, people she was fond of, those people who she worshipped next to every week, while they voiced potentially hurtful views. There was, she felt, no good outcome for her personally, in having those views expressed.

The church hall was full. Susan recognised many of the people as regular attenders on Sundays, but at least half the people were new. She realised that news of the debate had spread, and people were interested to hear what would be said. There were two women in the back row, both with very short hair, wearing baggy jeans and flowing shirts, and Susan wondered if they were a couple. Then she reminded herself that Ben and Kevin looked just the same as everyone else, and it was silly to try and determine orientation by dress choice. She had hoped to sit in the back row herself, but the family had spread themselves across two rows in the middle, so she followed Tom to a seat next to Ben and Kevin. Neil turned from his seat in front of her, and kissed her cheek. He leaned close to whisper in her ear.

"I contacted William – tell you about it later...Are you still going to Gran's tomorrow? To tell Aunty Elsie we've found her son?"

Susan nodded. "Yes, I've told them I'm popping in for tea at eleven. I'll let you know how it goes..."

Edward and Jack were sitting in the row in front, with Josie between them. Edward was talking to Josie, leaning close to her ear. Susan saw Josie giggle. Then Edward turned to greet Susan, giving her a wave which turned into a camp, weak-wrist, hand-flap – so she glared at him before looking down at her lap.

Susan heard people walking to the front of the hall, and looked up.

At the front of the hall, on a small stage that was used for nativity plays and occasional concerts, was a desk and three chairs. Rob – 'Black Rob' as her mother called him – sat in the middle, and was smiling at people. On his right was Fraser Campbell, who was also smiling at people. He usually welcomed people as they arrived on Sundays, and was one of those people who knew everyone and could chat for hours – a very personable, easy to like, sort of person, thought Susan, looking at him. A slight man, with a Scottish accent and a slightly too-long hairstyle, he was grinning round at people, showing his crooked front tooth, his eyes sparkling.

"Fraser Campbell looks like he's enjoying himself," whispered Tom. "Full of adrenaline I suppose."

On the other side of Rob was Stephen Porter. He was sitting up very straight, and although he was also attempting to smile, Susan thought it looked rather forced, as though he felt uncomfortable. Aged, she guessed, mid-fifties, he had a mass of curly grey hair. He was tall, and very well-spoken, and Susan thought he was some kind of civil servant, though she wasn't really sure. He was always pleasant, tended to speak with authority, and was respected, if not especially loved, by the church membership.

"I wonder which one is anti-gay, and which one is pro," said Tom.

Neil shuffled round in his seat. "I don't think you should view it like that Dad," he said. "It's not being 'anti-gay', it's saying what you believe the Bible is teaching."

"I stand corrected," said Tom. Then, lowering his head to Susan, he whispered, "I also need to learn to speak quieter."

Susan rubbed her ear where his breath was tickling and nodded. "Yes," she said. "You do."

She glanced towards the window. The light had faded and dark grey night was pushing against the pane. As she watched, a drop of rain touched the glass, sliding downwards, followed by another.

"Storm's coming," said Tom, following her gaze.

At half-past seven, Rob stood, and everyone shuffled to silence. Susan felt she could feel the tension in the air, the atmosphere was expectant, everyone keen to hear what would be said, each person hoping that their own view would be properly represented. She wondered how many people, like herself, were confused and hoping for clarity on the subject, and how many had already decided where they stood on the gay issue. Tom reached for her hand, and she held it, looking straight ahead, wishing she and her family were invisible.

Rob was welcoming everyone, saying how great it was that so many people had come to listen, and reminding everyone that this was a church debate, and therefore should be conducted in an attitude of love and respect. He also reminded people to turn their phones to 'silent mode'.

Susan reached into her pocket, and pulled out her phone. She decided that she was unlikely to be contacted by anyone – most of her family were in the church with her, and her mother and aunt would be in bed. She switched off the phone, and slid it back into her pocket. In the seats around her, she was aware that other people were fiddling with their phones, ensuring they wouldn't disturb the debate.

At the front, Rob was praying, and Susan lowered her head, though found she wasn't really listening. She could feel the tension in her body, her neck was stiff, and she forced herself to exhale, to lower her shoulders, to try and relax a little. "Otherwise," she thought, "I'm going to have a nasty headache by the time we're finished, and that's not going to help if I need to defend Ben afterwards."

When she looked up again, Rob was introducing Fraser, saying that he was going to begin the debate with his views on what the Bible teaches about homosexuality. Rob explained that following Fraser's speech, Stephen would speak, and then Rob would end the meeting, and people were welcome to stay for coffee and further discussion. He reminded people to listen with 'open ears' and to be willing to learn from people who might have a different understanding to their own. He then nodded to Fraser, and sat back in his seat.

Fraser walked to the front of the stage, glanced down at his notes, and then smiled at the packed hall. He began to speak, his voice confident, his clipped accent interesting and clear. Susan remembered that he was a school teacher, and thought that his pupils probably enjoyed his classes and found them interesting. She watched him, as he strolled around the stage, making eye-contact with the audience, engaging them. Susan found she was listening attentively, she forgot where she was, forgot about people looking at her, and strove to understand what Fraser was saying.

"To understand what the Bible teaches about homosexuality," Fraser said, "we have to begin at the very beginning – we have to start with Genesis." He reached down and picked up a Bible, opening it, seemingly at random, and holding it high. "We have to start in Genesis, because that is where we learn the pattern set down by God, the blueprint for early man that was designed to be continued throughout all cultures, and all societies. That is where we learn God's plans for mankind."

"Right back, when God created people, he established his covenant with them, he showed them what was best for them – what God himself intended for mankind. Genesis tells us, that God created man, and he created woman. We read that they became one flesh, and that, from that time on, marriage was established as a holy covenant. If we start at the very beginning, before sin came into the world, before people started to ruin everything, we can see that God established marriage. One man, one woman, bound together. There was nothing else – no variations. One man, and one woman."

Susan wondered why he kept repeating phrases. His voice was mesmerising, easy to listen to, almost hypnotic. She found she was believing him, everything he said made absolute sense.

There was a sudden flash of light from outside, followed by a crash of thunder, making Susan jump. A few people gasped, and there was a general stirring as people shuffled and shivered and looked towards the window. The weather outside was wild, and there was something isolating about hearing it roar against the window, shutting off the congregation from the world outside, forming a barrier. It was as though they were in a cocoon, unreachable.

Susan saw Tom and Jack exchange worried glances, and Jack lean to whisper something to Josie. Susan guessed they were worrying about their farms, wishing they were at home so they could check the animals and crops. "Not," she thought, "that they could do anything to change the weather, even if they were there."

On the platform, Fraser, unperturbed, began to explain other parts of the Old Testament. He discussed the story of Sodom and Gomorrah being destroyed, how the people were practising homosexuality, and so God destroyed the city. As he spoke, explaining his view, he also referred to arguments made by those who disagreed with him, disputing their logic.

"Of course, the reasons given in the Bible for the destruction of the cities vary – for example, in Ezekiel we read it was due to the people not giving to the poor. But early Jewish documents, which we use to verify and explain the Bible texts, make it very clear that it was the sin of homosexuality that was the cause for God's anger. This was why the city was destroyed."

There was another crash from outside, almost as if nature was providing the visual aids.

Susan wondered if Fraser was messing up what Stephen had planned to say, and glanced at him. But his expression was impossible to read; Stephen sat as if carved of stone, staring straight ahead.

"In Leviticus 18," Fraser was saying, "we read the laws that God gave to his people. These laws were to ensure they were a holy people, separate from those nations around them. He lists homosexual relations as one thing they should avoid, telling them that it is wrong. We read that if a man lies with a man, they have sinned – and the punishment in those days was execution – it was such a serious sin. There is no doubt here, no need to try and work out what the text is saying, it is clearly written for all to see. God wanted his people, the Israelites, to be different, a special race."

He was speaking louder now, fighting to be heard above the rain beating against the window. The water was racing down the panes, almost as if it was falling in a continuous flow rather than droplets. Outside, all was dark and wet, the wind flinging leaves and sticks and oceans of water against the window, determined to push inside and reach the people.

"So, you might say, that was all very well for the Israelites thousands of years ago, but how is that relevant today? Well, God doesn't change. Society might change, laws might change, but God does not change. And when Jesus came, when the old testament gave way to the new, we can see that the old covenants, given to those early followers, became the inheritance of all who believed in Jesus. *Christians* today are the promised race. Christians today should be living lives that are holy, separate from how the world lives."

Fraser paused, allowing his points to sink in, for people to understand. Susan watched him.

"Of course, some of the early laws were superseded when Jesus came. We no longer observe all the Sabbath laws, for example. However, homosexuality is also discussed in the *New Testament*. We cannot claim it is old teaching, no longer relevant. When we study the writings of Paul – given so that we can learn how God intends for us to live – we can see that the Bible very clearly condemns homosexuality.

"When Paul wrote to the Christians in Rome, he talks about people who have switched natural relations for unnatural ones. He lists sins – and we are all guilty of these, there is no one in this room who can claim never to have disobeyed their parents, never to have been insolent or boastful. However, clearly written, with all those other sins, is homosexuality. It is a sin, and we know this, because the Bible clearly says so."

Susan found she was staring at her hands, twisting her wedding ring round and round, while Fraser's words filled the hall. She didn't want to hear these words, they felt discordant, the opposite to her view of God. Yet neither could she dispute them – as Fraser was saying, the Bible clearly said so.

How, Susan wondered, could God allow people to be born gay, and then tell them it was sinful? How was that fair? It didn't seem right to her, it felt cruel and unloving. And yet, it was there, in the Bible, clearly written.

Tom reached down, squeezed her hand. She looked up at him, and he gave her a slight smile, his eyes full of sympathy. Susan clasped his hand in her own, and tried to listen to the rest of the debate.

"Now," Fraser was saying, "some people will, I'm sure, try to confuse things by claiming the words Paul used are unclear." He glanced towards Stephen, but Stephen showed no sign of responding, so Fraser ploughed on. "The Bible was not, of course, written in English, it was written originally in Hebrew and Greek, so what we are reading is a translation. Whenever something is translated, we need to be careful that the original meaning isn't lost. Anyone who has ever read anything translated online, rather than by a person, will know that it's easy to get the wrong meaning. So, there are people who argue that when we look at the early texts, the words used by Paul mean something other than loving, monogamous, gay relationships. They point out that he used words which are found nowhere else in Greek, in one instance a made-up word, possibly. They claim that these words have been *wrongly* translated as meaning homosexual relationships. They claim that Paul was discussing the promiscuous idol worship of the Greeks of the time, and that his words do not apply to those who would support same-sex marriage. They look at the passage in 1 Corinthians, and 1 Timothy, and they say: '*Oh, but those words don't mean what we mean. Those words, which look as if they are condemning homosexual acts, are really referring to when people used young temple prostitutes, which is child abuse, or to promiscuous homosexual acts. They don't apply to loving, same-sex, monogamous relationships.'*

"Now, I ask you," said Fraser, gazing round at the hall full of people, "would God allow something so important to be so vague? The Bible is from God. The Bible clearly states that homosexual practise is wrong. Why would God demand that someone has a theology degree before they can understand it? No! Those texts are clear, and homosexual behaviour can never be justified. It is wrong – because the Bible says that it is wrong."

Susan took a breath, forcing herself to breathe slowly. Fraser was saying all the things she had feared he would say. She could not fault his logic. Either the Bible was wrong – which she didn't believe – or homosexuality was wrong. Which meant, she had to face, that Ben and Kevin's relationship was wrong. However much she might be fond of Kevin, however much she could see that he was good for her son, and made him happy, and encouraged what was good in him; if homosexuality was wrong, then their relationship was wrong. It was completely clear.

In the seat in front, Susan could see Neil nodding, agreeing with Fraser's words. She glanced around, trying to keep her head still whilst moving her gaze to those around her, not wanting to attract attention to herself, but keen to gauge other people's responses. Some people had Bibles, open on their laps, others were taking notes, scribbling on scraps of paper or in tiny notebooks. Most were nodding, their faces serious. They all, it seemed, agreed with Fraser's words. Susan looked again at Stephen. Still he sat, motionless, his face blank, almost as if he wasn't listening.

"What can he possibly say?" thought Susan. "Fraser has already debunked his arguments, he's already pointed out that we can't rely on culture or translations to claim the teaching on homosexuality no longer applies. How can Stephen possibly defend his position?"

She sighed, wondering if Stephen would simply abdicate, concede that Fraser had won the debate. Surely, she thought, there was now no plausible defence of homosexuality, not when the Bible so clearly condemned it. Even the weather seemed to support his view.

Chapter Eleven

Fraser finished speaking, and went back to his chair. Someone at the back started to clap, and although initially it was only a couple of people, gradually more and more joined in, until, it felt to Susan, everyone in the hall was applauding Fraser. None of her family joined in, not even Neil, and Susan felt Tom squeeze her hand again.

As the applause died away, Stephen walked to the front of the stage. He looked assured, but unlike Fraser his body language wasn't relaxed. He didn't, Susan felt, seem *friendly*. She waited, wondering again if he would simply concede, agree that his arguments were hopeless, and the Bible was clear on this issue.

Stephen cleared his throat, and when he spoke, his voice was loud and clear. It was a pleasant voice to listen to, thought Susan, educated but not too posh, a voice with authority.

"To understand what the Bible teaches about an issue," began Stephen, "we have to start at the very beginning." He allowed himself the barest ghost of a smile, a flicker of recognition that he was copying Fraser's speech.

Susan leant forwards, surprised.

"We have to start in Genesis," said Stephen, "because that is where we learn the pattern set down by God, the blueprint for early man that was designed to be continued throughout all cultures, and all societies. That is where we learn God's plans for mankind."

Stephen crossed the stage to where the Bible had been placed, on the central table. He flicked through to the early pages, and held it high.

"In Genesis chapter 9," he said, his voice loud, "we read about Noah, a man of God, and his sons: Shem, Ham and Japheth. We read that Ham behaved immorally, and that Noah cursed Ham's son, Canaan. Now, we don't read very much in the Bible about Noah's sons, but we know from reading early Jewish documents, those used to support and verify the authenticity of the Old Testament–"

Susan saw him shoot another glance at Fraser, a half nod to show he was aware that he was repeating much of the other man's speech.

"–that the early Hebrew word for 'Ham' meant 'dark, black, or heat'. We can therefore be fairly sure that Ham, and his son Canaan, were men of dark skin. They probably developed into the race we now think of as black Africans, which is supported when we read where Ham's family settled, in Genesis chapter 10.

"The Bible clearly states, that Canaan shall be a servant to his brothers. We know, that the word used for servant, can also be translated as 'slave'. It is absolutely right, as shown by the Bible, that people should own people of black African ancestry as slaves, and that their role, as set at the beginning of time in Genesis, is to serve. Not to lead, but to serve. The Bible says this clearly."

People around Susan were shuffling, unsure what was happening. Susan was also confused – had Stephen confused what he was supposed to be speaking about? She glanced at Rob, expecting him to look worried or uncertain, but he wasn't. Rob was looking straight at Stephen, and he was smiling and shaking his head, as if he understood exactly why Stephen was saying these things, almost, thought Susan, as if he thought Stephen was being extremely clever. Rob's expression was one of admiration, not concern.

There was another blast of light from outside, another clap of thunder, as the storm began to roll back over the town. The rain, which had eased, began to drum, flung against the window as if trying to break through. Susan felt Tom stir beside her, and knew he was itching to leave.

"Later in Genesis," continued Stephen, "we see more examples of God's people owning slaves. Abraham, the founder of God's people, owned slaves, and this is not once condemned in the Holy Scriptures. In Exodus chapter twenty, in the Ten Commandments – which were given as a guide for how people should live – we see that slaves are again mentioned. Mentioned, but not condemned. It was *assumed* that God's people would understand the natural order set down by Genesis, that people would own slaves. Later, in Exodus 21, we read instructions – God's instructions – concerning slaves. So, a man could sell his daughter as a sex-slave, as laid out in scripture, and a man could beat his slave, his property, and as long as the beaten slave survived for at least a day afterwards, that was okay. You don't need a degree in theology to understand these things, they are clearly written, slavery is part of God's plan.

"Of course, some would argue that this teaching only applies to the Old Testament, and that it passed away with the coming of Jesus. However, this is illogical. In the time of Jesus, slavery was rife amongst the rich people, Romans were well-known as slavers, yet Jesus *never* speaks against slavery. In fact, Jesus uses slaves as an illustration in a parable, showing his acceptance of slavery. When we look at the things that Jesus *did* speak against, such as divorce, it is significant that he never spoke against slavery.

"If we move to the writers of the letters, we see more evidence. The letters were written to the early church, telling them how they should live. In Ephesians, slaves are told to obey their masters with fear and trembling. In Colossians, slaves are told to obey their masters. This is again clearly written in the Bible, we do not need a degree in theology to understand it – owning slaves is part of the rightful order of life."

Yet another roar of thunder, which seemed to resonate immediately over the little church, accompanied by a flash of light so bright it filled the room, searing the audience's eyes, making everything appear artificial, overly bright, then disappearing as suddenly so that all colour seemed to be leached from the room. Susan could feel her heart thumping.

"That sounded like a strike somewhere near," whispered Tom, sounding worried.

Stephen had paused, as if holding his breath, but now he recovered, and continued.

"No one would doubt that Paul was a Godly man, and his teaching should be used as an example to us all. We have in the Bible, clearly written, a letter from Paul to another Christian, called Philemon. We read that one of Philemon's slaves – Onesimus – had managed to escape. So does Paul shelter him? Does Paul let him continue on his journey? No! Paul sends him back, as a slave, to continue serving his owner. Paul pleads for his life, because an escaping slave could by law be executed, but he does not help him to escape. This is clearly written in the Bible, owning slaves is correct.

"Now," Stephen paused for a moment, and looked around.

No one moved, Susan wondered if anyone was even breathing – whatever was he saying? Susan could see that his argument was logical, that it did seem that the Bible condoned slavery. But surely, she thought, everyone knows that this is wrong, that a loving God could never create a race who were inferior, created only to serve. The logic went against everything she believed about a God who was loving and fair. The weather was forgotten, all attention was on Stephen and what he was saying.

"Now," continued Stephen, "I know that this teaching will be unpopular with some of you."

"Understatement of the year," muttered Tom.

"However, just because something is unpopular, doesn't mean we should reject it. Slavery was accepted for generations by Christians, it was an accepted part of life, it was 'the way that things were done'. Do we have the right to overthrow all that Christian tradition? Do we have the right to claim that we know best – better than our Bible-believing forefathers? Many practices evolved over time, so the practice of polygamy, of having multiple wives, was commonplace in the Old Testament, but frowned upon by the early church and gradually disappeared. But not slavery – slavery continued until relatively recently. And many of those who fought for its abolishment were little more than terrorists, they certainly were sometimes violent and often ruthless, many were not even Christians. So do we want to continue in their footsteps? Or do we want to return to the teaching of the Bible, and the example of the church of history?

"You might be thinking that slavery is unfair, that black people should not be forced into positions of submission. But actually, God's word is given to show us what is correct. Black people, being inferior, are better cared for when not placed into positions of authority. It is due to slavery that the Gospel first spread to Africa, slavery was a means to educate ignorant races. When a black person is in a position of servitude, they will be sheltered from the harder decisions in life, they will be given roles that are appropriate to them. It is when we wrongly place black people in positions of authority, that wrong decisions are made, and then we end up blaming those people who should have been protected in the first place. Black people were not created to be leaders, they were created to serve, and society would be better, healthier, more Godly, if we returned to those principles which are clearly written in the Bible. Thank you."

Stephen nodded at the audience, and retreated back to his chair. He sat, staring hard at the floor.

There was silence. No one knew what to say or do. On her right-hand side, Susan saw Mrs. Smith lift her hands, as though to clap, then slowly lower them.

Rob stood, and walked to the front of the stage. Susan was surprised to see that he was still smiling, still composed. The storm had died away, the rain providing a constant accompaniment on the window, but rhythmic, controlled, as if all the anger had gone out of it.

"Thank you, both Fraser and Stephen, for being willing to speak," said Rob, nodding to both men. "I think we will all agree, you have given us a lot to think about, and you have clearly studied the Bible extensively." He paused, as if considering what to say next. "I suspect that some of you might be wondering why Stephen chose to speak about slavery–" he turned to Stephen and said, *sotto voce*,

"Brilliant, by the way." Then turning back to the audience, Rob said, "I think it's best if we pause for refreshments, as planned. However, are there any questions first? Anything you want to ask our orators before we break for coffee?"

Instantly, John Carey was on his feet. "Stephen, how can you say those things?" he said, his voice rattling with emotion. "How can you possibly defend the cruel, the unchristian, *abominable* practice of slavery? How dare you stand up in church and say those things?"

"I can't," said Stephen, standing again. "I do not believe that the Bible means those things, I don't believe that God intended for black Africans to be slaves. I believe that slavery is wrong. It doesn't fit with my image of a loving God, it is inconsistent with the teaching in the rest of the Bible. I believe the passages I quoted, whilst appearing to be clear, are taken out of context, and misquoted to support an argument – an argument which the church believed for generations. I believe that they were wrong, that many Godly men and women, right back to the time of the early church, were wrong. I do not believe that God *ever* condoned slavery, nor do I think any person is ever meant to own another human being. I think a person's skin colour is irrelevant, a black person is no less likely to be a good leader than a white person – we are all equal." He sat down again, and folded his arms.

"But..." said John Carey, "But...why would you...I mean, what was the point of what you just said?"

Rob answered. Very gently, he explained that Stephen was making a point. "I think," said Rob, "that we need to consider the arguments that Stephen made, and the evidence that he used, and then decide how it applies to the debate about homosexuality."

John Carey went back to his seat, frowning.

Rob closed the meeting, and gradually, people began to move and talk.

"Well," said Tom, blowing out his cheeks and slapping his knees, "that certainly wasn't boring!" He looked at Susan. "You okay Love? Want a coffee? – I could do with a whiskey myself, but doubt that's going to be on offer...I don't want to stay long, better get home and check everything, but if you want a drink before we go…"

"Yes, thanks," said Susan, not quite sure how she was feeling – shocked more than anything, she decided. "Yes, I'd love a coffee. Can I wait here? I don't feel like 'mingling' this evening."

Tom nodded and headed towards the serving hatch, where a queue of people was waiting for coffee to appear.

Most people were standing now, walking around, greeting people, talking in quiet huddles. She could see Edward and Josie standing in the coffee queue, Edward was talking, Josie was laughing. Jack was standing with them, his expression dark. Susan sighed and stared down at her hands, not wanting anyone to approach her. She heard the chair next to her being occupied, and looked up to find Stephen Porter sitting next to her.

"Hi," he said, "I thought I'd come and say hello. Find out how you're feeling."

"Confused, mainly," admitted Susan. "You spoke very well, but it wasn't what I was expecting."

"No," he said, "I don't think it was what anyone was expecting. But that was the point you see, I didn't think going over all the same old arguments about same-sex marriage would help anyone. It's too hard to justify, if you start looking at how words are translated, or what the culture of the day was, then it simply becomes confusing. I was hoping to challenge people a little, to make them reconsider *why* they hold such strong beliefs, and hopefully to introduce a little doubt."

"Doubt?" said Susan. "Surely it's right that people are sure of their faith?"

"Of their faith, yes," agreed Stephen, "but not necessarily sure of their theology. Not to the extent that they start laying down laws for other people, saying who can belong and who can't."

There was a pause, and Susan listened to the rain, thinking that it was a nice sound now, comforting somehow.

"So, what do you actually believe? About being gay I mean," said Susan. "You never told us."

"No, I didn't, did I?" said Stephen, and smiled. He shuffled in his seat, as if uneasy, then turned to her, his voice low but decisive.

"Let me share something with you. Something personal...about my childhood. I grew up, many moons ago," he smiled, "I grew up with my brother, in a good Christian home. My brother, Jonathan, was a good friend, we had a lot of fun together as kids, got up to all the mischief that most brothers get up to – we argued and fought, of course, but at the end of the day we had a lot of fun together, and were always there for each other – like your boys seem to be." Stephen looked across the hall, to where Edward and Jack were, and smiled.

"We were both taken to church every Sunday from practically the day we were born, taught to pray, taught to study the Bible. It was a good upbringing, and it gave me a solid ground on which to build my faith. Our church was very traditional, but I can't really criticise, because it gave me a good grounding for the Christian faith. I learnt a lot about what the Bible teaches, it was a good training ground, and I accepted everything that I was taught and tried to live a good Christian life. I was completely involved as a teenager, part of the leadership committee of the Youth Fellowship, striving to become a Godly man..." He paused, as if struggling with the words. "But...I don't have a brother any more..." Stephen stopped, and swallowed.

Susan waited, listening to the rain, the steady hum of people in the background as they chatted. She felt sad, but also that she shouldn't move, shouldn't offer sympathy. Her role was to listen.

"Jonathan killed himself, when he was sixteen, and the note he left explained that he was gay, and although he had prayed about it, and fought against it, and he knew that it was wrong, he couldn't change. The guilt had built up inside of him, the belief that he was a bad person, that if he was a Christian, God would take away this sin, and God didn't, so he didn't know what to do. He was worn down by it, by constantly being taught that it was wrong, hearing nothing but condemnation or easy answers about 'coming to God and being healed' but being unable to change, and in the end, he killed himself."

Stephen stopped, looking down. He looked back at Susan, and continued. "I know, that at sixteen, he had other things going on, a bubble of hormones, all sorts of things that teenagers have to cope with. I've seen it with my own kids – it's hard being a teenager, isn't it? But I also feel, very strongly, that by preaching that homosexuality is a sin, we are condemning a whole lot of people to a life of guilt and shame. No wonder most gay people will never come to church, never listen to what the Bible teaches – because all they see is condemnation. Even today, many churches which claim to be inclusive, to welcome everyone, still believe that same-sex relationships are wrong. Gay people can attend the church, but under the surface of acceptance is an attitude of judgement, and there would be problems if they wanted to be part of the leadership team, or asked for a same-sex ceremony.

"So no, I never said what my own view of the Bible teaching on homosexuality is – because frankly, I don't think my own views would, or should, persuade anyone. There is evidence that suggests it's wrong, and there's conflicting evidence which shows those passages are being wrongly applied by the church. I don't think it's clear – just as I don't think it's clear in the Bible whether slavery is wrong. I personally think slavery *is* wrong, I don't see how it can possibly be justified, not if you look at the Bible as a whole. And I think the same applies to those who condemn same-sex relationships. God created people gay, because he wanted them to be gay, it is part of who they are, what makes them special. It's not a sin, it's a gift. But for centuries, Christians, good people, holy people, thought slavery was okay. I don't know why. Perhaps God waited, until people were ready to listen, before showing them it was wrong. Perhaps it was too big a step, but I don't know, because I'm not God."

Stephen grinned, but it was, thought Susan, a rather sad grin. "Sometimes the church forgets that, doesn't it? That we're not God. We like to think everything is clear, neatly wrapped up, we understand everything. But we don't, we can't. We simply have to live how God wants us to live, to do our best to follow his teaching. I think it's the same with the whole gay issue. Personally, I think the passages in the Bible that condemn homosexuality are too reliant on how they were translated, and it doesn't fit with my relationship with God – I don't believe he would create gay people and then tell them that it is wrong to be gay. I think the church is getting it wrong again."

Susan looked across the hall. Tom, carrying two mugs of coffee, was chatting to John Carey while spilling coffee on the floor. Neil was talking to Ben, and Susan saw them shake hands. She thought that Neil was looking emotional, as if their conversation was meaningful. Jack and Josie also seemed to be having an intense conversation, in the far corner of the hall. Susan saw Josie shake her head, and Jack moved back a step, his arms folded, his back very straight. Next to her, Stephen followed her gaze.

"I'm keeping you from your family," he said, starting to stand. "I just wanted to check you were okay – this isn't intellectual for us, is it?"

"No," said Susan, shaking her head. "And thank you – for the debate, and for what you told me. Thank you." She put out a hand, put it on his arm. "I'm truly sorry, about your brother. I expect he would be proud of you, if he could hear what you said tonight. It was very brave of you. Thank you."

He nodded and moved away.

Tom sat in his place. "What was that about then?" he asked, handing her a coffee with drips underneath.

"Nothing," said Susan, wiping the mug with a tissue.

Neil came over, and said he needed to leave, because it would already be late by the time he got home, and the weather was so awful he wanted to get going. Susan hugged him, and thanked him for coming, and sent love to Kylie. She whispered that they could speak later, by phone, about cousin William and what Neil had learned.

"Tomorrow, I will tell Elsie," Susan told Neil. "I didn't think one day's delay would matter, and I wanted to get this over with first."

Neil nodded, but Susan could see he was barely listening, and wanted to get home to Kylie. She kissed him again, and watched him leave.

Then Edward appeared, and said he'd wished he'd known what Stephen had been going to say, because he could have brought some anti-slavery signs. Susan shook her head, and kissed him, and told him to drive carefully.

It was late by the time Susan and Tom left the church. Susan's friend Esther had chatted, saying she had been shocked when Stephen had started to speak, and wondered if she should stand up and support her black husband. Eileen, standing nearby, had joined in, saying that she thought it was bad form really, to introduce such an emotive topic when we actually had a black person in the church, and she expected Susan felt the same, having a black daughter-in-law.

"After all," said Eileen, "he must have known that black people would be here. How could he say those terrible things – even if he does believe them to be true? Surely, given that the law in this country has changed and everything, surely he would just keep those views quiet, between him and God, and not start flinging them at people in such a *nasty* manner..."

Susan paused, thinking of all the hurts that had been flung at gay people, how much she had dreaded the debate, knowing her son was being judged. But she just smiled, and moved away.

At home, Susan went first to the chicken coop, walking carefully to avoid the puddles. All the birds were inside, sitting along the perch. She shone the torch inside checking for foxes who might be hiding, and all the chickens looked at her with their round eyes, their expression cross. Susan glanced to see they had food and water for the morning, and shut the door. Tom was coming back from the barn, and she walked across the yard with him, not speaking, but holding hands. The air around them was damp and cool, the storm had washed away the humidity of earlier, and Susan thought it smelt clean and new. A ragged-edged moon shone from behind racing clouds, and the yard was splashed with silver light as they crossed to the house, the sky grumbling over distant hills.

In the kitchen, Susan wondered whether she wanted another drink before she went to bed, but decided she was too tired. There were crumbs littering the table from their hurried meal, and Susan reached for a cloth, wiping them onto her hand and carrying them to the bin. Another yawn stretched her jaw, and she closed her eyes. She opened them, and saw her phone, where she had left it bulging in the pocket of her coat. With a sigh, she pulled it out, and glanced around the empty kitchen, before heading towards her bedroom, ready to sleep, turning on her phone as she walked.

There were 22 messages.

Chapter Twelve

As Susan stopped, surprised by the messages on her phone, she heard Tom calling her from upstairs.

"Sue! Susan! Have you turned on your phone? Your mother has been phoning – Aunty Elsie has been taken into hospital. There's a message on my mobile."

Susan stopped, suddenly cold. Her fingers were shaking as she fumbled with the phone, pressing buttons so she could phone her mother. She listened, then the phone beeped, telling her that it was unable to reach the other phone. She tried again, with the same non-result, so decided instead to listen to the messages. Perhaps her mother's phone had run out of battery.

Susan stood in the hallway, leaning against the bannister rail, as she strained to hear what her mother had said. There was message after message – all from her mother's mobile – so Susan listened to the most recent one. Dot's voice was distant, as if she hadn't held the phone close enough to her mouth, and she was shouting – as she always did when she used a telephone. The last two messages said very little, were simply asking where Susan was. So she scrolled back, to the first message, and listened to them in order.

Susan could hear the alarm in her mother's voice, the panic, then the tears. Dot had called to say something was wrong with Elsie and she had phoned for an ambulance. Then nothing but crying.

There was another message as Dot left the house: "Hello, Susan, me again. They came, they're taking us to hospital..." There was a brief conversation, away from the phone, and Susan could hear a man's voice, but couldn't decipher the words, followed by her mother again. "Yes, we're going straight to Pembury – the new one – you know, near Tunbridge. I'm going too." Her voice faded, so Susan had to strain to make out odd phrases, as if the phone was away from her mother's face. "Yes, I'll get my coat...no, I don't think so..." and Susan realised she was listening to her mother's conversation with someone else, possibly the man she had heard. The message ended.

Susan listened to the next one, and could barely hear her mother above the sound of an engine and a siren: "...on the way..." she heard, and "...not sure what they're doing..." and "...makes you feel travel-sick..." and "Where are you? Are you coming?" There was a crash, which sounded like thunder, and Susan remembered the storm, realised she was listening to messages sent a few hours earlier.

The next message was breathless, and tearful, with no background noise. "We're here. They've taken Elsie into a room, and I'm in the waiting area. They think she's had a stroke. Are you on the way? Why aren't you answering? I don't know what's happening and I'm frightened..." Her mother's voice cracked, and the message ended.

Susan swallowed, fighting her own tears, scrolling to the next message.

"Hello? Susan? Are you on the way? I've called Cassie, she's coming. The doctors are still with Elsie, I'm not allowed to see her yet. I'm just waiting. It's a waiting room upstairs, near the ward I think...Are you on the way?"

Susan knew her sister Cassie would take a couple of hours to reach the hospital. She glanced at the phone again. There were still several unheard messages, but she could listen to the rest on the way – if the worst had happened, if Aunty Elsie...but no, she wouldn't think about that, not until she needed to. Tom was hovering next to her, his face concerned, not interrupting.

"We need to go to the hospital – Pembury." said Susan. "Will you drive me?"

Tom nodded, and went to find his keys.

Susan felt as if she was dreaming, as if nothing was real. Her hands weren't quite steady, and everything seemed very clear, overly bright, as she used the toilet, found her coat, picked up her bag. It was as if her mind was numb, she was focussed entirely on leaving the house and getting to the hospital, beyond that all was blank. Tom didn't say anything, but she was aware of him moving around her, locking doors, going into the kitchen. Susan felt a scarf being draped across her shoulders, and as they left the house, Tom passed her a travel mug, full of hot tea.

"Drink it while we drive," Tom said, holding the car door open for her. "It'll be good for you."

Within minutes, they were in the car, drawing away from the farm. It would take them an hour to reach the hospital, even with the clear roads. It was raining again, and Susan heard the steady sweep of the windscreen wipers as she once more began to scroll through the messages.

"Don't get on the motorway until I've listened to all the messages," she said to Tom, glancing up from her phone. "Then, if...if there's nothing we can do at the hospital, we can go to wherever Mum is..."

Tom nodded. His face was in shadow, suddenly lit as a car came towards them, his expression solemn. Susan turned back to her phone, holding it against her ear as she sipped the sweet tea Tom had made for her.

She listened to the next message: "Susan? I'm still here. They've given me tea. A nurse came...she was very young..." the next few words were lost, and Susan imagined her mother, juggling her phone and her handbag and a cup of tea in a plastic cup, possibly standing in a corridor. She couldn't hear any background noise, and she wondered if her mother had put the phone into her bag. Then Dot's voice drifted back, as if Susan was listening to a radio and the volume was being turned up and down. "...a little room...told me she's had a stroke...but they don't know if..." There were more words, but Susan couldn't decipher them.

The next message was full of static and bubble, and Susan thought she really was hearing the inside of her mother's handbag.

There were two more messages, asking where Susan was, and Dot saying she had tried all the boys' phones, and only one had answered, and that had been a man she didn't know, so she must have phoned the wrong number.

The following message was clearer, and Susan could hear a humming noise in the background, and faint noises, as if other people were in the room. "Susan? It's me again. I'm with Elsie, they've let me sit with her...she's asleep...but her colour's good. She has...tubes and things..." Susan heard her mother sob, and imagined her reaching into her bag for a tissue. She heard the sound of nose blowing, and a swallow, and then, quite clearly, her mother said: "They said they're sure now, and it was a stroke. But they said I did well to get her here so quickly..." Susan could hear the pride in her mother's voice, knew that it would matter to her, that she had done the right thing. The message continued: "And they won't know for a little while how she will be – it takes time for the brain to heal after a stroke... for them to assess the damage..." Susan nodded in the car, knowing her mother was repeating words she had been told.

"But for now she's safe, there's nothing else they can do," the message continued, "so I'll just wait here, for you and Cassie. You are coming, aren't you?"

The call ended.

There were several more messages, each one asking Susan where she was, and were the messages reaching her. She turned to Tom.

"It sounds like Aunty Elsie has had a stroke," she told him. "From the most recent messages, I think she's going to..." Susan paused, swallowed, not wanting to voice her fears. "She seems, at the moment, to be okay. And she's in Pembury, so let's go there. I'll try Mum's phone again..."

Susan rang her mother's phone, but her screen simply told her that it was unable to connect, so she tried her sister's phone instead.

Cassie answered on the second ring. Susan heard wind roaring into the mouthpiece, and guessed Cassie was somewhere outside. "Hello? Susan?" said her sister.

"Hi Cassie – what's happening? Are you with Mum?" said Susan.

"I've just arrived," Susan managed to hear, though the words were indistinct and breathless. "I've parked, I'm going towards the hospital now. From what Mum said, Aunty has had a stroke, but I don't know any more than that. Mum's battery was running out, so I haven't been able to talk to her for the last half an hour. Are you coming?"

"Yes," said Susan, glancing at the clock. "We should be there in about 40 minutes."

"Less than that," said Tom, swinging the car into the fast lane.

"I'll see you soon," said Susan. The phone was silent, and Susan realised she had lost signal. She tried to phone Neil, then gave up, and typed a text, telling her sons the situation, and saying she would phone them when she had some news. The car lurched as Tom avoided a car that had joined their lane without indicating. Susan stared at the screen, waiting for the signal bar to reappear, feeling the car sway, listening to the rain and the wipers, and the hum of the engine.

As soon as her phone had signal, she pressed 'send' and the message was sent to each of her sons. Then she sat back in her seat, and stared hard at the lights that flashed past, and felt grateful to Tom for not speaking, and tried to not think about what news might be waiting for them at Pembury.

Chapter Thirteen

Susan's phone rang as they reached the hospital car park. She saw Neil's name, and answered as she unclicked her seatbelt and fumbled to open the door. Tom came round to help her, and she climbed down from the Land Rover saying hello and telling Neil they had just arrived. The car was muddy and wet, and she noticed that her coat touched the side, a streak of brown clinging to the hem. She sighed.

"Mum?" said Neil, as Susan delved into her pocket for a tissue and tried to wipe some of the mud from her coat. "I got your message – are you all right? How's Aunty Elsie? And Gran?"

"Hi Neil," said Susan, following Tom across the car park. It was still windy, and her hair was dancing around her face, her coat rippling as the wind tugged at it. She was shouting into the phone, hoping Neil could hear her, whilst trying to keep up with Tom, who was striding ahead. "We've only just arrived, so I don't know anything yet. I'll phone you once we know..."

"But what about William?" said Neil, interrupting her. "Have you told William? Aunty Elsie is his mother – *his mother!* – If he's been searching for her for the last few years, should we tell him? Should we try to get him there, in case...you know..." Neil's words seemed to echo across the car park before being whipped away by the wind. Susan heard the urgency in his voice, understood his concern.

Susan stopped. She had forgotten about William. She stood, in the middle of the car park, the wind pushing against her, driving rain into her face. When she blinked, her eyelashes were heavy, as if she'd just stepped from the shower. For a long moment, she simply stood there, thinking. Her mind was racing as she tried to assimilate this new information and decide what she should do.

William. How could she have forgotten William? After all this time, all these years, this might be his only chance – Elsie's only chance – for a conversation. Should she phone him? Or was it better this way? Would the shock of meeting him be too much for Elsie?

Ahead, Tom had stopped and turned. He saw she was standing still and walked back to her.

"Susan?" he said, peering into her face, his expression creased with concern.

"It's Neil," said Susan, still holding the phone against her ear. "He asked whether we should tell William. Whether he ought to come to the hospital, quickly. Just in case."

Tom shook his head as if trying to force this new information inside, overwhelmed by the focus of delivering his wife quickly to the hospital, he now needed to make a decision which could potentially never be changed. He shook his head again, and Susan realised that she would need to make the decision herself.

"Not yet," she said into the phone.

"Sorry?" said Neil, shouting, even though she could hear him clearly.

"Not yet," Susan shouted, over the sound of the wind rasping across the microphone, trying to make her son hear. "Let me go inside first, and see what...what the situation is. I'll phone you back. When we know..."

Susan ended the call, already hurrying towards the building, trying to not think of possible outcomes to 'the situation'.

The hospital sprawled in a hollow. It was below the car park, and the pathway ran towards the main entrance, white and wide, with room for wheelchairs and walking sticks and worried patients. Even now, everything was brightly lit, as though the black sky was painted above a film set, unreal, temporary, the clouds that scurried overhead projected as an ever-repeating sequence.

Susan followed Tom to a large revolving door, searching for signs or people that might guide them. The door was locked, inside, in the gloom of the waiting area, there was an information desk. They peered through the window, searching for clues as to which direction they should walk. An ambulance screamed past behind them. More cars slid into the car park. But inside, all the public areas seemed dark and deserted.

"We need to go round to the A&E department," said Tom, "Casualty – that must have people still working."

He led the way, along narrow pathways, through another car park, to the door used for emergency patients. They were met at the door by two young men, one bleeding from the head, and they followed him inside, avoiding the drops of blood that splattered the corridor. Inside, all was bright, and busy, and – Susan felt – unwelcoming. There were no signs, nothing to tell them what to do or where to go.

They joined a line of people waiting at the reception desk. For a while, they stood there, a straggling line of people, all being ignored by a woman sitting behind a desk, who was writing and checking a computer. Susan wanted to scream or shout, to tell them to hurry up. Around them were people sitting or lying on hard plastic seats, the air filled with the quiet murmur of voices, the occasional gasp of pain, all underscored by the continual groans from a woman in the corner who was clutching her arm.

Eventually the woman behind the desk looked up, and began to deal with the people in the queue: sending them into rooms or telling them to take a seat. When it was their turn, they were questioned by an abrupt woman, and directed to the Acute Stroke Unit. Long corridors stretched ahead of them, their shoes noisy on the shiny floors, past coffee shops and newsagent kiosks full of shadows that formed strange shapes, threatening and dark, in the empty hospital. Susan shivered, feeling that they were trespassing, would be told to leave. They hurried on, into a lift, doors hissing shut, machinery whirring, the air falling beneath them. Then out, into the semi-lit gloom of another corridor, through more glass fire-doors that resisted when pushed and swung back abruptly, spitefully bashing their heels. They saw Cassie, standing the other side of a final glass door, and they slowed.

For a moment, Susan wanted to stop, wanted to delay the knowledge that was waiting for her through those doors. Images of Aunty Elsie through the years rose up, forcing their way into her head, choking her throat. Images from childhood, when Aunty had made cookies with her and iced them to hide the burnt bits, pictures of playing in the garden, the physical memory of snuggling on her lap while she was read a story. More recent memories: Elsie at the beach, the gleam in her eye when she laughed, the enthusiasm when she was included in family life, the loving, happy *essence* of Aunty Elsie that had somehow refused to be contained in her tired body, and had seeped out in her giggles and her wild hair and the sparkle of her eyes. For one moment, holding her breath, Susan did not want to know if that was finished, she wanted to hug her ignorance to her like a shield, to hide from reality.

Then, with a deep breath, Susan walked through the door that Tom was holding open, and into the arms of her sister.

Chapter Fourteen

Cassie was older than Susan, and although the three years between them had diminished over time, she was still the older sister. There was something secure about hugging her, knowing that she was there, and Susan felt that whatever happened, if Cassie was there, it would be all right in the end. Cassie would sort out anything that needed to be sorted.

Elsie was in a room in the Acute Stroke Ward, and she was asleep. Susan was told that they could see her, but only two visitors at a time, and only during visiting hours, which had finished. Dot, as Elsie's next-of-kin, was with her, and had been allowed to sit next to her bed for a while, but the rest of the family needed to leave, and come back the following day, during visiting hours. They had been allowed in, to collect their mother, but not to visit Elsie.

The nurse who told them this was not unkind, Susan felt, though she was certainly not willing to compromise. The nurse told them that the consultant would do his rounds in the morning, and would make a decision about care for Elsie then. Elsie was the patient, and the hospital revolved firstly around the consultants, and secondly around the patients. The visitors, Susan realised, were tolerated by the staff, but were there by permission; they certainly had no rights, and their needs were not, in any way, the concern of the hospital staff.

The nurse was also unable – or unwilling – to offer much in the way of information. Susan was told that the family – or rather Dot, as next-of-kin, and whoever Dot chose to have accompany her – would be informed of the prognosis tomorrow, by the doctor. All they knew, at this point, was that Elsie had suffered a major stroke, but was now stable. Susan wondered, rather bleakly, what 'stable' meant.

There were a few chairs lining the corridor, and the nurse suggested that they wait for their mother there, then she collected her folders and files, spoke to her colleague at the desk, and whisked away, with an air of limited time and too many patients and not enough energy. Susan watched her until she disappeared behind the first fire-door, then settled back in her chair and turned to Cassie.

"How's Mum?" said Susan.

Cassie screwed up her face, considering. "I think," she said slowly, "that she was okay – given the circumstances. She phoned me, and luckily I had just finished work, so was able to come straight away. I'll reschedule things, so I can stay with her for a couple of days. When I arrived, they had just taken Elsie for the scan, and–"

"What scan?" interrupted Susan. "We don't know anything. I haven't managed to speak to Mum, I only know what she told me in messages, and it was hard to understand most of it."

"Ah, okay. Well, I'll tell you what I know."

Cassie ran her hand through hair that was straight and shiny, any grey strands carefully coloured; it looked as if it had been recently combed. It made Susan wonder what her own hair looked like, still damp from the weather and possibly with straw in it. She reached up a hand and began to comb it with her fingers while Cassie talked.

"So, when I arrived, they had taken Elsie for a CT scan, so they could confirm she'd had a stroke, though I think by then they were fairly sure she had. Apparently there are two kinds of stroke though, and they needed to confirm which kind it was, so they could give her the correct medication."

"What was it?" asked Tom.

Cassie shook her head. "I-skie something," said Cassie. "Not entirely sure, to be honest."

"What made Mum call an ambulance in the first place?" said Susan, "Did Aunty collapse or something?"

Cassie shook her head again. "No, I think it was because she started to talk weird. They were watching telly, and Mum asked Elsie something, and when she answered, she spoke in this funny garbled way, and Mum couldn't get any sense out of her, so she panicked, and called an ambulance. Lucky she did, because I think the speed helped – the doctors could do more early on, before there was lots of damage...or something."

Cassie paused, and Susan realised her sister was piecing together what she herself had been told, probably by an anxious mother, in snippets of time while they waited.

"And how are you?" asked Susan, looking at her sister. Cassie always managed to appear immaculate, and this evening she wore a navy suit and high heels, her coat was neatly folded across her knees and a small briefcase rested by her feet. Susan stared at the shoes, thinking that she wouldn't be able to walk in such high heels, and would probably end up in casualty herself, with a broken ankle, if she had worn them to rush here.

Cassie opened her mouth, to start speaking, then shut it abruptly as the door opened, and Dot emerged.

Susan took in her grey face, her tangled hair, the coat in her hand that was dragging on the floor, and rose to meet her.

"Mum?" she said, as Cassie guided Dot to a seat between them.

Dot sat, perched on the chair as if she didn't intend to stay. Susan saw red-rimmed eyes, and hands that shook, and she reached across and hugged her mother, feeling the bones in her shoulders.

"Elsie's asleep," said Dot. "Let's go home."

***

Susan returned to the hospital the following day. She had collected her mother and Cassie as soon as she had fed the poultry, then dropped them at the entrance while she went to park. Even this early, the hospital was busy, and the only car park with spaces was up on a hill – too far for her mother to have to walk after her exhausting evening.

As Susan walked back to the main entrance, which was now flooded with daylight and people, she yawned. Last night, as soon as they had arrived at the farm, Tom had disappeared to check the animals, and Susan had gone to bed. But she hadn't slept well, her mind full of the church debate, and worries for her aunt and mother. When she had finally drifted to sleep, her dreams were peopled by black slaves, and outcast gay people and everyone spoke with crooked mouths, and she was hurrying to get somewhere, before it was too late, while black crows wheeled overhead. She woke feeling more jaded than when she'd gone to bed.

Susan walked through the revolving doors, into the main entrance of the hospital. There was a woman, headscarf wound around her scalp, makeup carefully applied, heading into the bowels of the hospital. A young man passed Susan, using his crutches to swing his feet in front of him, more like a gymnast, she thought, than someone with a disability. A harried woman pushing a man in a wheelchair was struggling to push the button next to the automatic doors, and Susan detoured to help her, before going to join her family where they were waiting. Dot was sitting on one of the chairs, a fat bag on her lap, and she was hunched over it like an owl guarding chicks, her thick-stockinged legs crossed in front.

"Hi," said Susan, leaning down to help her mother stand. "Ready?"

They walked along the corridors, and Susan thought how different they seemed to the night before. The newsagent was now open, people filing in, squeezing past display stands, emerging clutching newspapers or fiddling with the cellophane wrapper of greetings cards. Dot stopped, and stared into the shop.

"We should buy some flowers," she said.

"You're not allowed to take flowers to hospital patients anymore," said Cassie, shaking her head. "Something about the germs that grow in the water and that flesh-eating virus that patients can catch."

Dot started walking again. "Oh," she said, sounding defeated.

They passed the coffee shop, the aromas enticing and warm, a line of people standing against the counter, couples slumped at tables. Cassie led the way, striding confidently ahead. Susan walked behind, her arm looped through her mother's, so she could support her if she slipped. There was something fragile about Dot today, her movements were slower, and there were shadows in her eyes.

When they arrived at the entrance to the ward, the nurse greeted them. Susan wondered if the woman had been working all night, or if they had caught the end of one shift and the beginning of the next – but she didn't like to ask. The nurse recognised them, and suggested that one could wait outside, while the other two went to see Elsie, and then they switch places.

"You go first," said Cassie, moving to sit on one of the seats that lined the wall. "I need to make some phone calls for work, so I can do that while you and Mum sit with Elsie for a little while. Then we can swap places."

Susan nodded, and followed the nurse into the ward.

Elsie was in bed, propped up by huge pillows. She looked, thought Susan, as if she had shrunk and grown very old overnight. Susan wasn't even sure, had she arrived alone, if she would have recognised her aunt. There was something unfamiliar about seeing her in a hospital gown, her hair uncombed, her face pale.

Elsie was awake, and her eyes tracked them as they approached, looked up at them as they loomed over the bed. Susan bent down, and kissed the wrinkled cheek, smoothed the hair from her forehead.

"Hello Aunty Elsie," she said, "how are you feeling?"

Elsie stared at her, not blinking, not looking away – but she didn't speak, or smile. Her expression was one of intense concentration. Susan wondered if she recognised them.

Her mother was busy, unpacking items from her bag.

"We've brought you your proper nightie," said Dot, holding it up. "And a hairbrush – looks like you need to use it. And your bathroom stuff – I suppose the nurses help you to wash, do they? And I brought some magazines, and those word-wheel puzzles you're so fond of. And I brought you the rest of those biscuits you bought – I don't like them, and there's no point in them going to waste."

Elsie watched, her eyes following each item as it was taken from the bag, held up, placed on the bed or on the cabinet beside her.

The biscuits were in an open packet, dribbling crumbs as Dot lifted them onto the bedside cabinet.

"Have you got a plastic bag for those Mum?" said Susan. "Or a container? So they don't go stale?"

Dot stopped, looking uncertain. "They'll be all right," she said, "Elsie can eat them."

Susan glanced at her aunt, thinking it unlikely she'd be eating biscuits any time soon. But she could see her mother was worn out, with nothing in reserve for fussing with biscuit containers. So she smiled, and nodded, and instead of answering she reached for her aunt's hand, and held it.

Elsie's fingers closed around her hand, almost like a baby gripping a finger. Susan used her thumb to stroke the paper-thin skin, smoothing across the wrinkles, trying to warm and comfort her.

"Do you want to put this nightie on then?" Dot asked holding up a wrinkled cotton nightdress patterned with birds and flowers. "I could go and find a nurse, ask someone to help..."

"Why don't I go," suggested Susan, "while you sit with Aunty for a little while." She leaned towards her aunt. "I will be back in a minute," she said, very loudly and slowly.

"I don't think she's deaf," muttered Dot, going to sit in the large blue chair that was next to the bed.

Susan left, in search of a nurse. She felt as if she wanted to be doing something, anything, that might help her aunt. Seeing her, lying there so helpless, made Susan feel lost, as if she was drowning and couldn't remember which way to swim for shore. She passed the ends of beds, all hidden by curtains, some with people groaning, some silent; low-voiced chatter drifting from others.

In the centre of the ward was a nurse's desk, two women in blue bustling behind it. A third woman appeared, carrying a needle balanced on a small oval dish –

she leaned over the desk, checking something, then gave Susan a brief smile as she passed her, hurrying away.

"Excuse me," said Susan, approaching the desk. She felt as if she were trespassing again, being an inconvenience, getting in the way.

One of the nurses looked up, gave a small efficient smile with no warmth to it.

"Yes, can I help you?"

"I was wondering, would it be possible for my aunt," Susan half-turned, and pointed towards Aunty Elsie's bed, "for her to wear her own nightdress?"

"Elsie Heath?" said the nurse, checking her records. "Yes, that should be okay."

She looked up at Susan, and something warm entered the nurse's face, something human touched her expression. "Why don't you leave it on the chair, and when we next wash your aunt we can dress her in it? I expect she'll feel more comfy in her own clothes.

"Now, have you seen the doctor yet? I expect Mr Taylor would be able to have a little chat, if you've got any questions?" She pointed to the end of the ward, where there were several doors. "Why don't you take your mother into Room 4? I'll go and ask Mr. Taylor if he has time to explain things before he leaves."

Susan thanked her, and walked back to Aunty Elsie's bed. Her mother was sitting, where Susan had left her, staring at Elsie, tears coursing down her cheeks. Dot wasn't moving, and her crying was silent, an agonised helplessness of water that streamed, unchecked, and fell in fat blobs onto her cardigan.

"Oh Mum," said Susan, going to her, putting arms around her, hugging her close. "It'll be all right," she whispered, rocking her mother forwards and backwards as if she were a child. "Elsie's safe now, she'll soon be better," said Susan – saying what she hoped was true, with absolutely no idea whether that was right or not.

Susan pulled away, wiping her mother's cheeks with her hands. She wiped her wet hands on her jeans, and forced a smile.

"The doctor can see us, if you feel up to it? He can tell us how Elsie's doing."

Dot nodded and stood.

"We'll be back in a minute," Dot said to Elsie, then followed Susan to Room 4, collecting Cassie on the way.

They crowded into the little room, Susan told her mother to sit down, her and Cassie leaned against the wall. There was a table, and two chairs, and no room for anything else – it was, thought Susan, more of a cubicle than a room. There was no window, and she wondered what it would be like to work in this place, somewhere that was so detached from the outside, no weather, no seasons, no fresh air, no natural light. She frowned, feeling a headache behind her eyes, knowing that a walk across the fields would clear it.

When Mr Taylor appeared he was very tall, very thin, and very young. Susan saw Dot's eyes widen, and knew she was wondering how this boy could possibly be a doctor. He bent to shake Dot's hand, nodded towards Susan and Cassie, before folding his angular body into the chair. He rested one ankle on his knee, and balanced a sheaf of papers on his foot. He wore blue socks, with tiny motorcycles emblazoned along the top.

"Right," he said, "I am Michael Taylor, and you must be Elsie Heath's family." He glanced up at them, gave a small smile.

"It's like he's read a policy on how to behave," thought Susan, "–introduce yourself, smile, give information, answer any questions, leave..." Perhaps, she thought, it was necessary to have a strategy, when all day long you are having to deal with stranger's worst fears, explain horrible things about the people who they love. Perhaps it's the only way you can cope, to become slightly less human, so that the inner core of you, the human bit, doesn't get broken.

She stared at him, taking in the shaggy brown hair, the tired eyes, the short fingernails on bony hands.

"Elsie was admitted last night..." Mr Taylor was saying, reading from his notes, "and was given a swallow test and a CT scan, and we took bloods, which is normal procedure when we suspect a stroke. The scan confirmed an ischaemic stroke caused by a thrombus in the middle cerebral artery..."

He glanced up. Susan saw him notice that the women were looking confused, and he shut his folder.

"Your sister has had a stroke," he said to Dot. "She had a blood clot, in her left hemisphere, and it caused some damage. But luckily, she got here nice and quickly, and we managed to treat her before there was further damage. It looks, from the scan, as if we won't need to perform surgery, and can treat her with medication. Do you have any questions?"

Dot shook her head. "No, thank you," she said.

"Mum, you do have a few things you'd like to know," prompted Cassie, frowning. She looked towards the doctor. "What's the prognosis?" she said. "Will Elsie make a full recovery?"

"Well," said the young Mr Taylor, frowning, his words measured. "It's early days, we'll know more in a week or two. Elsie will need medication, and some physio – to get her mobile again. You have probably noticed the right side of her body is affected, she'll need some help to get that moving again...And we don't yet know how much speech was damaged..."

"Yes, I was wondering about that," said Dot, looking at Susan, not the doctor. "Can she understand us? Why isn't she answering?"

"We'll know more in a few days," repeated the doctor. "The left side of the brain, where the clot was, is the part that controls speech. I expect that Elsie can understand most of what you say, but it might take time for her to be able to respond. She may have to learn how to use her speech muscles again – have to remember how to make sentences and words, and then learn how to make her mouth say them."

"So, would an iPad help?" said Cassie. "Then she could type her answers, not have to say them."

"Well, it might..." said the doctor, clearly not willing to commit. "But we don't know yet the extent of the damage. If Elsie is unable to form words into sentences, cannot create the words in her mind, then giving her an iPad is not going to make much difference. It might be worth trying in a few days, when we know more. Was she proficient on computers, before the stroke? Does she know how to use an iPad?"

"No," said Susan.

"And I doubt the stroke has made her brain suddenly able to use one, has it?" said Dot.

"It was just an idea..." said Cassie, her voice trailing away.

"Yes, and a good idea at that," said Mr Taylor, coming to her rescue. "But at the moment, we simply don't know. Always worth a try though, isn't it? It certainly can't hurt to try."

He gave another smile, and sort of bounded out of his chair. "Right, was there anything else?" he said, clearly keen to leave.

The women shook their heads.

The doctor nodded at them and left, closing the door behind him. Susan felt that she had been in the presence of a small whirlwind.

"Do you think he's qualified?" said Dot. "He looks like he should still be at school."

Chapter Fifteen

Susan first met William Evans at the hospital. There had been long discussions with Neil, weighing the risk to Elsie's health against the possibility that time might run out. In the end they had agreed that Neil would meet William first, and if Neil felt comfortable, then he should be allowed to visit the hospital to see Elsie. Elsie however, would not initially be told who William was. He would be introduced as a friend.

"Won't she think that's odd?" said Ben, when Susan explained the plan during a rare lunchtime when they had all coincided in the kitchen at the same time.

"Possibly," conceded Susan, carrying a plate of bread and cheese to the table. "But to be honest, Aunty Elsie has so much happening to her right now, having to come to terms with learning to speak and move again, I think she'll hardly notice."

"Have you seen him yet? This long-lost cousin of yours?" said Tom through a mouthful of sandwich. "Any pictures on Facebook or anything?"

Susan shook her head. "I've hardly had time to live my own life these last few weeks," she said. "I certainly haven't felt like stalking anyone else's!" She glanced at the clock.

Jack looked up sharply. "Stalker?" he said, frowning. "Stalker...I wonder if..."

"What?" said Ben through a mouthful of tomato.

"Nothing," said Jack, turning back to his meal. "Nothing. It's just something Gran told me is beginning to make sense now, I thought she was imagining it at the time, but maybe she wasn't..." His voice trailed away. No one was listening anyway.

Susan was gathering her lunch and wrapping it in a piece torn from the roll of paper towel.

"I might eat the rest of this in the car," she said. "I told Neil I'd meet them there at two."

"You ought to be careful," said Tom, frowning at her over a mug of coffee. "You've done nothing but rush around since Elsie's stroke – try to plan an afternoon doing nothing at some point. Or you'll make yourself ill."

Susan nodded at him, grateful he had noticed, but fully aware that there simply wasn't time for any time off. Not if she was to keep everything stable. And 'stable' was precious, she realised, as she slid into her car and placed her lunch on the seat next to her. She shook her head, longing for days that were 'normal', days when she was bored, when there was nothing turbulent waiting around the corner.

"The trouble is," she thought, turning into the lane, "we don't realise the value of 'normal' until everything has been turned upside down." Susan gripped the steering wheel and took a breath. She couldn't start thinking about how precarious life was, not now when she was about to meet a stranger. She needed to put her emotions on hold until everything had settled down again. "Because it will," she reassured herself. "Nothing lasts forever, not even the bad times." She took a bite of cheese, and drove to the hospital.

***

Neil was waiting in the foyer, walking towards her when Susan entered. Behind him was a man. He was very tall, with thick grey hair and he was wearing a blue sweater and jeans that looked as though they had been ironed. Then the man looked at her, and Susan stopped, shocked.

"He looks like Edward!" Susan stared at the man, this stranger, who had the same profile, the same way of ducking his head when he smiled – and as she grew closer, she saw the same blue eyes – as her son. "I didn't expect that," she thought. "It never occurred to me that he might look like one of us..."

"William, this is my mum, Susan – your cousin," said Neil.

The man came to Susan and shook her hand, smiling. She found she was blushing.

"Goodness," she thought, "this is odd."

"It's so very kind of you to allow me to see my mother," said William, releasing her hand.

Susan looked at him sharply, but she couldn't detect any sarcasm in his expression, he looked sincere.

"Of course," she said, feeling defensive. "We're trying to do what is best for Aunty, so she recovers quickly. We felt that a shock might be dangerous for her, she's very frail."

The man nodded, and they walked towards the ward.

"I really am, very grateful," William continued as they walked. "I've been looking for Elsie – my mother – for months. I managed to find her name, but it's not an uncommon one, so there were several possible candidates. I tried to find their addresses, just through using telephone numbers and Google searches, and Facebook..."

His voice trailed away, and Susan glanced at his face, which was pink, and he was looking down, as if embarrassed by his own behaviour.

"I even tried to visit some of the women," he was saying, his voice very soft. "I thought that perhaps, if I saw her, I might recognise her. I wasted a lot of time, driving to various places, trying to see people. But then, whenever I was there, actually at their homes, I just felt like a stalker, I found I couldn't trespass on their time, on their lives, and so I left again, without making contact...often without even knocking at the door...and then the DNA results appeared, and finally, I had a match, I felt that I was beginning to find out who I was."

Susan smiled, hoping that she had made the correct decision in allowing this.

It seemed further today, this walk that Susan had done most days for the last two weeks. Now that Cassie had gone home, it was mostly Susan who drove Dot each day to visit Elsie – though sometimes Jack or Ben were able to help.

"We're only supposed to have two visitors at a time," explained Susan, as they waited for the lift to arrive. The doors swooshed open, and they stepped inside. "We thought I could go in first, and say hello, tell Aunty that

Neil wanted to pop in, and has a friend with him. Then if you both come in, together, so Aunty thinks you're Neil's friend. We'll have to hope a nurse doesn't notice there are three of us – if they do, we'll just apologise and Neil can leave."

William nodded, but didn't speak. Susan knew that Neil had already explained the plan to him, wasn't sure why she was saying it all again, knew she was speaking simply to fill the space. She looked across the lift at him, saw him push back the hair that had fallen over one eye in a gesture she had seen Edward do many times.

They stepped from the lift and walked to the ward, their feet loud on the shiny floor.

"I left Dad sorting out another new lot of calves," said Susan. "He was checking the ear-tags all morning, making sure they matched with the passports. I'll have to help him feed them later, it takes ages when they're all still on milk, it's much easier once we can give them fodder." Her voice was overly loud, her words too fast. Susan didn't really know why she was talking, certainly neither man was really listening, were simply nodding politely, their faces blank. But she felt she should say *something* to this cousin, try to make some sort of connection. Neil had already explained the situation of his birth, there was no need to go over that again. But what do you say to someone who you've never met before? Someone who so closely resembles your son that you can read his every look, but who you know nothing about...how can you catch up with fifty years of conversation in an afternoon?

A nurse passed them, hurrying with a clipboard.

They slowed behind a patient in a thick green dressing-gown, who was struggling to walk with a frame, a relative walking beside them. Susan didn't feel they should ask to pass, but she felt her frustration growing with every stumbling step the man took, his slippers slapping onto the floor, the pause before he jerked the frame forward, then adjusted his weight, before taking the next step. The man beside him noticed them waiting, and smiled in apology. Another step; another pause; another jerk of the frame.

They reached an alcove, the corridor widened, and Neil led the way past the patient.

They reached the ward, and Susan looked furtively for the nurses, feeling like a criminal. There were two at the central station, but they knew Susan, did no more than glance in her direction as she walked towards Aunty Elsie. Neil and William waited near the plastic seats, waiting for a signal from Susan.

Aunty Elsie was sitting in the blue chair beside the bed, her right hand curled on her lap, her right leg stretched in front, the foot turned inward. She looked up as Susan approached, and smiled with the left side of her mouth. Susan's heart clenched at the lop-sided expression, she wondered if she would ever get used to seeing it.

"Hello Aunty Elsie," she said, kissing her aunt's forehead.

There was a curtain, patterned with great orange swirls, and Susan tugged at it, half-pulling it across the runner so it gave some privacy, before sitting beside Elsie. She noticed that her aunt's hair hadn't been combed, and her pink cardigan was twisted on her shoulder, as though she had been dressed in a hurry.

"Let me smarten you up a bit," said Susan, reaching in her bag for a comb. "Neil's outside, with a friend. He wants to pop in and say hello..." She began to pull the comb through her aunt's hair, teasing the knots from the curls, watching them bounce back into place. She straightened the cardigan, and used a tissue to wipe her aunt's chin.

Elsie made a sound, a sort of grunt, her mouth stretching awkwardly over elongated vowels, which Susan took to be a "thank you".

Susan noticed a shadow, and looked up to see Neil and William standing at the foot of the bed, hovering near the end of the curtain. Neil walked forwards, into the space, and kissed his aunt, before sitting on the bed.

"Hi Aunty Elsie," he said, "how are you doing?" He swung his legs, and placed his hands flat on the mattress, looking comfortable. Susan wasn't sure that visitors were supposed to sit on patient's beds.

Elsie made a sort of gurgling grunt, and Susan wished people would stop asking her aunt questions. She knew it was the natural thing to do, but it pained her to hear her aunt struggle to form words, and she knew the person didn't expect a reply. It was, she thought, like when you're lying on the dentist's couch, and he starts to ask you how your family are, when he knows you have a mouth full of tools and cannot possibly speak coherently.

"This is my friend, William," said Neil, glancing in William's direction.

Susan watched, not breathing, as Elsie moved her head towards William. She saw her aunt gaze at him, then look back to Neil. William moved forwards, and stood opposite Elsie, on the other side of the bed. He was staring. Susan saw him, absorbing the shape of Elsie's head, staring at her eyes – blue like his but watery and red-rimmed. Susan watched him take in the mouth that drooped on one side, the narrow shoulders, the hand with the claw-like fingers that rested in her lap. He stared, without reserve, and Susan felt suddenly angry, feeling that he was invading her aunt's privacy, he should look away, appear less interested. Aunty Elsie was not a spectacle to be observed.

Neil coughed, breaking the spell.

"So, Aunty," he said, "Did Mum tell you that she talked to the nurse, and they say you can come out, for Noah's christening? If you'd like to? Dad said he'll collect you, and the hospital will lend you a wheelchair, and you can come, just for the service because we don't want to tire you out. Then Dad will pop you back, so you can rest. Would you like to?"

But Elsie wasn't listening. Elsie was staring back at William.

"She knows," thought Susan, a cold itch creeping under her skin, turning to fire that filled her whole being with heat. She watched her aunt, as Elsie stared, mesmerised by William, her mouth opened, but no sound. Tears filled her eyes, balanced there, shining on the lids, before streaming down her cheeks, wet rivers that flowed down, dripping from her chin.

Susan moved forwards, a tissue in hand, and began to wipe her aunt's face. Elsie lifted her left hand towards William. He moved around the bed, sat next to Neil, took her hand.

Beyond the garishly patterned curtain, there was a clatter from the ward, voices humming, the whir of a machine. The doors to the ward batted open and squeaked closed. Footsteps in heels clicked past. Someone coughed. But beside Elsie's bed, a pantomime was being played out in silence, no words spoken, no emotions expressed beyond the pressing of hands, the water-filled eyes; the faces filled with sorrow, regret, love, all tangled together in a single look. Susan watched as William took Elsie's hand, his slender fingers covering the wrinkled flesh until it was quite hidden. Then, reaching forward, he placed his other hand on Elsie's shoulder, looked into her eyes, and said, very quietly so Susan barely heard him: "Hello."

Nothing else. No name, no 'Mum'. Simply that one word, spoken with so much warmth and longing and relief that Susan felt it was almost a palpable thing, something that filled the space around them and touched and warmed all of them.

Susan glanced at Neil, who was also staring, watching, enchanted by the scene. Neither of them moved or spoke, not wanting to break the spell, disturb the mood. They stayed, like statues, absorbing the scene.

It was a nurse who ended it. Rounding the corner of the bed, pushing a trolley rattling with drugs in tiny pots and syringes balanced on oval dishes, she stopped.

"Only two visitors at a time please," she said, the authority in her voice chasing away the mood.

Neil and Susan both stood. There was no doubt now, no deciding whether William should be allowed access to Elsie. They had both shown that – there was something stronger than logic joining them, and Susan felt suddenly in the way, an observer, while the main characters were the ones who knew the script.

Susan leaned towards Elsie, threaded an arm around her shoulders, feeling the softness of her, smelling the familiar scent that clung to her cardigan.

"Shall I wait outside, with Neil, for a few minutes?" said Susan, her voice soft, gazing at her aunt for a sign, an expression that would show what she wanted.

Elsie nodded, the slightest incline of her head, her eyes still locked on William's face, as if, thought Susan, after all these years she needs to absorb every last detail.

"I'll come back, in a few minutes," said Susan, glancing towards William.

He looked at her, blinked away the tears that had hung for a moment in those blue eyes.

"Thank you," he said, his voice low and warm. "I would like that – if you don't mind?"

Susan shook her head, hoping she was doing the right thing, and followed Neil to the plastic seats at the entrance to the ward.

"I'm not quite sure what happened there," said Neil, as she sat beside him. "Did Aunty Elsie recognise him?"

"I don't know...she seemed to know who he was though," said Susan, "almost as if she has been waiting for him."

"Do you think it's a sign?" said Neil, frowning. "Do you think she might die now?"

"No," said Susan, too quickly. She didn't want to think about that, couldn't bear to consider that somehow, seeing her son was something Elsie had been waiting to do, and now her wish was fulfilled, she might leave them. "No," she said again.

The plastic seat was hard beneath her, and she shuffled, trying to arrange her bones so they didn't rub uncomfortably against the rigid chair.

"The doctor said she's doing really well, and if there was someone able to care for her at home, she'd have been released by now," said Susan, determined to convince Neil that Elsie was getting better, not preparing for death.

"You make it sound like prison," muttered Neil.

"Discharged," said Susan. "I meant discharged."

"Though," she thought, "it feels like a prison at times, this place with no weather."

They waited, not speaking, for twenty minutes. Susan pulled a magazine from her bag, but although she turned the pages, was aware of photos of celebrities whose names she didn't know, she couldn't read it. Her mind was a fuzz of emotion. Waiting, she thought, was not like pausing. You cannot rest when you're waiting, you are too alert, too noticing of the time that is passing.

Beside her, Neil was staring at his phone, scrolling through emails, his thumbs flying across the keypad.

After twenty minutes, Susan stood. "We should go back now," she said. "We don't want to tire Aunty Elsie, it's time to say goodbye. Mum will come later, she needs to rest now."

They walked back to the bed, not caring if another nurse told them to leave – they were leaving anyway. William was sitting in the chair, next to Elsie. Susan saw he was holding her hand, talking, and as they approached, she saw Elsie smile at something, her shoulders shaking.

"He's made her laugh," thought Susan, smiling, a sense of relief flowing through her. Perhaps it had been all right after all, perhaps they hadn't made a mistake in allowing William to come.

When Susan stooped, to kiss her aunt and tell her that Dot would be coming later, Elsie caught hold of her arm with her good hand. Susan watched her mouth moving, wordless, but her aunt's eyes were clear and blue. There was something in that look, something which Susan understood.

**

The sweet smell of baby milk met Susan at the door of the shed. It was a small space, crammed full with sacks of calf milk, and buckets and any farm equipment that needed to be kept clean. A brick-built building, it was easier to keep it dry and free of rodents than the barns. When it was new, Susan remembered that they had kept it clean, almost an extension to the house, but over time, the dust from the milk powder had drifted down to coat the cement floor, and the sink in the corner had become grubby and unwashed. In one corner, attached to the wall, was the fat water-heater, the wires and pipes running through the wall behind it. There was also the sink, with a cold-water tap, and an extremely dirty tea-towel hanging beneath it.

Tom was mixing milk for the latest batch of calves, but the smell – sugary and creamy – always took Susan right back to the days of feeding her own babies. Not, she thought, that she had fed them bottled milk very often, unlike Kylie, she had fed her babies herself.

"Even the calves get fed proper milk-substitute," thought Susan, "none of this soya rubbish..."

Thinking of Kylie made Susan frown, so when Tom looked up to greet her, he saw her dark expression and assumed the hospital visit had gone badly.

"Oh dear," said Tom, turning back to stir the bucket on the floor. "Meeting your cousin didn't go well then?"

Susan watched as Tom finished mixing the milk – the powder completely dissolved; she saw him use his wrist to check the temperature.

"Your cousin not who you were hoping for?" Tom said, lifting two buckets and walking towards the door.

"Oh, no," said Susan, shaking her head, her expression clearing as she followed him to the barn. "William was... nice. Seemed like a nice man. He looked like Ed, which took me by surprise – very nice looking. And he was kind to Aunty. I think she recognised him."

They reached the barn, and the calves grew restless as they realised they were about to be fed. The calves nearest to the door began to push each other, competing to watch as Tom lifted the first bucket, pouring it into the container for them to drink. The calves pushed forwards, the first few latching on to a teat, eyes shut as they began to suck. There was a spare teat abandoned in the middle, and none of the other calves could reach it, so Susan stretched forwards, to force one head back to it, allowing another calf to feed at the end of the row. The hard black head clung on, determined to not be moved, and Susan had to use both hands to force it along the row. Other calves pushed forwards, their long grey tongues encircling her arm, searching for food.

Tom was emptying the second bucket into the next feeding container.

"Elsie knew him, did she?" said Tom, sounding surprised. "I thought the plan was for your cousin to see her – just in case – but for her to be kept in the dark. Did you change your mind?"

Susan shook her head. "No, we didn't say anything, William kept to the script. But Elsie...Elsie sort of stared at him, and cried, and wanted him close. She knew. I'm sure she knew."

"And this William was all right? Not a psycho?"

Susan picked up an empty bucket and followed Tom back to the shed. She watched as he began to scoop milk powder from the sack into the first bucket, adding water from the water heater. It was a cool evening, and the steam billowed round his hand. Susan took the bucket from him, and began to add cold water while Tom scooped powder into the next bucket.

"He seemed nice, actually," said Susan, thinking of William, with his blue eyes, and the way his hair flopped over one eye, just like Ed. "And he was very nice looking."

"You already said that," muttered Tom, reaching for another bucket.

Susan giggled. "Lucky I'm attracted to short, bald chubby men then, isn't it?" she said.

"Not so much of the 'chubby,' thank you," said Tom, grinning back at her.

They filled four buckets with milk, and carried them across the yard to the barn. Both dogs were with them, tracking each step as they circled around, hoping they would spill some. When Susan put down a bucket, Molly sat, attentive, watching closely, eager for drips of milk. The calves in the far pens were restless, pushing against the bars, rubbing alongside each other, trying to reach the milk they could smell.

Susan stood for a moment, noticing the smell of hay and straw that mingled with the heat from the calves and the stench of their poo, overpowering the sweet milk. The calves were sucking, concentrating with their whole being on eating; the dogs were licking up drips; Tom was scattering fresh hay into the pens, leaning across the bars to throw armfuls onto the bedding.

"This is life," thought Susan, savouring the moment, knowing it was far removed from the ordered sterility of the hospital. "I think I would rather die here, amongst the dirt and smells and sounds of life, than stuck in an airless room with no colour."

Then she shook her head, telling herself that no one was going to die, took a breath, and followed Tom to the shed for the next lot of milk.

Chapter Sixteen

When Jack went to collect Josie for the christening, she wasn't ready. She answered the door, with makeup in place, a thick towelling dressing-gown wrapped around her, tied with a fat knot at the front.

"You wearing that?" said Jack, grinning.

"Very funny," snapped Josie. "I don't know what to wear," she whined, walking away from him across the white tiled floor. "Everything looks awful. All my dresses are like tents, and trousers look even worse..."

She turned, and Jack saw she was genuinely upset.

"I don't think I can come," said Josie, "just go without me. It's a family thing anyway, no one will miss me. And they'll all be looking smart and pretty, they don't want some giant woman wearing a tent taking up space..."

"Josie," said Jack.

Josie stopped, staring at him, her eyes challenging him to say something silly, some trite remark that she would shoot down in flames.

Jack said nothing. He crossed the hall, and took her into his arms, and held her. He could feel her tension through the thick towelling of the dressing-gown as she held herself stiffly upright. He tugged her closer, knowing that trying to reassure her would be flung back at him, that telling her no one would notice what she wore would be twisted into taunt.

"I want you there," he said at last. "Please come – for me."

At first, Jack thought Josie would still refuse, tell him he was only pretending, say that it wouldn't make any difference. Then he felt her relax slightly, her back became less upright, and he knew that he had won.

"Wear your blue dress," he said, remembering the outfit she had worn to a restaurant recently. "I like that one," he said – which was a lie, because he could barely remember it. But Jack honestly didn't care what Josie wore, he never noticed clothes anyway, he simply wanted her next to him, part of his family.

Josie nodded, and went to change, running up the stairs, thumping into her room. Jack stood at the bottom of the stairs, listening to the creak of her wardrobe door, a bang that sounded like a chair had fallen, followed by a curse, then footsteps, still hurrying, as Josie appeared again on the stairs, pulling the blue dress straight, carrying shoes in one hand.

"Mum met that man who's her cousin," said Jack as Josie descended the staircase, hoping to distract her from her appearance before she could launch into a wail of self-loathing about her current outfit.

"Really?" said Josie, reaching down to put on her shoes.

Jack looked up at her, noting that with heels, Josie was taller than him. He put an arm round her waist, and kissed her cheek, before heading towards the car.

"Yes," said Jack, "Mum met him at the hospital.

"William – he's called William," added Jack, remembering. They left the house, and crossed the yard to where the car was parked.

"Mum said he met Aunty Elsie," said Jack, "and that it was like Elsie knew who he was, even though they didn't explain it to her." Jack opened the car door for Josie, because he knew she liked that, and had told him in the past that it made her feel special, like a woman.

"I'm not sure why Josie has this idea that she's not feminine," thought Jack, watching as Josie climbed into the car and reached for the seatbelt. He shut the door and went to the driver's side. "She might be big, but that just means more curves," thought Jack, and grinned.

"What are you smiling at?" said Josie, her tone accusing.

"Nothing," said Jack.

"Was he nice then, this William?" asked Josie.

"I think so, from what Mum said. She seemed to trust him with Aunty Elsie, anyway, and Neil has invited him today – to the christening – so you'll get to meet him."

"I wonder what he looks like," said Josie, staring at the fields as they passed.

Jack was silent. He remembered that his mother had said William looked very like Edward. But Jack found he didn't want to tell Josie that, he didn't want to mention Edward at all. He stared ahead, as if he hadn't heard, and concentrated very hard on driving.

***

When they arrived at the church near to Neil's house, they parked in a street full of cars, edging into a space between a smart blue hatchback and an old Fiesta with moss growing on the outside. They walked back towards the church, hoping they weren't the first to arrive, checking their watches.

Jack opened the door to the church, and looked inside. There was a woman, arranging flowers at the front, foliage falling over the altar, a bucket with more flowers at her feet.

"Hello?" said the woman, turning when the door opened, holding a dahlia stem. She smiled, looking confused.

"Uh, hi," said Jack, peering behind the door, in the hope that for some reason his family might all be sitting at the back of the church. It was empty. "We've come for the christening," he said to the woman, who was now coming towards them, water dripping from the flower onto the floor.

"Neil and Kylie Compton?" Jack added, hopefully.

The woman shook her head. "I'm sorry," she said, "I don't know them. I wasn't told there was a christening today...what time does it start?"

"Well...now," said Jack, his heart sinking, a heaviness creeping through his stomach. "I think we must have the wrong day, or time, or something..."

The woman was level with him now, Josie had come in, and was standing beside him.

"Hello," the woman said to Josie.

"Have you got the invitation, with the address on it?" the woman asked Josie, clearly having decided that Jack was not to be trusted.

Josie read out the name of the church: "St. Andrews Church...Church Road..."

"Ah, well, this is St. John's," said the woman, beaming. "St. Andrews is in the next street, at the top of the hill." She walked to the door, and pointed.

There was a church tower, above the line of rooftops, about half a mile away.

"Thank you," said Jack, and turned, pulling Josie with him.

"You idiot!" said Josie when they were outside.

"Do you think we can walk there?" said Jack, hurrying down the road, past the line of cars, towards their own. "We'll never find another space, there are too many cars in this city."

"No," said Josie, staring at the long road, which wound around a corner and out of sight. "I'm wearing heels. You'll have to drive, and hope we're lucky."

They climbed back into the car, and Jack did a multi-point turn, jolting the car forwards and backwards until they were facing the other direction.

"Lucky this isn't a driving test," muttered Josie, as the car lurched onto the kerb. Jack ignored her.

They drove back down the road, around the corner, to the junction with the correct road. The road, which was called Church Road rather than Church Street, joined on the right – but it was a one-way street, with the traffic moving in the opposite direction. Jack stopped at the junction, staring at the red no-entry signs.

"Do you think we could risk it?" he said, glancing at the time. The road was clear, lined with parked cars but nothing moving, no traffic. To enter the road legally, he would have to drive all the way back to the main road, and go along the high street. There really wasn't time, especially given the number of people who would be shopping on a Saturday morning.

Josie leaned round him, scanning the road. It curved up the hill, semi-detached Victorian houses on both sides, red-bricked with bay windows under pointed eaves. They had tiny gardens, mainly filled with large shrubs. The road was lined with parked cars, and at the top, near the corner, they could see the church.

"Look, there's a space," said Josie, pointing to a small space next to a yellow skip.

Jack looked up the road, waiting. No cars were coming. He glanced in his rear-view mirror. Behind him, there was a white van approaching at speed; in front, at the junction with the main road, a red Mini was turning into Church Street. He glanced up Church Road again – it was still empty – no traffic on the road, no movement from within the houses. The Mini was now driving towards them, Jack took a breath, pressed the accelerator, and zoomed around the corner, into Church Road.

Engine revving, he raced up towards the space, passing the skip, stopping slightly beyond, level with a parked car, ready to position into the space. As he glanced forwards, pulling up the handbrake, a lorry appeared around the corner ahead, a giant on the skyline, driving down the middle of the road.

Josie gasped; Jack spun the wheel, twisting in his seat, looking behind, steering the car back, towards the space. He looked forwards. The lorry loomed nearer, filling the horizon.

"He's on his phone!" said Josie, "Hurry up and get out of the way before he hits us!"

Jack glanced forwards again, saw that Josie was right, the driver of the lorry was staring down, as if reading a text or adjusting his music. The lorry was moving at speed, swaying from side to side, confident that the road ahead would be clear, almost upon them, as Jack revved their little car, hurtling the back end into the space, almost touching the edge of the skip before slamming on the brakes, jolting to a stop. The lorry careered past – Jack didn't think the driver had even noticed them, so intent he seemed on his phone. Jack watched in his mirror, as the lorry reached the end of the road, paused for a second, then roared around the corner. He turned to Josie.

"Sorry about that," he said.

Josie shook her head.

Jack shuffled the car, edging forwards and backwards, until the car was aligned straight with the pavement. The back of the car was overshadowed by a large blue sofa which overhung the skip, and the front bumper was almost touching the red car in front. But they were in the space, and only a few hundred yards from the church, and they were late.

Jack and Josie climbed from the car, Jack glanced up at the sofa on the skip and hoped it wouldn't fall, then locked the car and followed Josie towards the church.

They walked quickly, Josie's heels clicking on the paving stones, past the houses, which were all red brick, though as they hurried Jack noticed tiny differences. "I wonder what it would be like, to live so close to your neighbours," thought Jack, staring at the houses as he passed. Some had tiles hung across the upper walls, others had black and white stripes in the eaves, or ornamental gingerbread cutouts decorating the porches. All the houses seemed to have large shrubs in the front gardens, which towered over the low brick walls, and seemed overly large for the size of garden. "It must be weird," he thought, "to have strangers living practically in the same space, to have your home joined to another one, with only a single wall separating you. I wonder if you can hear, if a couple are shouting at each other. I wonder how much privacy you actually have..."

Jack noticed his parents' car, covered in mud, standing near the church.

They arrived at the church. The doors were shut, and Jack and Josie looked at each other.

Jack took a breath, and pulled open the door. The sound of singing welcomed them, and he walked into the building.

The church was old, with a modern extension over the porch. As Jack walked inside, he could smell the wood from the ancient pews, and he saw tall white arches in the walls, and that the floor was patterned with black and white tiles. It was a long building, the family occupied only the front few rows, with empty pews stretching to the back.

It was impossible to walk soundlessly, and as they tapped their way to the front, everyone – or at least, it felt like everyone to Jack – turned to watch them. The hymn finished, and people began to sit down. Jack noticed that the two families had arranged themselves separately, either side of the aisle, as if at a wedding. Kylie's family were all sitting on the left, turning their dark faces to watch as Jack and Josie walked to the front. On the right of the aisle sat Neil's family: Jack could see Aunt Cassie next to his grandmother sitting four rows back with a tall man with grey hair. A wheelchair was in the aisle, next to the pew, and Jack could see the back of Aunty Elsie's head. In the second row were his brothers, who were all grinning at him, Edward pointedly looking at his phone to check the time, Ben and Kevin laughing. Jack's parents were in the front row, with Neil and Kylie. Susan smiled, looking relieved when she saw Jack.

Jack moved into a seat behind his aunt and grandmother. There were spaces in the rows nearer the front, but he felt more comfortable at the back. This was unconnected, he told himself, to the fact that the empty seats were next to Edward. The congregation settled back, and the vicar continued with the service.

***

There was a lunch reception following the service. Neil and Kylie had hired caterers, and the church hall had been arranged with chairs clustered around low tables, paper tablecloths and vases of flowers. The flowers reminded Jack of the woman in the other church.

"We had bit of trouble getting here," Jack told Ben, as he followed him along the edge of the buffet table. "We went to the wrong church."

Ben leaned across the table to take some potato salad. Most of it landed on his plate.

"How'd you manage that then?" asked Ben.

"Josie was map-reading," said Jack.

Josie, who was standing behind him, dug him in the ribs.

"Then Jack nearly killed us with a head-on collision with a lorry," she said, reaching for the potato salad spoon. It was smeared with mayonnaise, so she used her napkin to wipe the handle before spooning a heap onto her plate.

"This would be nice with some ham," Josie whispered.

"Or sausage rolls," added Ben.

Jack took his plateful and a plastic beaker of something described as punch, and went to an empty table. He looked around the hall.

Kylie's family had spread themselves around a few tables near to the buffet table. There were more of them than the Comptons, and Jack could hear them laughing and the steady hum of conversation. Two small boys had dropped a tiny tomato on the floor, and were kicking it between them under the table, in a variation of table football. Kylie's mother noticed, and told them off. They waited until she turned to the person next to her, and then continued, kicking the tomato across the garish carpet. Jack noticed Kylie's father remove a small flask from his pocket and add something to his beaker of punch. Jack considered moving to their table. He looked up as Josie came to join him.

"That must be your Mum's cousin," whispered Josie, gesturing towards a tall grey-haired man.

William was speaking to Neil.

"Thank you so much for inviting me to such an august occasion," Jack heard William say. "It was terribly decent of you to allow me to trespass on your day. Lovely to finally meet the rest of the family..."

Jack glanced at Josie. "I think he had a different sort of upbringing to the rest of us," said Jack.

"Yes, but he seems nice," said Josie. "I think he's rather sweet – and he's very nice looking."

"Is he?" said Jack, scowling. "He's old."

Jack saw his mother approach Neil and William, and noticed that his mother was blushing. "Weird," he thought, watching them. Jack knew his father had taken Aunty Elsie back to hospital, as soon as the service had finished. People had filed passed her, patting her shoulder in a consolatory manner, almost, thought Jack, as if she were a kitten. He wondered for a moment whether not being able to speak properly also meant that a person couldn't think, and was now retarded in some way, or if their brain functioned in every other way as it always had, and whether perhaps Aunty Elsie thought people were rather strange in petting her, and perhaps taking a liberty by patting her. People did not, generally, touch other people, but there was something about a wheelchair which seemed to make touching acceptable.

Jack realised he was staring into space while he thought, and he looked back at the group beside him. Neil was speaking, while William and Susan listened, and Jack saw them both nod in agreement. He watched in horror as his mother turned towards him and Josie, gestured to William, and then proceeded to lead him over.

"Oh no," he whispered to Josie, "I think we're about to be introduced."

"Jack," said Susan, looming over him, "I'd like you to meet William, my cousin."

Josie was staring at her plate, and Jack knew she was wondering if she could sidle away. He would rather like to sidle away himself, but instead he stood, and offered his hand.

"Hi, William, pleased to meet you," said Jack, shaking his hand. "Why don't you join us?"

William sat next to Josie, and smiled at them both – more, thought Jack, like the host than a visitor. There was something supremely confident about William.

"Tell me about your farm," said William, turning his very bright eyes towards Josie. "Susan tells me that you're thinking of starting a dairy herd? You will have to use layman's terms I'm afraid, as I'm rather a novice, but I'm terribly interested in your plans."

Jack saw Josie blush as she struggled to swallow a mouthful of brown bread. It stuck in her throat, and she coughed, turning an even darker crimson, reaching for Jack's cup of punch. She swallowed, and began to speak, telling William about the farm. Jack wondered if she would refer to her father, but she didn't. She simply told William about the herd, and how they were struggling to make the farm pay, and some of the ideas which he, Jack, had suggested.

Jack looked down at his plate, wishing she would stop talking. William was asking pertinent questions, seemed genuinely interested, and Jack could hear Josie's voice becoming more confident as she began to explain the situation – their situation – which Jack felt was private, and not for discussing with strangers, even if they were physically related by blood. He lifted his fork and poked at the potato salad despondently, thinking that it looked slimy where the mayonnaise had melted, and the speckles of chives that had once clung to the potato were now in a slippery heap on his plate. He chased a tomato around his plate with his fork, not wanting to use his fingers while William was there, then gave up, put his food on the table and folded his arms.

William was eating with delicate bites, using his napkin to wipe his mouth, only speaking when each mouthful was finished. Jack thought it was effeminate, this obsession with manners, and deciding to use his fingers after all, reached for the tomato. As he bit into it, the tomato exploded, showering his shirt with tiny seeds and pink juice. Josie glanced at him and chuckled.

"You'll never get that stain out," she said, and turned back to William, who was asking her about the buildings at the farm, and what they were currently used for, and whether Josie had ever thought about branching out, into something other than farming.

"Well, it can be hard to get permission for change of land use," Jack heard her say.

"I'm going to see the baby," said Jack, standing. "Be back in a minute."

Jack walked across the hall, to where Kylie and Neil were sitting. He didn't actually have much desire to see the baby, cute though he was, but he did want to get away from William. There was something slippery about him, something too polished, that Jack didn't trust. He also didn't like the way all the females seemed to gravitate towards William, even Josie seemed eager to talk to William, and Josie rarely spoke to anyone. Plus, the more he thought about it, the more he was beginning to think that stalking his grandmother – because that was what it amounted to, was a dodgy thing to do. Gran had been anxious, almost frightened when she first mentioned 'being followed' to Jack, and although he had dismissed it at first, told her she must be imagining it, now that he'd seen William and how like Edward he looked, something inside Jack felt defensive, as if William was going to cause trouble.

Baby Noah was asleep in the crook of Kylie's arm, a long train of christening gown flowing under the plate of food she was attempting to eat.

"Hi," said Jack, peering down at his nephew. "Do you want me to hold him for a minute, so you can eat?"

"Oh thanks, yes. I can do most things with one hand now, but it would be nice to have a break."

Jack sat, and Kylie eased the baby from her arm onto Jack's lap. Neil looked up from his own food and nodded, his face grey. Jack wondered if Neil had a headache, then turned to look at his nephew. The baby was warm, and Jack thought it was similar to holding a heavy hot-water bottle. As Noah slept, he made tiny snuffling noises, and his arms twitched.

"He sounds like a piglet," said Jack.

"Smells like one sometimes," said Neil, "though I'm not sure you should really compare my son to pigs..."

"And the dress?" said Jack, staring at the lacy gown.

"It's a gown," said Kylie, her voice defensive, "and it's what my grandfather was christened in, and my father. It's traditional."

Neil met Jack's eye and grinned, but remained silent.

Jack glanced across the room, and his smile faded. Josie was still speaking to William, and Edward had joined them and was standing, leaning on the back of Josie's chair. Jack saw Edward say something, and both Josie and William looked up at him, laughing. Josie's cheeks were pink, and even across the room, Jack was aware that her eyes were sparkling, and she was holding herself differently, almost as if, Jack thought, she felt more womanly when she was with Edward.

"I see that you've met William," said Dot, interrupting Jack's thoughts. Her voice sounded harsh, and Jack looked at his grandmother in surprise.

"Don't you like him Gran?" he asked, hoping for a reason to dislike the man.

"He stalked us," said Dot. "Before he found Susan through that DNA thing, he stalked us. I saw him; twice I saw him. And I knew that I knew him, just couldn't think why. He looks very like his father you know, the way he stands...I don't know why he didn't introduce himself then, like a normal person would have. All that sneaking around, makes you wonder, doesn't it...I told you, didn't I Jack? I told you we were being followed."

Jack saw Neil look up, their eyes met, and Neil very faintly shook his head. Jack felt that there was a story here, something that wasn't being said. But Neil simply said, "I think it was a difficult situation Gran, William couldn't be sure if he had found the right Elsie Heath, he didn't want to approach the wrong one and cause a saga..."

On the other side of the hall, Jack's parents were talking to the vicar and a woman in a flowery dress who moved her hands as she spoke, like she was dancing. Kylie's family had swarmed back to the food table, and Jack saw that desserts had replaced the salads. There were mounds of muffins, and a pyramid of meringues dotted with raspberries. Someone was spooning a heavy sponge pudding into their bowl, a trail of melted syrup leaving a sticky line across the paper tablecloth. Two men were laughing loudly, people turned to look at them, and Jack saw Kylie look up and frown, then lower her face as if embarrassed. A shadow fell over him, and Jack looked up to find Josie standing next to him.

"Hi Josie," said Kylie, smiling at her. "Thank you for Noah's money-box, it's really sweet. I'll put it in his bedroom."

"Oh, that's okay," said Josie, sounding embarrassed. "Thanks for inviting me to the christening. Jack, I was wondering, would it be okay if I got a lift home with your mum's cousin? William has some ideas, about the farm, and he wants to look around a bit. And I need to get back really, to sort the cows, so it would mean you could stay longer, with your family...so it makes sense, if you don't mind, for me to get a lift with William? He suggested it, and I thought it was a good idea?"

Jack opened his mouth to object, and then shut it again. What could he say? He could hardly ban Josie from accepting a lift with William, and she was right, it would mean he needn't leave the christening before the rest of the family. But he was deeply unhappy, and something inside folded into a lump of helpless resignation. He felt, for no reason that he could think of, that this leaving, this sudden plan, was the heralding of something unstoppable, something that would sweep Josie away from him. Josie was blocking the light from the window, but Jack felt under a greater shadow than that, he felt as if something sinister was happening, something he was powerless to stop.

Noah, on Jack's lap, yawned, stretching his arms and arching his back. Jack looked down, as Noah opened his black eyes and stared, intently, up at Jack.

"Yeah, that's fine," Jack heard himself saying.

Josie kissed the top of Jack's head – a feather-light caress that he hardly felt, the sort of kiss that passes between people who have known each other for years and are not, he thought, in any way exciting. Then he watched, his stomach plummeting even further, as Josie walked from the hall with both William and Edward, deep in conversation.

"That was odd," said Kylie, frowning.

"Yeah, it was a bit," said Jack, feeling that this in no way described the turmoil of his feelings.

"Perhaps William's got some business to discuss," said Kylie, as she reached for Noah and took him from Jack.

Jack nodded.

Chapter Seventeen

When Susan arrived home from the christening and went into the kitchen, Josie was in there. Tom was checking the cows for the night, and Susan had come inside, wanting nothing more than to go to bed. She stopped when she saw Josie, her mind racing.

Why had Edward brought Josie back to the farm – was he trying to sabotage Jack's relationship? Surely not, although Edward wasn't a great one for rules, surely he would never mess about with Josie now she was firmly with Jack. But why then was Josie here? Why had she not waited, and come with Jack?

Susan stepped into the room, forcing herself to smile, quelling her fears until she knew for sure why the girl was there.

Josie was refolding the cloths in the linen drawer – which was a meaningless occupation – so Susan guessed she was waiting for her. Her heart sank. She crossed the kitchen and pulled a glass from the cupboard.

When Josie saw her, she stopped folding tea-cloths and pushed the drawer closed.

"Hello," said Josie, "I was waiting for you."

Susan nodded, glad that at least with Josie things would be direct, she wouldn't spend half an hour working up to what she wanted to say. She braced herself for whatever it was that Josie planned to announce.

"Can I ask you a question?" said Josie, peering into her face. "About...you know...God and stuff? Because you believe all that, don't you? About God I mean."

Relief flooded through Susan, and she suppressed a smile.

Susan filled the glass with water, and drank it, all down, in a single long drink. Then she refilled the glass and went to sit at the table. It still had crumbs where she hadn't wiped it before they rushed out to the christening, and she reached across, using her hand to sweep them into a single pile.

"Yes," said Susan, "I do believe in God. I'm not sure I could cope in life without him. What did you want to ask?"

She was tired, and she could hear the weariness in her own voice. "Why," she wondered, "do guests always arrive unannounced when you're exhausted? Why do people want to ask questions about God when you're too tired to even think? Things never happen when it's convenient..."

"Well," said Josie, sitting in a chair opposite Susan and frowning, "how do you know *what* to believe? I mean, the other night – that debate – doesn't that just show no one knows what the Bible really means? Doesn't it show that even if God is real – which I can't decide about, by the way – then it's all just guesswork? If we can't trust the Bible – and obviously we can't – then how can we *know* anything? What basis do you have for your faith? It all seems a bit, well...made-up to me."

Susan took another sip of her water. "I'm too tired for this," she thought, "God, you'll have to give me the words..."

She looked back at Josie, who was staring straight back at her, her grey eyes intent.

"We *can* trust the Bible," said Susan. "The Bible tells us that all Scripture is 'breathed out' by God – isn't that a lovely expression? And it was given to us so that we could learn about God, to teach us what is right and wrong, and to train us; so that we can become who God intended us to become. The problem is that none of us is perfect, and so we translate things differently. Perhaps God wanted it like that, so none of us could become conceited, and claim that *our beliefs* were absolutely the only complete knowledge about God. Because God is God, and although he wants us to come to him, we can never know him completely. If we did – if we knew everything there was to know about God – then he wouldn't be God. God is way beyond our understanding, and part of being a Christian, trying to follow him, is learning, gradually, who he is and what he wants for our lives."

Susan paused, and drank more water, not because she was thirsty but because it gave her something to do. She glanced at the clock, staring at the large round face, noting the time, whilst feeling that this conversation was important, possibly more important than all the words that had flown back and forth during the debate. Much of that had been an intellectual exercise, arguments to prove a point, an opinion; clever speeches, not necessarily important. But Susan sensed that Josie was honestly looking for answers about God, and that was more important than anything.

She looked back across the table at the young woman. Josie was sitting very upright, the dress she had worn to the christening was creased now, and her hair was bouncing around her head in unrestrained chaos; in contrast, Josie's eyes were very serious, and Susan realised she was being watched intently, as Josie waited for her answer. Susan stifled a yawn and placed the glass, very carefully, back on the table.

"Some of the Bible teaching *is* unclear," she began, "and if anyone claims they understand and can explain everything, then they are lying. But that doesn't mean that the important bits – the bits that tell us how God views us – cannot be trusted, because they can. You see, people were making a mess of the whole scripture thing, the whole reading and understanding God thing, so when Jesus came, he explained a lot about what people were getting wrong. Jesus said, very clearly, what was important.

"We can know, absolutely, that God loves us."

Susan looked across the table. Josie was scratching the surface with a nail, but she looked back at Susan when she said this.

"That's like Sunday-school kid's stuff," she said.

Susan shook her head. "No Josie," said Susan, "that's the most important thing that we, as adults, need to learn. Don't you want to be loved? Completely loved and accepted?"

Josie blushed, pink rising from her neck and flooding her face. "I do have someone who loves me," she muttered, embarrassed.

Susan paused, guessing that Josie was thinking of Jack, wondering if the girl also felt loved by her mother and feeling desperately sad that anyone could ever doubt something which should always be certain.

Susan reached across the table and touched her hand. "I know," she said, "but God loves you even more than that. God loves you completely, because he knows you completely. God knows everything you have ever done that was good, and it pleases him; and he knows everything that you've ever done that was wrong – he even knows the things you will do wrong in the future – and yet it doesn't change his love for you. He accepts every bit of you, and he longs for you to know him, to let him into your life. He doesn't want you to be alone, he wants to help with all the things you struggle with, he wants to teach you how to become who you were created to become..." Susan withdrew her hand and sipped her water, trying to sort the words in her mind.

"In the Bible, we read that God loves us. When Jesus came, he told people that God loves us. When we look at a raging sea, or a beautiful sunset, or a perfect rose, we can feel that God loves us..."

"Yeah," interrupted Josie, "I kind of feel like that when I watch one of the animals being born – like it's a sort of special."

Susan nodded. "When we try to respond to him, to that love, when we spend time thinking about God, talking to him, then we can properly know that God loves us.

"But there's more to it than that. We can know that God loves us, and never do anything about it. We can treat it like a free offer at the supermarket, something that's worthless, and we never bother to collect it. God doesn't want that, he wants us to have a relationship with him, to think about him, to learn about him. That requires effort, it requires a conscious decision on our part. There is nothing we can do to earn his love, his forgiveness, but we do have to be willing to accept that love.

"And I think that part of that is reading the Bible and studying it, knowing that we don't have all the answers, and asking God to show us what it means.

"When Jesus was with people, he used parables – stories – and his disciples got irritated, and asked him why he didn't just say things plainly, so everyone understood. But Jesus explained that he wanted those who were serious, who would put in some effort, to understand. I think that's what the debate was about. It's not about *not trusting the Bible*. It's not about doubting who God is, it's about doubting our *own understanding*. It's about using our brains to try and decide what it is that the Bible is saying, to learn how to understand what God wants. So we can try to live how God wants us to live.

"Because when you know, for sure, that someone loves you completely, it changes you, and you want to try and please them. I guess that's why I'm struggling with all this gay stuff. I want to please God, and I'm not entirely sure how to best do that. But it's not about doubting the rest of the Bible – well, not about doubting any of it really – only doubting my own understanding of bits of it.

"And I'm sorry if it's confused you. I'm sorry if the message – the important message – that God loves you and wants to be involved with your life, has got muddled. That was never the intention – of any of us. We are struggling with passages that we don't fully understand, perhaps we'll never understand them. But that doesn't detract from what we do understand. It simply shows that we're not there yet, we don't yet fully understand God. But like I said at the beginning, I don't believe we ever will, not fully, because God is God and he can never be fully understood. We have to keep working on the bits we can understand..."

Susan yawned. All the tiredness inside rose up, in one huge aching sigh, that forced her mouth open and came out in a long, jaw-stretching, yawn.

Josie stared at her for a second, and then stood up. "You must be knackered," she said, "and the cows will want their morning feed in less time than I want to think about, it's time to go to bed. Tell Jack I'll see him tomorrow, it's too late for me to wait any longer.

"But thanks, for explaining. I'll think about what you've said."

Susan also stood, carrying her glass to the sink.

Susan nodded, thinking that she *was* exhausted, and much too tired for this conversation. But she was also loath to miss an opportunity, to let the moment pass without some gesture of help. She looked at Josie, with her round face and mass of untamed hair, and smiled.

"Do you have a Bible Josie?" she asked.

Josie nodded, "Yeah, somewhere. I got one when I was kid, I think when I was christened."

"Let me give you another one," said Susan. "It'll say all the same things as your one, but they're all translations – they weren't written in English to start with, and some of the newer translations are easier to understand. There's no point reading one which was written when people said 'thee and thou' when you can read one that says 'them and you'!"

Susan went quickly from the room into the parlour. There were shelves either side of the fireplace, and she knew there was an old Bible there, a bit tatty, but a modern version. She carried it back to the kitchen and passed it to Josie.

"Here you are," she said. "I don't need it back, so you can keep it. And I wouldn't start at the beginning if I were you, some of those first books are quite hard to understand. Start in about the last quarter – the bit called the New Testament. They're a bit easier."

Josie glanced at the book. She looked slightly awkward, as if she wasn't sure that she wanted to take it. But Susan didn't give her the option to refuse, she felt that although she was too tired for an in-depth conversation, the answers were there, in the book, if the girl was serious enough to look for them.

"If Josie honestly wants answers," thought Susan, watching as the younger woman squeezed the Bible into her coat pocket, rolling it slightly so it fitted, "if she really wants to know about God, then she'll find what she's looking for in the Bible. It's not much use asking people, because we usually get it wrong, and it's certainly no use asking me, tonight, because I'm whacked. But if she genuinely wants to know, she'll find what she's looking for in there..."

Susan leant forward, and kissed Josie lightly on the cheek, then watched as the young woman left.

Chapter Eighteen

When Jack arrived back at Netherley Farm, it was late. Tom and Susan had left ahead of him, to sort the cows and shut up the poultry, but Jack – now that Josie had abandoned him – had no responsibilities for the evening. Neil had suggested that Ben and Jack might like to join him at the local pub for a drink, and they had stayed there until it closed, talking and drinking insipid lager-shandies – because they were driving.

As soon as Jack was home, he pulled out his phone and pressed the app to find Josie. He had checked it, several times during the evening, while Ben bemoaned having to live at home and the hours of his job, and Neil bemoaned the lack of sleep that came with having a baby and how even now, months and months after Noah had been born, he still hadn't enjoyed a single night of unbroken sleep. Whenever Jack searched for Josie – to check she was safely home, he told himself – the app simply told him her location was unavailable. Jack had even gone to the Gent's, and locked himself into a cubicle so he could phone Josie, to check where she was, but all he heard was the rather embarrassed: "Hi, this is Josie, please leave a message," of her answering phone. When he emerged from the cubicle another man was there, standing at the urinal, and he looked at Jack, with laughter in his eyes, clearly having heard the message from behind the locked door. Jack had glowered at him, to show his distaste for the man having broken the unspoken rule about never making eye-contact when in the Gent's, and escaped back to his brothers.

Now, at home, Jack lay on his bed, a tumbler of whiskey in his hand – because he fancied a 'proper' drink, trying Josie's number again. There was still no answer. Jack frowned, considering his options. He knew, in the logical part of his brain, that probably Josie had turned off her phone and forgotten about it. But there was a nagging ache inside of Jack, something that whispered about Josie perhaps wanting to be evasive, perhaps not as contended with her relationship with Jack as Jack hoped. Perhaps, perhaps, Josie was beginning to look elsewhere. Perhaps Jack, now he had helped Josie over the turmoil of her father's death, was surplus to requirement. Perhaps Edward, with all his charm and easy manners and good looks, was who Josie still hankered after.

Jack rolled onto his side, and pulled the duvet over his clothes. He knew he had drunk too much really, even with the lagers diluted with lemonade, and that driving home had been a slight risk. He had been careful of course, kept the music off so he could concentrate, and kept the speed strictly within the limits, to avoid being stopped by a random patrol car. He didn't usually drink and drive, his father had drilled them thoroughly when they were young, but Jack had felt that after a meal, even one without meat, and on familiar roads, he would be safe enough. He certainly didn't feel any effects of alcohol, and was able to think as clearly as ever.

Across the room, barely visible in the darkness, was the shadow of his desk. Jack stared at it, his eyes gradually discerning the shape of it, the edge of his chair, the deep indigo of the space beneath. He had sat at that desk for hours as a teenager, struggling with homework, or playing a computer game whilst pretending to be struggling with homework. Jack remembered when it first arrived, when his father had heaved it up the stairs, announcing that Jack was old enough for his own desk, somewhere to keep his things.

Jack reached for his bedside lamp, snapping it on, squinting as the light flooded the room and stung his eyes. The desk came into focus, jumping from the obscurity of darkness into the clarity of the soft yellow light. Jack thought about the hours he had spent, swinging on that wooden chair, the piles of books, and papers, and football card pamphlets that had been stacked there. The desk was still coated with papers – farm business papers, and old magazines, and a photo of Josie, stuck on the wall behind with Blu Tack. It was the photograph that Jack was searching for, trying to see across the room from his bed. The photo was wonky. Jack stared at it, absorbing Josie's face, the embarrassed grin she always wore in photographs, the way her hair stuck out randomly at the sides. The photograph was dusty, and the edges curled up in resistance to the central heating, but the face, the expression of Josie, was very clear. It made Jack focus, reminded him of why he cared, of how much he cared.

"I love her," Jack thought, despairing at the thought even as he owned that it was true. She was like his counterpart, they thought the same, shared values, enjoyed the same humour. Yet even while Jack faced the reality of his own feelings, the knowledge that Josie was slipping away struck him afresh. "She always liked Ed," Jack admitted. "Always. When we were kids, and Jose hung around the kitchen door, all big-eyed and blushing, it was always Ed she was hoping to see..."

Jack thought of his brother, with his easy smiles, those blue eyes shining from even features. Ed had inherited all the good looks of the family, he was taller, slimmer, with thicker hair, than Jack. Growing up, Ed had always been a whole leap ahead of Jack – Ed and Neil were the 'big boys' the ones who were nearly grown up. When Neil and Ed had started to have girlfriends, Jack had watched with bemusement, wondering why his brothers were bothering to shower more often, to care about what clothes they wore. Now it was different of course, now they were all grown up the age gap had shrivelled away to nothing; but something of the hierarchy remained, a feeling that Ed was somehow better, and that he, Jack, was a step or two behind.

As Jack considered Josie and Ed together, as he remembered that look as they both walked from the room, deep in conversation, something in Josie glowing – in a way that it didn't glow when she was with Jack – he felt something similar to despair wash over him.

"And there's nothing I can do," thought Jack, rolling onto his back with a moan. "Anything I do will only make it worse, will only force her to choose to leave me...it's best to do nothing, to let things settle, give her chance to make her own decision...best to do nothing..."

Jack stopped.

He swore, and sat up, then swung his legs out of bed and stood up.

This was what he always did when there was a problem – this avoidance thing, this refusal to take any action. He was, he realised, the perfect example of the archetypal ostrich with its head buried in the sand. If he looked back over his past, from childhood to the more recent years of adulthood, whenever there had been a problem, Jack had always done absolutely nothing. Always. He never acted, never tried to escape, he simply waited, eyes shut, waiting for the worst to be over.

"But not this time," said Jack, surprising himself by speaking aloud. "Not this time..."

His mind was suddenly clear, if not with a plan, then certainly with a determination – he *would* sort this out, he would find out once and for all how Josie felt, and he would do it this very minute, before time weakened his resolve.

He grabbed his car keys from the corner of the desk, and opened his door. It might be well past midnight, and Josie was sure to be asleep, but this couldn't wait any longer. It was time to sort things out, once and for all.

The landing outside Jack's room was dark, but there was sufficient light from the moon outside the large square window for him to grope his way down the stairs. He crept along the hallway, and gently lifted the latch on the kitchen door. The dogs were waiting for him on the other side of the door, all black and white fur, turning in excited circles, pleased to find someone awake. Jack put out a hand and stroked their ears.

"Shh, quietly does it," he whispered. "You two go back to bed, it's still night-time."

Jack crossed to the boot-room door and pulled on his coat and an old pair of trainers that had been kicked into the corner. They were dusty, fluffy balls of dog hair sticking to the laces. He dusted them off, and tied the laces. It was surprisingly difficult to tie the laces, and took him two attempts. He opened the backdoor, and walked towards his car.

The sky was clear, a round moon staring down, casting shadows across the yard. As Jack approached his car he could hear an owl hooting, the cry melancholy, as if pleading with him to return to bed. For a moment, Jack stood still, debating whether it was worth driving the short distance to Broom Hill Farm, when the walk would take less than ten minutes. Something scuttled across his path, probably a rat, and Jack shivered, pulled his coat closed and bent to open the car door.

The engine sounded unnaturally loud when Jack turned the key. The headlights reflected back from the stone wall that ran around the perimeter of the yard, and Jack turned in his seat ready to reverse. The car jolted forwards, Jack stamped hard on the brake, was flung forwards against his seatbelt and narrowly avoided hitting the wall. He threw back his head and laughed, a loud harsh sound, then shaking his head in despair at his own ineptitude, he found the reverse gear and backed away from the wall. The headlights lit objects as they touched them: the side of the house, the gaping hole of the barn doorway, the gate – which was red in daylight but now appeared grey. When the headlights moved away, everything dissolved back into dark grey, cold and unfamiliar.

As he pulled out into the lane, Jack turned up the heating and flicked on his music. It was less lonely with music.

Jack could feel his heart pounding, the blood racing through his veins. He was excited, keen to resolve his uncertainty, eager to confront Josie. He pressed the accelerator, and the grey silhouette of the hedgerow slid past, the silver road scurrying beneath him. At one point, near the bend by the large oak tree, Jack lost control of the car, oversteering and sending the wheels stuttering onto the bank, the tyres sliding over the wet grass, one wing shuddering into the bush, before Jack swung the wheel back round, and bumped back onto the tarmac.

Suddenly he had arrived, the entrance to Broom Hill Farm looming into view on his left. Jack slowed down. As the wheels of the car slowed, so too did Jack's heart, and some of the passion seeped out of him. He drove slowly up the driveway, wanting to postpone his conversation, fearful that it might be the end of something rather than the beginning. It occurred to Jack that *knowing* might not necessarily be good, it might not hasten the end of uncertainty, but rather the end of the relationship.

By the time the car crawled into the farmyard, Jack was at the point of returning home without seeing Josie. He drove to a corner near the house, and switched off the engine. In front of the car, in blackness, was the house. There were no lights. All the windows in the house were black, the occupants asleep. Jack folded his arms, and stared into the gloom. He didn't want to go home without resolving his insecurities, but neither, now he was actually here, was he confident that waking Josie was such a good idea.

Moments passed, and Jack sat in his car, staring at the dark house. There was no upstairs light, no movement, nothing to encourage him on his mission. He wound down his window and the harsh night air flooded in, cooling him; the faint night sounds floated towards him – the hollow cough from a nearby cow, the whisper of branches moving in the wind, a far off car, and an owl, possibly the same one as earlier, pleading with Jack to return home.

After an age, Jack pulled out his phone.

"We need to talk," he wrote, "I have something important to discuss."

He sent the text.

He waited. Nothing changed. No lights appeared, no answering message flashed across his phone; Jack alone was awake, and he began to feel rather foolish. All the energy that had motivated his heroic expedition had left him, and Jack felt that instead of being decisive and strong, he had actually behaved impetuously without sense. His bed suddenly felt very attractive.

Jack started the car, and drove home. He walked through the excited dogs in the kitchen, up the stairs, and into his room. Then, fully dressed, he pulled the duvet up to his chin, and slept.

Chapter Nineteen

Jack woke to a headache and a message from Josie. The light was streaming through the curtains which he had neglected to close properly the night before, and he could hear a cockerel shouting that it was daylight and the world should be awake. His mouth felt like the bottom of the chicken coop, and Jack grimaced as he pushed himself up on one arm to read his text.

"I have something to discuss too. Let's meet in the kitchen @10. That ok?"

Jack glanced at the clock. Josie knew that he'd agreed to cut some of the hedges this morning, before he went to Broom Hill. It was almost seven o'clock, so he'd have to hurry if he was to meet her at ten.

Jack swallowed a cup of tea and some aspirins as he struggled into his overalls. His father had helped him to mount the hedge trimmer on the tractor yesterday, before they set off for the christening – it seemed a long time ago now. Molly swept around Jack as he pulled on his wellies, her soft tail brushing against him.

"Not this morning girl," he said, ignoring her beseeching eyes and excited body as she turned circles around him.

The tractor was waiting, the long arm of the hedge-cutter resting on the ground. Jack climbed up into the cab, his head pounding, and started the engine, then pulled the lever which caused the cutter to rise up, a mechanical arm waving at the world. The tractor juddered and throbbed, his head kept time, and Jack drove to the field. Jack flicked on the windscreen wiper to clear the view, and it swung, the pendulous motion sweeping dust and dirt from the glass, backwards and forwards, as he drove.

The hedge had grown over a metre in the last two years, a tangle of stalks and brambles and shrub. Jack set the trimmer to the right height, drove forwards until the head was touching the branches, then turned on the rotating cutters, which spun within the shield of the hedge-cutter, spewing stumps of wood and leaf as they ate the top of the hedge. The noise was immense, a great clash of metal on metal as the cutter chewed through the top of the hedge, the noise drilling into Jack's skull. He edged forwards, hoping the aspirin would kick in soon. Behind him, the cut limbs of the hedge stood like bare bones, almost as if Jack was skinning the top of the hedge, leaving skeletal remains. Only from a distance did the hedge look neat, lowered to sensible height, the brambles controlled.

Towards the middle of the hedge was a sapling, surrounded by branches and weeds. Yesterday, Tom had chopped that section of hedge by hand, separating the new tree from the branches of the hedge. As Jack approached the gap, he withdrew the arm of the cutter, ensuring the sapling could continue growing. Then he continued round the field, grinding and chopping and shredding the hedge, his headache keeping time, so that by the time he had finished, Jack felt exhausted. He drove straight to Broom Hill, and parked the tractor in the yard. A light rain was beginning to fall, misting the air.

Jack walked towards Josie's kitchen, rubbing his hand through his hair so that flakes of leaves and twigs fell as he walked. He banged on the door, and walked inside. Josie was waiting.

"You look rough," said Josie, looking up as he walked in. She was standing by the kettle, wearing overalls similar to Jack's, and socks. Her hair was damp from being in the fields, and it stuck out at strange angles, her cheeks were pink from the cold, and her eyes were shining.

Jack moved to kiss her, feeling the warmth of her cheek, wanting nothing so much as to bury his head in her neck and forget about the day, and his headache, and his worries. He breathed in the smell of her, her lemon soap and fresh air mingled with the sweet smell of hay.

Josie moved away, the gesture awkward.

"Tea?"

Jack nodded and sat at the table. He noticed that a toe was poking from one of Josie's socks.

"So, what did you want to discuss?" asked Josie, tipping water over teabags in mugs. Her voice sounded light, but artificially so, as if she was making a supreme effort to appear normal, to make this discussion civilised.

"No, you first," said Jack.

Josie passed him a mug, and he took a sip. His headache was already receding, and the caffeine would help.

Josie sat opposite Jack, her face serious. She lifted her grey eyes and looked into his face.

"Don't be angry," she said.

Jack took another sip of tea. He wondered if Claire, Josie's mother, was in the house, or whether they were alone. "I'm never angry," he said.

"Yes, you are, especially when it's anything to do with Edward..."

Jack scowled. "Edward," he said.

"Yes, but just listen, please. I'll tell you everything, but don't interrupt, I need you to hear it all, before you say anything – so I know you understand, properly understand."

Jack nodded. His headache was lifting, but his stomach had tightened with dread. He didn't want to hear what Josie was going to say, didn't want to stay and listen while she explained what could only – if it involved Edward – be bad news. He lifted his mug, using it to shield his face, so that Josie wouldn't be able to read his expression, and he could hide his reaction to whatever this news was. He glanced at the window, noticed it had started to rain properly now, large drips chasing each other down the pane, and he thought that it was lucky he'd finished cutting that hedge, before it had become too wet, and that he hoped he'd remembered to shut the cab window properly or the seat would get wet. Then he dragged his mind back to the kitchen, took a breath, and forced himself to look back at Josie. He wasn't sure if he wanted to tell her to cut straight to the conclusion, to tell him immediately if it was over between them, or whether he wanted to delay her speech, to preserve these last few shreds of belonging, being part of her, for as long as possible, clutching at the few minutes he had left before he knew.

"Okay," he said.

Josie put down her mug and sat back in her chair. Jack could see that she looked tense, and she swallowed, glanced at the rain, then looked back to him.

"Jack," she said, her voice low and calm, "I know you've tried – we've both tried, but things aren't going great, are they?"

Jack held his breath, something sharp was caught in his throat and his mouth was dry. He could hear the rain, a steady patter against the window, and a car driving along the lane, its tyres muted and hissing on the wet road. Inside the kitchen was silent, and he wondered if Josie too was holding her breath. He felt himself nod, and in that nod, that feeble assent which showed he agreed, he knew he wasn't good enough for her, Jack felt the last of his hopes slide away.

"I know you've had all these plans, I know you've been keeping track of every penny we spend, tried the maize maze, started to get the milking sheds going again, paid to inseminate the heifers – but we have to face it, the money is draining away even faster than it was before. We're running out of time, aren't we? Something has to change..."

"The farm!" realised Jack, *"She's talking about the farm!"* Jack felt something shift, an easing of tension, and he took a deep breath. He swallowed a mouthful of tea, and lowered his shoulders, waiting. He still wasn't quite sure what Josie was about to tell him, but there was a chance, a chance, that this might simply be a business conversation, and nothing to do with their relationship at all. There was, he told himself, still hope.

"Anyway, yesterday, when I met your uncle, he asked me about the farm, and he already knew some things, because your mum had told him, but he wanted to know more..."

"He's not my uncle," interrupted Jack.

"Your *sort-of-uncle*," said Josie, shaking her head. "As I was saying, he asked me lots of details, like he'd already been thinking about it, and then he asked – quite bossily, actually – if he could come and see it. He said he was interested in some of the buildings, the ones we aren't using at the moment. And Ed was there, so he came too. I think," Josie paused, frowning. "I think that they'd already been talking about things, those two, and they'd already made their plan. So I might have been the last to know...

"Anyway, they came, and they looked, and..." Josie leant on the table, staring across at Jack, "...they want to start using one of the barns to make gin! William would run it, Ed would manage it and be *the interface with the customers*...or something like that. Like I said, I think they'd been planning it already, before they asked me about it. Probably they already asked your dad and he said no, I don't know..."

"Gin," said Jack, not sure he was understanding correctly. "William and Ed want to make gin."

"Yes, apparently, it's all the fashion at the moment – well, we know it is, look at how many gins you get offered now when you go to a pub for a G&T. But there's money in it too, if you have a gin factory – more money than in farming, anyway."

Josie stopped, her eyes searching Jack's. "So, what do you think? Given how rubbish the finances are and everything, if we can get the change of land use sorted, shall we go for it? Shall we let William take over one of the barns – he's already picked one actually– and let him and Ed run a gin factory? I mean, I know it's early days, I know we need to look properly at their numbers and everything, and we might not even get permission anyway, but do you think it's worth a try Jack? Shall we go for it?"

Jack opened his mouth, then closed it again. He was having trouble processing the information, his main focus being on the number of times Josie had said "we" when referring to the farm, as if she was assuming that Jack was part of it, and would continue to be part of it. Plus the plan involved Ed, specifically Ed working near to Josie, which was possibly the wrong thing to focus on, but it was one of the things spinning around Jack's head. He lifted his cup, noticed the tea was finished, and put the mug back on the table, his hands wrapped around it as though for comfort. Josie was staring at him, her face on one side, her expression, which he knew oh so well, one of curiosity, waiting for his, Jack's, opinion.

"Well? What do you think?" prompted Josie.

"I think," said Jack, the words escaping from his mouth before he had time to think about them, before he had time to arrange them into the right sequence, before he had even properly considered if it was what he intended to say: "I think we should get married."

Jack then watched, aghast, as Josie's face dropped. He saw something close to fear shadow her eyes before she lowered her head, shaking it decisively.

"No," she whispered.

Chapter Twenty

Dot stared at Elsie across the room. They were in their own sitting room, in their terraced house, and the room was dwarfed by both the metal-framed wheelchair and the large commode which had been moved into a corner of the room, next to the dresser. Dot was trying to ignore the commode.

"I've got you an early Christmas gift," said Dot, forcing her mouth into a smile. She wanted to give Elsie the gift while they were alone, before the occupational therapist – a *man* for goodness sake! – returned. This was Elsie's first trip home, and Dot swallowed, knowing that she felt nervous.

At first, when the ugly van had arrived and the bossy young man in the short white coat had wheeled Elsie up the path, Dot had wanted to get rid of him as soon as possible. The man – Stephen, he'd said his name was – had spoken very slowly, as if reciting from a list learnt by heart. He told the sisters that this was Elsie's first home visit (as if they didn't know that) and that several more would follow before she was allowed home to live (like she was some sort of prisoner being allowed privileges, this was her *home* for goodness sakes). He reminded them that Elsie was able to stand unsupported, and was beginning to walk again, and that she could swallow perfectly well (like she was a baby) but her speech needed further development (like that wasn't obvious).

The man, this Stephen, had then walked over the whole house, writing things on his clipboard. He even went upstairs, into Dot's own room, and the bathroom, and the kitchen – though when he had started to open cupboards,

Dot stopped him, asked if he really thought where she kept the baked beans really mattered, and he had told her that yes, if Elsie was to be completely independent they might need to reconsider the placing of certain products. He muttered to himself as he went: "Stairlift eventually, but could sleep downstairs initially, needs a rail in shower, rail next to commode, rugs will have to be removed, ramp at both doors..." Dot followed him round, wishing that he would go, and leave them on their own. She knew that they were to be left, for two hours, to see how they coped, and then *Pushy Stephen* would return and drive Elsie back to hospital. These home visits were to be repeated, for longer periods, until both Dot and Elsie felt comfortable with Elsie returning home for good.

Dot felt that the thing she was *not* comfortable with, was having her home intruded upon by a pushy man with a clipboard, invading her privacy and treating her home like a public building.

However, now that they were alone, having watched Stephen reverse the ugly van out of the parking space and off down the road, Dot felt suddenly worried. What if something happened? When she looked across at Elsie, she saw the same insecurity reflected in her sister's eyes, the same realisation that after weeks and weeks of nurses and doctors and social workers, they were now on their own, and if anything *happened* there was no one to help.

"He'll be back soon," said Dot firmly, "so you might as well have your present now, before he tells me it needs a ramp or a handrail or something..."

Elsie smiled her lopsided smile.

Dot took the gift-wrapped parcel from the dresser, and put it onto Elsie's lap, planting a kiss on her cheek. "Happy Christmas," she said, "hope you like it. Ben helped me buy it."

She hovered next to Elsie, waiting to see if she would manage to remove the Christmas paper by herself. Elsie secured the gift with her right hand, tucking it under her claw-like fingers. She then used her left hand to tear away the paper. Dot took it from her and screwed it into a ball.

Elsie stared at the box on her lap.

"It's an iPad," said Dot. "I thought you could learn to use it, and then you can send messages." She didn't add that this might help everyone to understand the garbled words that Elsie tended to say, or that she had copied the idea from Cassie. She simply said: "Ben helped me buy it, and he's done all the setting up, so it's ready to use, shall we turn it on?"

Elsie turned it over, then looked up.

"Where's the 'on' button?" she slurred in her new, indistinct fashion.

"It's on the top," said Dot, showing her.

Elsie attempted to press the tiny button, but the iPad slipped from where it was secured under her right hand, and Dot caught it before it slipped to the floor. Dot pressed the button for her, and the screen turned white before shining with a variety of coloured icons. Dot showed her which ones to use so that she could send messages.

"Look, this one with an envelope – that's for messages, emails...and the speech-bubble one is for a different sort of message." Dot pressed the screen and a line of faces and names appeared at the side. "Ben added those," explained Dot. "They're your contacts. Look, you touch one...and then touch that bubble there...then use those letters to write a message..."

Dot watched, as Elsie slowly pressed the letters in turn, gradually writing 'thankyou' on the screen.

"Now, how do we send it?" said Dot, trying to remember. "Is it that one? No, that's a picture of a thumb. Try the arrow...yep! That's it, the message has gone. Oh, who did you send it to? Jack. Oh, well, that will confuse him. Never mind. Do you like it? I expect it will take some getting used to, but some people love them, it might be useful. Shall I turn it off?"

Dot lifted the iPad from her sister's lap and turned it round, looking for an 'off' button. There did not appear to be one. She tried pressing several buttons, but the screen remained bright until eventually, she found the button at the top, and the machine clicked and the screen went black. She passed it back to Elsie.

Dot watched, as Elsie stroked the screen, turning the iPad over and over, examining it. She placed her thumb on the large circle at the front, and the screen suddenly glowed again, the words: "What can I help you with?" appearing.

"Oh! What have you done now?" said Dot, taking the iPad back. She stared at it, wondering why it was still reacting after she had switched it off. "I don't know what's happened now," she said and looked at her sister in bemusement. "We'll have to phone Ben and..."

At once, the iPad started to click, and then, from nowhere, came Ben's voice.

"Hello? Gran? Did you phone me?"

Dot dropped the iPad onto Elsie's lap and backed away. Both the sisters stared at it in alarm.

"Ben?" said Dot, staring at the screen, which was now showing a photograph of Ben. "Ben? Is that you?"

"Yes. Hello Gran. You phoned me." There was a pause. "Did you give Aunty Elsie the new iPad?"

"Yes," said Dot, nodding. She glanced at her sister's face, then lowered her head so she was speaking directly onto the iPad. "But we didn't phone you, we were trying to turn it off. It did that by itself."

They heard Ben laughing. "Never mind Gran," he said. "I'm at work, so I can't chat now. Just put the iPad on a table, and I'll sort it out when I get home. Bye now, bye..."

There was a click.

For a moment, the sisters stared at the iPad, not moving. Then very tentatively, Dot used both hands to lift it from Elsie's lap. She carried it, two-handed, over to the dresser, and slid it into a drawer.

"I think we'll leave it there until we've had another lesson from Ben," she said, closing the drawer with a clunk. "We don't want to find other people can hear what we're saying in private, do we?"

Elsie nodded.

Dot looked at her, and then, without warning, the realisation that her sister was not going to be chatting to her any time soon, that they only had another hour before Elsie was whisked away back into hospital, overwhelmed her. She felt sadness wash over her like a wave, the whole world felt unsteady, as if nothing could be relied upon anymore, and Dot realised afresh how terribly lonely she was without her sister. She went back to Elsie, and held her hand and leaned against her side, awkwardly over the uncompromising edge of the wheelchair.

"Get better quick Els," she whispered, "I want you back here with me, where you belong."

She took a breath, and straightened. "Right, now how about a nice cup of tea before Mr Bossy gets back? Have you got your straw thing for drinking with? Lovely, I'll go and put the kettle on."

Halfway to the doorway, she stopped.

Dot felt the burden of unspoken words, words which she knew needed to be said, and which, if left unsaid might never be resolved. Time had become finite, time with her sister did not now seem like an eternal thing, but rather something fleeting, to be treasured, something which might turn out to be more fragile than she had expected. She felt the barrier of the unspoken words, separating her from her sister, making Dot different somehow, almost as if her spirit had become deformed, and she realised that she could no longer rely on having time later to speak, *later* might be a luxury that was denied them. She stopped walking towards the kitchen, and turned back to Elsie, forcing herself to speak, to release the feeling of guilt she had been carrying.

"And I'm sorry," she said, dry-throated, her hands finding each other and twisting together, as if she could wring out the guilt.

Elsie looked up at her, her lopsided face confused. She grunted.

"I'm sorry for making you give up your baby. It seemed best, at the time, but I can see now, that perhaps it hurt you..."

The memories flooded back, images, one after the other, flowing through her mind like a film, each one stirring her emotions, so she recalled the exact feelings, the same fears, that she had experienced over fifty years ago.

"We were so worried, me and Grandmother, when you started to walk-out with that man," Dot whispered, more to herself than to her sister. "I never wished so hard that Mother was still alive, that there was someone else to direct you. I never trusted him, you see, I could see in his eyes that he wasn't serious, was just messing you about; you were so in love, so blind to his character, you couldn't see his faults – even when we tried to warn you, to protect you. Oh, and he was a looker all right, with those eyes that saw right through you, and his winning ways and lovely manners. But there was something not right about him – he scared me a bit, if I'm honest. I was never so happy as when you told us he had left, even though it was sad to see your heart broken like that, but hearts mend...at least, I thought they did, back then."

Dot's voice grew quiet, less certain, and she paused for a moment, remembering.

"Then when you told us you were pregnant, we didn't know what else to do, we knew he would never come back to marry you, we wanted to save you from the disgrace. So Grandmother found Mr and Mrs Evans, and they were a nice young couple, we trusted them to look after the baby properly..."

Dot paused. She wanted to say that the Evans would have cared for the baby better than the teenaged Elsie could have. But that seemed wrong now. Now, Dot wasn't so sure, the confidence of a previous era had passed.

"And now there's this William who's turned up. I'm not sure if I trust him...looks too much like his father for my liking, but I can see a bit of you in his face too, he's got your eyes...so perhaps he'll take after you more, and then he'll be all right..."

Dot paused again, remembering those feelings of mistrust, that premonition of trouble, she had felt when she had first seen William, when he was just a man that she half-recognised. She still wasn't convinced that he wouldn't prove to be trouble, as fickle as his father had been. But she realised that it was up to Elsie to decide how she wanted to proceed. Dot had already forced her to give up her baby, she no longer had the right to insist on anything else. She took a breath.

"But anyway, I'm sorry for my part in it. If I was wrong, which I can see now, I probably was. I was trying to protect you – that's what families do, isn't it? But now, after all this time, I need to say sorry. That's all." She took a breath, feeling that something had shifted in her mind, that words which had needed to be said, had now been spoken. It was done.

"Right, I'll make some tea."

Dot hurried to the kitchen. It wasn't until she filled the kettle with water, that she realised her cheeks were wet with tears.

Chapter Twenty-One

After that awful morning, when the thought had gushed out of Jack only to be thoroughly rejected by Josie, Jack had done a lot of thinking. Josie had been clearly shocked by his proposal – aghast even, almost frightened by it. She had been very definite, and told Jack that she loved him, and she most certainly considered that their future was together, and thank you very much for asking, but no, she not want to get married, ever, to anyone. They then discussed the business proposal that William was offering, they agreed that Josie would look into applying for a change in land use after she had spoken to her landlord, and Jack would ask Neil, who understood numbers and budgets better than anyone else, whether he thought it was sound financially. They could then discuss it properly at a later date. They did not agree to discuss marriage again.

However, as time passed, what had initially been a sudden blurt of emotion, was now almost an obsession with Jack, and he was thinking of little else. Jack knew, without doubt, that now he had suggested it, he did, very much, want to marry Josie. It made their relationship secure, it formalised the bond, and he even felt that any concerns he might have over Josie's past feelings for Edward would diminish to nothing if they had the security of a wedding binding them together. It was the ultimate 'hands-off' to all other men.

A plan began to emerge when Jack went to his grandmother's house to deliver a Christmas gift. As he drew up at the kerbside, he was surprised to see Aunty Elsie, standing next to the open front door as though about to enter. Jack parked the car, and hurried to help her. Elsie was wearing slippers, and a brown coat, and was facing the door, standing precariously on a new ramp and leaning heavily on a walking frame. She appeared to be concentrating very hard on trying to lift her leg, so that she could step inside.

"Hello Aunty Elsie," said Jack, "I didn't expect to see you outside." He moved towards her, his hand outstretched.

"Don't help her!" came a shout from the depths of the hallway as Jack moved towards his aunt.

Jack peered into the house. His grandmother was standing inside, arms folded across her chest, watching Elsie as she struggled to negotiate the ramp.

"She won't learn if you help her," said Dot. "She's got to do it by herself, otherwise they'll never let her move back home again."

Jack stepped back, hovering as close to Elsie as he dared so that he could catch her if she fell, but far enough away that his grandmother wouldn't shout at him. He watched, as laboriously, inch by painful inch, his aunt made her way up the ramp, and over the threshold into the house. He realised he was holding his breath, and exhaled once she was fully inside.

"You can come inside now," said Dot, and Jack followed his great aunt inside.

They went into the living room. It was very crowded. All the furniture had been squashed together, so it had a higgledy-piggledy look, similar to a furniture showroom. A wheelchair had been squeezed between two sofas, and next to the window was a small Christmas tree. Christmas cards covered every surface, even along the top of the television, vying for space with what looked like boxes of medical equipment. The room was very warm, and condensation was misting the window. There was a new chair, very high-backed, and Jack went to sit in it.

"I wouldn't sit there if I were you," said Dot, "it's Elsie's commode."

Jack moved quickly away, sat in an armchair near the window, and began to struggle out of his jacket and scarf and sweater, thinking that it was akin to sitting in a sauna.

Elsie inched her way into the room and gradually lowered herself onto a chair by the door. She looked exhausted.

"Hey, well done you," said Jack, beaming at her. "I didn't realise you were making such good progress."

Elsie shook her head, but her eyes looked pleased.

"Does it smell in here?" demanded Dot, from where she was standing, behind Elsie's chair. "I can't tell anymore, whether all this stuff..." she waved her hand to indicate the commode, and the high chair where Elsie sat, and the grab-handles that had been screwed onto the wall in strategic positions, "...whether it smells. Does the room smell like an old people's home, or does it just look like one?"

Jack obediently sniffed the air and shook his head. "No Gran, you're fine," he said. Though, if he was honest, he could detect the tang of something in the air, something medical that spoke of body fluids and disinfectant, mingling with the left-over smells of dinner. Jack glanced around the room, thinking how much it contrasted with the beautiful everything-in-the-right-place house designed by Josie's mother. Even he could see that this room was cluttered with ugly furniture which overshadowed the few remaining items from the original sitting room. The equipment that had arrived with Elsie might be functional, but in no way was it pleasing to look at.

"I suppose all this is to help you get around?" Jack said to his great aunt. "There's certainly a lot of stuff – is it just here temporarily? Then will you give it all back, make the room like it used to be, without all this...equipment?"

"No!" said his grandmother, something sharp in her voice. "It's here to stay."

Jack glanced at her face, suffused with rage, and he realised with a sudden sinking of heart, how tactless his comment was. This equipment, the ugly furniture and rails, were a permanent part of Elsie's entourage, and they would remain for as long as Elsie did. Jack coughed, wanting to cover his mistake.

"I've brought round gifts from me and Josie," said Jack, pulling two packages from his bag and placing them under the tiny tinsel tree in the window. "I won't see you on Christmas Day, because I'm eating with Josie and her mum. I gather you're staying here, and Cassie's coming to cook lunch? And you're seeing William in the afternoon, and Mum and Dad will pop down too?"

Dot nodded. "That's right. Elsie's coming here for the whole day." She gazed at her sister, looking concerned. "I hope it won't be too much for her." She looked at the gifts that Jack had brought. "Very kind of you and Josie to buy us presents," she said.

"Well, it was Josie really," said Jack. "She likes doing things like that. It's only something small."

"She's a good one, that one," said Dot, nodding to herself. "Time you asked her to marry you, I should say. Don't want to let her get away."

"Thanks Gran," said Jack, not wanting to have this conversation. He was very used to his grandmother being outspoken, but this was a little too near the truth. "Besides, Josie doesn't want to get married...I think it's because her parents weren't very happy together..."

From her chair by the door, Elsie said something indistinct. It sounded, to Jack, as if she said, "She can't be arsed." Jack frowned, not really sure how to respond.

"So, how does it feel to be home again Aunty Elsie?" said Jack, deciding to move the conversation forwards.

Elsie banged her fist on the edge of the wheelchair in frustration, and said, slightly louder, the same sentence:

"She can't be arsed." —Or at least, that's what it sounded like to Jack. He stared at his grandmother for help, it felt wrong to simply ignore Aunty for a second time, but he really had no idea what she was saying...could a stroke cause Tourette's?

Dot said, "Elsie wondered if you'd asked her – Josie I mean. Have you asked her why she doesn't want to get married?"

"Well, not exactly," said Jack, feeling relieved, "because I know why. Like I said, her parents weren't very happy, so she doesn't want to get married."

But later, when he was thinking about the conversation, and how difficult it had been to understand Aunty Elsie, Jack realised that actually, he didn't know why Josie was against getting married, not really. He assumed her reason was linked to her parents, but he didn't really know, not for sure.

So Jack decided on a plan. He decided that rather than repeat his request and ask Josie to marry him again, instead he would ask her why she had refused him. Perhaps, if he understood the problem, he could help to sort it out. Maybe, he thought, there was a way through this.

***

The week before Christmas, Jack showered and changed into smart clothes, and went to collect Josie. They had decided that rather than exchange gifts, they would treat themselves to a meal in a restaurant. It was rare for them to actually go out, and because of the unfamiliar clothes and the importance of what he planned to say, Jack had butterflies dancing in his stomach as he arrived at Broom Hill Farm.

Josie met him in the yard. She was wearing a long coat – a gift from her mother, and when Jack leant to kiss her cheek, she smelt of perfume. Jack decided, as he turned the car, that he preferred the smell of hay, but he was pleased she had made an effort. The evening was cold, and Jack drove slowly, looking for potholes in the country lanes, avoiding a mangy fox that slunk alongside the road searching for food, straining to see beyond the headlights, into the night.

They left the car behind the station in Marksbridge, and walked along the High Street to the Indian restaurant near the river. The shops were closed, their windows festive: blinking fairy lights hooked onto pelmets, green Christmas trees frosted with glitter, merchandise stacked in a muddle with gaily wrapped parcels to entice shoppers inside, an unspoken promise that they would find that elusive gift right here, in this shop. Jack held Josie's hand as they walked, their breath misted by the night air, their eyes absorbing the lights strung across the road, the decorations, the anticipation of Christmas.

There were two large steps up to the restaurant door, and inside was a small area designated to people collecting takeaway meals. A man was slumped in the corner, flicking

200

through a sports magazine whilst checking his watch every thirty seconds. A tall Asian man approached Jack, and they gave their name, and followed the man down a step and into the restaurant. They were shown to a table in the centre of the room, which was not what Jack had been hoping for, but he didn't like to ask for a different table, and instead he slid onto the chair and waited while the man flicked open the folded napkin and spread it across Jack's lap. A different waiter appeared with tall menus, and asked what they would like to drink. Jack asked for a beer, which was unusual when he was driving, but he felt he needed some extra courage this evening.

"I think I'll just have tap water, thanks," said Josie.

"Really?" said Jack, feeling this was unhelpful. He looked at her, trying to decide if she was hoping to avoid the calories or the cost. "It's a special night, why don't you have a proper drink? A glass of wine or something – don't leave me drinking on my own."

Josie agreed to have a beer, which Jack decided was better than nothing, and he turned back to his menu. His stomach was churning with tension, and his mind was racing with possible ways to start his conversation. Should he wait until the food arrived, or start as soon as they'd got the order in? And should he edge into it, or simply ask the question, ask Josie what the problem to marriage was, and then sit back and listen to the answer? And what if her reasoning was adamant, should he try to argue, or wait and hope to change her mind later?

"I think I'll have the chicken korma," said Josie.

Jack really did not want to eat anything.

"Good idea, I'll have the same," he said. He didn't much like chicken korma, but he couldn't face making a different decision.

A couple arrived at the table next to them. Jack watched them take their seats. The woman was slim and blonde, and wore a silk blouse that gaped when she leant forwards. He looked back at Josie, who was watching him, her eyes dancing, so Jack lifted his beer and took a long drink. Someone knocked the back of Jack's seat as they made their way to the washrooms, jolting Jack, who choked on his beer.

"Sorry, sorry," he spluttered, gasping for breath and stretching to put his glass back on the table. The edge of the glass caught a fork, tipping sideways like a leisurely pendulum, beer frothing over the edge and seeping into the white tablecloth. Jack dived forwards to catch it, knocking his knife, which spun from the table and clattered to the floor. The tablecloth was now brown and soggy, and very little beer remained in Jack's glass. He sighed, wondering if things could possibly get worse.

The waiter returned, fussing with cloths and clean cutlery, moving their side plates and lifting the soggy cloth, which dripped on the carpet, and replacing it with a smooth white layer. Eventually he left, the table was put to rights, and Jack smoothed a fresh napkin over his lap and stared up at Josie.

"Sorry," he said again.

"Are you okay?" she said, "You seem nervous."

"Yeah, I'm fine," said Jack, forcing a smile and trying to ignore the pressure in his chest and the constant flutter of nerves in his stomach. He was beginning to think this was a bad idea, the wrong environment entirely for a serious conversation, and that one of the barns or a field would be so much better, more private, familiar...

But then Jack reminded himself that if Josie didn't want to discuss, she would simply walk away, and that, to a certain extent, she was trapped here, in a restaurant, bound by social norms to at least listen, and they rarely ate out, it made the occasion significant, special. Jack took a long drink, watched while a waiter arranged dips and a plate of poppadums on the table, and then began to speak, his tone low, leaning forwards slightly so no one else could hear.

"Actually Josie, I was hoping, as we're here, somewhere a bit special, that perhaps we could, you know, have a proper conversation...about us...our relationship..."

Josie looked up from the poppadum she was breaking into pieces, her eyes wary.

"What do you mean?" she said, "I thought we'd sorted that."

"Well, no, we didn't, not really," said Jack, determined to continue. "You didn't explain, not properly, why you said no, why you don't want to..." Jack paused, whispered: "...marry me."

"It's not you," said Josie, all in a rush, as if trying to reassure Jack and escape from the conversation all at the same time. "It's nothing to do with you, really it's not. If I was going to get married," Josie too was whispering, leaning across the mango chutney, "then of course, of course it would be you that I'd want to marry. Honestly Jack, it's not you, it's me. I don't want to, not ever."

"Because of your parents?"

Jack saw a flicker of surprise in Josie's face, her eyes widened for the briefest moment, and she frowned, then lowered her eyes and started to break her poppadum into pieces.

Jack waited. He had promised himself, that however long the pauses were, he wouldn't fill them, he would wait for Josie to answer. He had read in a detective novel – which was not perhaps the best source of human psychology – that if you waited, and refused to speak, then the other person – in the novel, the person being interrogated – would eventually talk. Although he realised this situation was entirely different, he had decided to adopt the same strategy, and to say very little in the hope that Josie would reveal what her objections were. If he understood *why* she didn't want to get married, then he might be able to persuade her.

"No," Josie said eventually. "It's got nothing to do with my parents, though they weren't exactly a stellar example... but no. It's me, I just don't want to."

Jack waited.

The waiter returned, and removed the side plates and dips. Josie looked around the restaurant, stared across to the window, fiddled with her napkin. Jack watched her, waiting. He drank some more beer, and wondered if, as he'd split most of it, he could order another one, even though he was driving. The waiter reappeared, pushing a trolley, and began to place bowls of rice and hot dishes of creamy korma on the table. When he left, Josie lifted the spoon and put some rice on her plate, then covered it with the meat. Jack tore a piece of naan bread, and dipped it in the sauce.

"I would hate it," whispered Josie, at last, staring at her plate of food. "Not the *being* married, but everything else, all the fuss, everyone staring at me. Even being engaged – people wanting to see the ring, everyone wondering why you would want to marry a fat lump like me, laughing behind their hands, thinking that goodness! who'd have ever thought that Big Jose would land herself a husband? Wondering if I'm pregnant and you're being forced into it..."

Jack reached across the table and caught hold of Josie's hand. Some of the sauce bounced from her fork onto the white tablecloth, seeping into the snowy material like a bloodstain.

"Stop," he said, "just stop. That is nonsense, all of it. No one would think those things, any more than they would wonder why you were agreeing to marry a short bloke with premature balding issues and a rubbish credit rating! Honestly Josie, people don't think like that, no one does. And anyway, it's got nothing to do with anyone else – we could elope if you wanted to, just go away somewhere on our own, and tell people when we got home that we were married. It's not the fuss that's important, it's the...I don't know, the commitment, the promising, the letting the rest of the world know that we're together and it's permanent, not just until you find a better option."

Josie was still staring at her plate, her face was very pink and she was shaking her head.

"You make it sound so easy," she said, "but it wouldn't be like that. My mum would want me to have a church ceremony. *Your mum* would *definitely* expect us to get married in a church. And what would I wear? I'd look like a giant lemon meringue pie walking down the aisle! And they'd expect bridesmaids, and I don't exactly have many female friends, if you haven't noticed, certainly none who would want to wear a long pink dress and follow me down an aisle. And it would be really expensive, which we can't afford – in fact, I would resent having to pay for a wedding reception, watching all our friends and family get wasted at our expense when we could use the money for animal feed. And they'd all expect us to go on a honeymoon, and how can we leave the farm for a week, when we can't afford to pay a manager?"

Josie paused, and for the first time since her monologue had begun, she looked up, straight into Jack's face. He read fear and embarrassment and a determined refusal to be put in an unwanted situation in her eyes, and he understood.

Jack began to eat, his mind racing, his heart lighter. Although he couldn't, at present, think of a solution to Josie's objections, they seemed to him to be very flimsy. Not wanting a wedding dress? – *Of course* she wouldn't! Josie practically had a panic attack every time she had to leave the house in something formal, so a long white dress and a crowd of people staring at her was bound to be terrifying. But he could find a way round that, he was sure he could.

Jack helped himself to more rice and tore another lump from his naan bread. He indicated to the waiter that he would like another beer, and took a mouthful of korma. The sweet coconut taste was rich and cloying, but it wasn't too bad when washed down with a mouthful of bitter. He glanced up. Josie was eating slowly, alternating korma and rice with naan bread, her eyes scanning the room. She saw Jack watching her and raised her eyebrows.

"If," said Jack, placing his glass very carefully on the table, "if I promise not to make you do any of those awful things, and if I promise to protect you from what your mother and my mother will want us to do – will you consider it? Will you? I've been thinking – in fact, I don't think I've stopped thinking since I asked you – and this matters Josie. It really matters to me. I don't think…"

Jack paused. He had about to say he didn't think he could continue with a relationship that wasn't going anywhere, but he managed to stop in time. This wasn't the moment for ultimatums, especially ones that might not end how Jack was hoping.

"I don't think I want to look at a future without you in it, and for me, that means we should be married. It's a forever thing, and I want to be with you forever."

Josie placed her cutlery on the table and folded her arms, her head on one side, thinking.

"Do you think it's possible?" she said.

Jack nodded. "I do."

"No dress?"

"Absolutely, nothing long and floaty; I promise." Jack grinned, feeling that he was winning.

"And no bridesmaids?"

"Well, maybe only Steve..." grinned Jack, thinking of the farmhand with his muddy boots and ripped jeans.

"Ha! Can you imagine," said Josie, laughing too now, catching Jack's mood. "And no big reception? No speeches?" She paused, suddenly serious again. "No big spaces where my dad should be, and no expensive bash full of alcohol being drunk at our expense..."

"Absolutely," agreed Jack. "Just us, and perhaps a bottle of something nice...like beer."

"And no church?"

Jack's eyes narrowed, as he considered. This one would be harder – Josie was right, the parents would make a fuss.

"I'll do my best," he said.

There was a long silence, filled only by the lilt of Indian music that was whining from the speakers, and the mumble of conversation from other tables. Josie was staring at Jack, and he was holding his breath, hardly daring to hope.

The couple on the next table received their food, and Jack, in the corner of his eye, could see dishes of steaming vegetables being placed in front of them. The waiter was hovering, checking everything was correct, asking if they needed anything more, his shadow falling across Jack and Josie's table, in their space. Jack wished he would leave. Josie was still staring at him, her mouth pursed, while she considered.

Another person jogged the back of Jack's chair, on the way to the washrooms. A blast of cold air swept past them as the front door opened to another customer. Jack waited.

After what felt like an age, she nodded.

"Okay then," she said. Then slowly, Josie's face was suffused with a pink glow and a gigantic smile. "Okay then, Jack Compton, I will. I will."

Jack beamed back. Everything inside was singing and laughing and dancing.

"Right," he said. "Marvellous. Good decision. Now, have you finished eating or do you want pudding? I want to get out of here so I can kiss you properly."

Josie's eyes widened. "Of course I want pudding," she said.

Jack grinned and looked for the waiter, all the time wondering how, exactly, he was going to tell the mothers that they were not going to be married in a church.

***

At home, peeling off her dress and sitting on her bed, Josie allowed herself to think about the lump that had formed in her stomach. It wasn't indigestion, it was fear.

"What have I committed to?" she wondered.

Josie stared at her nails, chewed almost to nothing, the cuticles pink and sore. She picked absently at patch of dried skin, her mind fluttering over the evening, and Jack, and what she had agreed to do, and how she felt. *How she felt* was the hardest to consider, because if she was honest, that was the bit she didn't understand.

"I love Jack," said Josie, her voice low, as if saying the words, hearing them said out loud, would remind her, somehow make it more true. "But he doesn't excite me," whispered her traitorous mind, "he doesn't make me laugh like Edward does, he doesn't make my heart jump, he doesn't make me – tingle."

She pressed her lips together and sucked her teeth, feeling them dig into the soft pink of her lips, her eyes narrow. Was it okay to marry someone who you loved more like a brother than a lover? To commit to them because they made you feel safe, and special, and because you needed them to help you in the life you had chosen? Or was it selfish, when you knew, deep inside, that you were attracted to someone else?

Josie flung herself back on the bed, arms above her head, staring at the ceiling. There was a draught leaking from the window next to her, stirring the curtain, trailing cold air across her naked stomach. She turned, rolling onto her side, pulling the duvet over her shoulder, hiding her body, snuggling into the warmth.

"I love Jack," she said again, a whisper this time. "I love Jack and I *cannot* hurt him. He wants me to do this, and being married to him won't be so bad, will it? We'll have fun together, I like his company, I value his opinions, and he'll always look after me, he'll always be there. . ."

"But I'll be settling for second best, taking what I can get, not what I want," her thoughts reminded her, insisting she face the truth, refusing to lie.

"Oh, I don't know!" she wailed, pulling her pillow across her face, stuffing the fabric into her nose so she could hardly breathe. "It's too late now anyway. I already said I would. I can't back-out now, can I?"

Chapter Twenty-Two

"Oh," said Susan. "Oh, I see. And you've decided have you? The two of you have made the decision, and that's final? The rest of us don't matter?"

They were standing in the kitchen, Susan and Jack and Tom, on different sides of the table, staring at each other. There was a candle on the table, the last remaining decoration from Christmas, left to finish burning before Susan washed out the glass and reused it as a vase. The rest of Christmas had been boxed up and returned to the loft as soon as the new year had arrived.

Susan had been cleaning when Tom and Jack popped in for tea, and while the kettle boiled, as though it was a casual thing, something of no consequence, Jack had said that by the way, as they were both here together, he and Josie were planning to get married and it wasn't going to be a big deal, just a quick service in a registry office, they had decided ages ago, before Christmas actually, and they should probably tell people now because they were hoping to arrange it for a couple of weeks – not that it really affected most other people, as it was just going to be them, and a couple of witnesses...

"Claire knows, does she?" asked Susan, folding her arms and looking at Jack. "Josie's mother is happy about this, is she? Just the sort of wedding she's always dreamed of for her daughter, is it? Or doesn't it matter what other people think?"

Tom moved to sit at the table. He looked up at Susan, shaking his head to silence her, which made her want to shout at him. Instead she turned, and poured water into the teapot.

"What's brought this on then?" she heard Tom say, his voice slow and calm, as if he was trying to understand something difficult. "Is Josie pregnant?"

"No Dad, and you shouldn't ask that," said Jack, sounding cross. He sat down, and Susan carried the tea to the table and then stood, leaning back against the worktop.

Jack was flushed, and he wasn't quite managing to meet their eyes when he spoke, so Susan could tell he was uneasy, that perhaps this plan wasn't completely of his own making.

"It's what we want," said Jack, leaning back on his chair in an effort to appear relaxed. Susan didn't think it was a very convincing performance, and wondered what he really thought.

"It only really affects me and Josie, and we've decided that we want to be married, but we don't want a lot of fuss. And neither of us are religious, and it costs less if we don't use a church, and so..." he paused, as if unsure how to continue.

"And Claire?" repeated Susan, feeling sure that Josie's mother would have objected.

"Claire isn't exactly pleased," said Jack, lowering his head. "But it's not her wedding, it's mine and Josie's, and it's what we want. Just the two of us, and a couple of witnesses, no fuss."

Susan stared across the kitchen at Jack, rage surging through her, her mouth pursed as she fought to remain silent, to not say anything she would later regret. Without warning, her eyes filled with tears and she whipped round to hide her face, staring at the wall while clutching the sharp edge of the worktop with both hands.

"It's not fair," she thought, a great tide of disappointment rising within her, swamping her anger until only a huge sadness filled her. She struggled to control her feelings, to discern which ones should be expressed, which she should strive to ignore, aware yet again that being a parent, influencing her children, was an almost impossibly difficult task. Behind her, she could hear Jack as he drank his tea, could almost feel his eyes as he watched her back, so she kept very still, her face averted, her back straight, until finally she felt in control, able to speak quietly and not betray the incredible hurt that was unfolding inside.

"I would have thought," Susan said, still staring at the wall in front of her, "I would have *hoped* that you would want your family there, to share something so important. You don't live in isolation, you weren't raised in isolation; you're part of a family that loves you, and that involves some compromise on your part too."

Susan turned to face Jack, surer now of her response, feeling her way through the words, keen to express her view whilst hiding the turmoil of her feelings.

"Your family has always been there for you Jack, we've always supported you, loved you, tried to help you. We might have got it wrong – I *know* we sometimes got it wrong – but we did our best, and we love you. But you have to give back something too, it's not a one-way thing, this being part of a family, and something that's this big, this important, should be shared with the people who love you. You say that this wedding is yours and Josie's, and that's all that matters. But actually, that's not fair. You and Josie are part of something bigger: your families. You can't just ignore that, not without..."

Tom and Jack were both silent, waiting.

Susan paused. She had been about to say, *"Not without changing the relationship and showing everyone that you don't value them."* But that sounded too harsh, too much like a threat.

Instead she said: "Not without hurting them."

Jack was looking down, fussing Molly's head, looking as if he was hardly even listening. But Susan knew that this is what Jack always did when things were unpleasant, he always removed his thoughts and concentrated on something else, avoided confrontation.

"Jack," said Susan.

Jack looked up, met her eyes.

"Jack, please think about this some more. I understand that Josie doesn't like being the centre of attention, and that this will be hard for her, but please. It can be small, it can be a quick ceremony in a registry office–" Susan paused as her voice broke, her disappointment that one of her sons would choose to not be married in a church cutting through her. She coughed, forced herself to continue, to only argue the points she thought she could win. "But please invite the family, please let us all be part of it. It's the beginning of a whole new stage of your life, and we want – we *should* – be allowed to share that."

"And people could come back here after," added Tom. "Mum can make some food for everyone, save the cost of a big do."

Susan frowned at him, not sure she wanted to be lumbered with catering yet again.

Jack looked back at the dog's head and sighed. "Okay, I'll talk to Josie again, see what she says...

"Who's that?" he asked, as a car pulled up in the yard and Molly rushed away, tail wagging, towards the door.

"It's Neil and Kylie," said Susan, taking a breath and remembering that today had meant to be fun, a treat, and that before Jack had landed his news on her, she had been full of anticipation and excitement. "I'm looking after Noah for them, just for a few hours, remember? I did tell you."

Tom was getting up, joining Molly at the door, calling hello as the door opened, and Neil and Kylie and a lot of bags stumbled into the room, Neil carrying a folded highchair, Noah perched on Kylie's hip, laughing at Molly who was spinning in excited circles. Jack stood, saying he had better get back to work.

Susan smiled and went to take her grandson, hugging him to her as he wriggled to be free.

Jack laughed, and put out a finger to touch Noah's nose as he passed, calling greetings to Neil and Kylie as he returned to work, as if, thought Susan, he didn't want to chance the possibility of their conversation extending to include his brother, and was glad of the sudden change of mood, the perfect excuse to end their debate.

Neil opened the highchair and Susan secured Noah into the straps before moving to the kettle.

"Do you have time for tea before you go?" Susan asked Neil.

"Just a quick cup, thanks," said Kylie, delving into one of the bags and pulling out a small green square of paper. "Here's a mint teabag for me," she said, passing it to Susan.

Susan unwrapped the paper, wrinkling her nose as the smell of peppermint rose up. "Not proper tea," she thought.

Kylie was unfolding several sheets of white paper covered in careful writing. Susan could see bullet points, and under-linings and words highlighted in orange and yellow highlighter.

"I've written out instructions," Kylie was saying, smoothing the pages with her hand. "Shall I read them out?"

Susan carried the tea to the table and reached for the papers.

"Let me read them," she said, "and I'll ask if there's anything I don't understand."

Kylie pulled a fat plastic container from the bag, and went to put it in the fridge. "There's bread and cheese for Noah's lunch," she said, waving the box towards Susan before placing it on a shelf next to a box of eggs. "He just makes a mess if you give him sandwiches, so I cut the bread into little pieces, and give it to him on his tray with squares of the cheese – soya cheese, of course – and he eats it by himself."

Kylie came back to the table and pointed at some words highlighted in orange, half way down the first page. "Don't forget to wash his hands first, of course. And there's a jar of fruit, for his pudding. I usually give him a spoon to hold, so he thinks he's helping, but I hold the jar and feed him, otherwise it all ends up in his hair and on the floor."

Susan nodded, thinking that she had raised four sons, she was fairly sure she remembered how to feed a baby. But she said nothing, simply smiled and nodded, and wished they would drink their tea and leave so that she could enjoy looking after her grandson. As Kylie talked, her instructions washing over Susan like a waterfall of words, Susan watched the younger woman. She saw her hands with their manicured nails – trimmed short since Noah's birth but still shaped and varnished – as Kylie waved them around, pointing at the fridge, indicating an instruction on the list, miming the feeding of her son. Susan stared at her, waiting for her to finish, for an end to the flow of numbers to phone in an emergency, and the possible problems, and where to find medication if Noah should fall or cut himself or suddenly develop a temperature. She glanced up, and realised Tom was watching her, his eyes amused, telling her that this was funny, that this overcautious mothering was to be tolerated with patient humour, that it didn't matter – it in no way reflected an inability on her part to care adequately for her grandson. Kylie was explaining how to administer the Heimlich manoeuvre on a baby, in case Noah should choke on the pieces of bread and soya cheese, which he was to feed himself using his fingers, and which would not be made into sandwiches because he would just make a mess...

Susan began to feel they were now on a loop, and moved to the work surface.

"Would you like more tea before you go?" she asked.

Tom chuckled, a deep sound that rumbled in his chest, causing Neil and Kylie to both look up sharply.

"I'm off now," he said, "time to get back to work. Always more hassle when the cows are inside, I need to get some silage cut for them to eat – no soya cheese for them!"

Kylie was staring at him, looking as if she wasn't sure if he was making fun of her.

Neil put their empty mugs in the sink. "Come on Kylie, let's make tracks." He moved to kiss Susan's cheek. "Thanks for having him Mum, we'll phone if we're going to be later than planned."

"But we won't be," said Kylie, looking worried. "We won't be later than three o'clock."

"Well, don't worry if you are," said Susan, thinking that it would be rather nice if there was a big traffic jam, and they couldn't get back until late so she could bath Noah and put him to bed – Tom could get the old cot down from the loft, and she was sure to have some baby clothes somewhere that would fit, and...

Kylie kissed Noah, who squirmed in his seat and leaned over the side, letting her know that he wanted to be released. Susan removed the harness and carried him to the door.

"Wave bye, bye, to Mummy and Daddy," she said, feeling the weight of him on her hip.

Noah opened the fingers of one hand and Susan raised it, so that he was waving. They stood in the doorway, watching as Neil and Kylie got in the car, waving as it drove across the yard and disappeared down the lane. The last thing Susan saw was Kylie's worried eyes, as she stared back through the rear window, watching her son.

"Right," said Susan, a bubble of tension leaving with the car and a burst of happiness taking its place. She leaned forward and kissed Noah's cheek. "Let's go and watch Grandpa in the barn," she said.

They walked around the barn, Noah balanced on Susan's hip, the weight of him tucked into the curve of her waist, in the place she had carried her own boys. They looked at the cows, Noah leaning forwards, stretching two-handed towards them, arms straight, as if he would break away from Susan and fly over the space between them to where the cows stood watching him. Then he stretched downwards, lurching his body weight towards Molly who was circling their heels, and then forwards again, towards a cat that slunk along the top of a fence.

When Susan's arms were tired from trying to balance her lurching grandson, they went into the house, and Noah was fixed into his highchair while Susan made coffee. He banged two teaspoons contentedly on the plastic tray of his chair, and then attempted to cram both into his mouth.

Susan carried her mug into the sitting room, then returned for Noah, placing him in the centre of the rug, while she sat on the sofa, sipping the bitter liquid and watching him. In front of him was a plastic crate, the lid to one side, and Susan watched to see what he would do. Noah sat on the fat cushion of his nappy, rocking gently forwards and backwards, while he considered. The plastic mast of a sailing ship protruded from the crate, and the curved yellow of a racing track. Susan had carried the crate down from the loft, wanting to introduce her grandson to the toys his father and uncles had loved. She knelt down next to him, placing her mug on a table out of his reach.

"Look," she said, lifting the pirate ship from the crate, "this belonged to your daddy when he was a boy." She rummaged in the depths of the crate, finding plastic pirates shaped like corks, and lined them up in a row. Noah was trying to pull a tuft of nylon fibre from the rug.

Susan set up the road, and pushed a blue car with red wheels along its length. Noah leaned forwards and picked up the car, stuffing it into his mouth. Susan gently extricated it from his damp fingers, wiping the long line of dribble that clung to the wheels on her jeans. She set up tiny squares of plastic fencing, and filled them with balloon-shaped animals, making the sound of each one. Noah stared at her, entranced, breaking into giggles when she snorted like a pig. She ran the pig up his leg, and his giggles became great gurgles of delight as he tried to grab the pig. When Susan released it, Noah stuffed it into his mouth.

As Susan pulled out toys, set them up, moved them within Noah's reach, she watched him. Her eyes drank in the sight of his chubby fingers, his smooth dark skin, the thick lashes around his chocolate-button eyes. She learnt the smell of him, the feel of his warm body leaning against her, the weight of him on her lap, the sudden lurches as he strove to reach something. This tiny bundle of humanity, a package of unstoppable energy as he explored his environment, wound his way into her heart so that, had she been asked, her feelings for her grandson and her own children would have been inseparable, they were so entwined. When Noah began to tire of the toys, Susan placed them back into the box, counting each one aloud – because that's how children learnt numbers, and who knows whether Kylie – with her painted nails and soya cheese-substitute – did such things? Then she bundled Noah up in her arms, sank into the depths of an armchair, and began to read. The storybook was about a farm, and the pictures showed a tiny yellow duck on each page, which Susan dutifully found and pointed out, until she realised that Noah was asleep and breathing small puffs of warm air over her arm. She folded the book, and simply sat there, not moving, enjoying the feel of the baby and the sounds of his sleep. Nothing, she decided, was more important today than this.

When Noah woke, pink-cheeked and fretful, Susan took him into the bathroom to change his nappy before carrying him back to the kitchen for his lunch. She strapped him into his highchair and placed a couple of plastic farm animals on his tray, which he immediately flung onto the floor in the general direction of Molly, and then strained to reach.

"I am not spending all day picking those up just so you can throw them down again," said Susan, as she moved to pick them up and place them back on the tray.

Noah, as predicted, threw them back on the floor. Susan feigned despair, and picked them up again. She took a wet flannel and washed Noah's hands, then began to prepare the food that Kylie had left, cutting the bread into squares, removing the cheese from the packet. The cheese smelt oily, and when removed from the packet it sat in a heavy grey lump on the plate, looking solid and unappetising. Susan cut a small piece from one corner, and tasted it, feeling the plasticky texture, grimacing at the artificial taste; she spat it onto her hand and threw it into the bin.

"Molly!" she called, and cutting another square of cheese, she threw it towards the dog.

Molly came forwards, smelt the soya cheese, lifted her head to look at Susan as though asking why she was being summoned, and then moved back to her basket. The turgid lump of cheese lay where it had fallen, untouched, glistening on the tiled floor.

Susan stared at the soya cheese, and then her grandson. "I am not feeding you that," she whispered. She looked out of the window, checking to see who was near the house. The barn door was open, and the red tractor was missing from the yard. There were no people in sight.

Susan went to the fridge and pulled out a block of mild cheddar. She placed it on the plate, and slid the knife along one edge, cutting a slender finger, then returned the block to the its wrapper and hurried to put it back into the fridge. She looked at the slice of cheese. It appeared very yellow in comparison with the soya cheese. She looked at Noah, then at Molly, then back to the cheese. Another glance out of the window confirmed no one had returned; there were no witnesses.

"Right," she said, her voice low as if Noah and Molly were co-conspirators, "we'd better have this eaten before anyone else arrives." She wrapped the soya cheese in three layers of paper towel and threw it into the bin, then cut the cheese – the *real* cheese – into small cubes and placed them, with the bread, on Noah's tray. She watched him while she prepared his beaker of drink.

Noah stretched out a thumb and forefinger towards the food, and curled them around a lump of cheese. He squeezed. The cheese oozed through his fingers. Molly moved from her bed and sat beside the highchair, waiting. Noah moved his hand towards his mouth and smeared the cheese around his lips and into his mouth. Susan saw him pause as he tasted the cheese. He chewed, his face thoughtful, then he reached for another piece. Ignoring the bread, Noah ate the cheese, piece by piece. When it was gone he looked at Susan and gurgled.

"No, you can't have any more, you'll be sick," she said, "eat your bread."

Feeling triumphant, Susan waited until Noah had eaten the bread, then used the wet flannel to thoroughly wipe the tray and his fingers. "Hiding the evidence," she thought, smiling. She gave Noah a plastic spoon to hold and began to spoon mouthfuls of fruit puree from the jar that Kylie had left. The boot-room door opened, and she heard Tom kick off his boots and hang his coat on the peg.

"Just finished in time," she whispered to Noah, who stared up at her, his mouth ringed with orange.

"Have you enjoyed your morning?" said Tom, coming into the kitchen and sitting opposite her.

Jack arrived, washing his hands in the sink and saying he was just going to grab a sandwich before he went to Broom Hill, and what time was Neil coming back? He didn't mention their conversation of earlier, and Susan decided that she too didn't want to continue the discussion. She'd had her say, it was up to Josie and Jack to decide what to do.

They sat around the table, cutting slices of bread from the loaf and making them into sandwiches. It was rare that they all coincided for lunch at the same time, and Susan felt that Noah was like a magnet, drawing them together. She smiled at him.

Noah stopped twirling the spoon he was playing with, opened his mouth, and projectile vomited across the table and onto Jack's plate.

Jack jumped up, swearing.

Susan jumped up, and reached for Noah. She fumbled with the catch to his harness, her fingers sliding over the slippery plastic, as wave after wave of vomit was heaved from his small body.

"Grab the washing-up bowl," she told Tom. "Quick!"

"I don't think I want to ever have children," Jack was muttering while washing his hands, which had been splattered.

Noah stopped being sick and slumped against Susan. She sat for a moment, waiting for his stomach to settle before she moved him. He looked at her, his eyes full of misery, and hiccupped.

"Poor little mite," she said, stroking the damp hair away from his face.

"You wouldn't think that much sick would fit into such a tiny body," said Jack, drying his hands. "I think I'll go straight to Josie's – I'm not hungry anymore." He looked down at Noah. "Is he going to be okay? That's normal is it? Babies do that do they – or is he ill?"

Susan shook her head, not quite trusting herself to speak.

"Babies are sick all the time," said Tom, "I doubt if he's ill."

Susan was checking Noah, placing her hand on his forehead to check his temperature, looking at his face. His eyes seem to have sunk into his head, and his face looked taut, which Susan thought was probably due to sudden dehydration. The baby stared up at her, his eyes huge and full of trust, his little body exhausted.

Tom was beginning to wipe the table, throwing the food into the dustbin, stacking the plates into the dishwasher.

"It stinks," he said, making a face. "I wonder what brought that on?"

Susan didn't answer. She picked up Noah, and carried him to the bathroom. She had two hours to make this right before Neil and Kylie returned.

When Noah was bathed and dried and dressed in a clean nappy and wrapped in one of Susan's jumpers, she made a bed for him on the floor of the sitting room, moving sofa cushions onto the floor and folding sheets and blankets, so he was snug and warm and couldn't roll off. She placed all his clothes into the washing machine and turned it on. Tom was still in the kitchen, eating a sandwich.

"Lucky I'm not squeamish," he said between mouthfuls of bread. "It still stinks in here. It smells almost cheesy, doesn't it, like he's had milk..." Tom stopped and looked at Susan.

Susan filled Noah's beaker with warm water from the kettle and carried it into the sitting room. She sat on the floor next to Noah, and stroked his forehead. The baby was sleeping, exhausted from the effort of expelling his lunch so dramatically, but he had no temperature, he looked peaceful.

"I'm so sorry," whispered Susan, feeling wretched. "How could I have been so stupid? What was I thinking?"

But deep inside, she knew exactly what she had been thinking. She had been thinking that she knew so much better than Kylie, that her own way of raising children was the right way, and that Kylie was wrong to feed her child things that Susan would never have considered suitable. She had ignored Kylie's instructions, and done what she had wanted; and it hadn't been Susan who had suffered, it had been Noah.

When Noah woke, Susan gave him sips of water and played with him. Gradually he began to look less wan, and after a while Susan fed him fingers of toast – made from the bread Kylie had left – which Noah chewed with enthusiasm until he was full and then began to drop them on the floor, giggling when Molly snaffled them up. By the time Neil and Kylie arrived, their baby was healthy and cheerful, and Susan considered whether she could avoid mentioning that Noah had been sick at all.

"But he might be ill," she reminded herself, "so Kylie needs to know."

"Noah was sick, after lunch," said Susan as she gathered Noah's things and put them in his bag.

Kylie was holding Noah, and she pulled back, to look at his face, frowning.

"Oh dear, I hope he hasn't got a germ," she said, her voice worried. "He's only just got over a cold."

Susan shook her head. "I don't think so," she said, "he seemed fine all afternoon." She watched Kylie as the young mother examined her child, everything coloured by whether her son was ill. Susan felt another rush of shame eat into her, her stomach tightened into a ball of guilt, and she swallowed.

"Thanks for looking after him Mum," Neil was saying as they picked up the last few items and prepared to leave. "It was really kind of you."

Susan forced herself to smile. "I enjoyed it," she said and went to wave them off.

As Susan watched the car drive away, she felt a muddle of emotions.

"Next time," she thought, as she walked to the barn to find Tom, "next time, I'll pay more attention to the volume of instructions that Kylie writes, because," she thought, scratching the cheek of a cow as she passed, "I am not the mother..."

Chapter Twenty-Three

Josie hurried to change into clean clothes after Jack had left for the evening. Her heart was racing, she could feel it, thumping in her chest, an annoying tick in her neck; and her stomach was churning so much she wondered if she might be sick. She sat at her dressing table, staring across the muddle of hairbands and pens and unread books and letters with their jagged-edged tops – most of them bills. Her face stared back, paler than usual, with a tight lipped smile and worried eyes.

"Oh, it doesn't matter!" she scolded herself, noticing the vast expanse of cheek and jowl. "He knows what I look like already, nothing is going to change his mind on that score!" She picked up her eye-liner, ran it over her eye-lids, defining her grey eyes so they looked even larger in her face, standing out from the pale background: "Like dirty puddles," she muttered.

Her room was a muddle, a physical representation of her thoughts. Behind her, hanging on the door of the wardrobe was *the dress*. The dress she had bought with her mother on that day of tension, of "stand up straight, it will take inches off your waist" and "no, I think you're right, white is absolutely wrong for you." They had gone to the shops together, an attempt at a shared mother-and-daughter experience, something to unite them. Josie had resented her mother's advice, even whilst knowing it was correct, and longed to be told, just once, that she pretty rather than managing to hide her flaws.

The dress was silver, with a tight-fitting bodice, and a skirt that skimmed her hips – and her bulging stomach – and finished just below her knees – so at least only her fat calves would be on show. Josie turned, and glared at the dress. It looked not-too-bad, she knew that, especially now she had lost some weight, and with the help of underwear which would squash every bulge into compacted order, so that she would be unable to breathe or sit comfortably. The underwear was on the floor, rolled into a giant sausage when she peeled it off earlier in the day, and left there, amongst dirty socks and kicked-off shoes and a magazine with a skinny bride on the front.

"Smoke and mirrors," thought Josie, staring at the garments. "Giving people what they expect. Not too lumpy, wearing something special, making vows which will last forever, because that's what he wants, what they all want."

Tomorrow – a few short hours away – she was due to wear that dress, hold a posy of flowers, look the part.

Josie glanced at her phone. It was time. She sat for a moment, listening for sounds of her mother, keen to escape from the house without being heard.

There was silence.

She looked back at her reflection: the round face, the frizzy hair, the large eyes.

Another glance at the time. She would be late. If she was going to meet him, actually go through with this crazy plan, she needed to leave.

Josie pulled a sweater over her head, smudging her eye-liner but not noticing as she moved to the door, opening it wide enough to listen. Still no noise. She slid onto the landing, holding her breath as she took the stairs, one at a time, all the while listening, not wanting to meet her mother, not wanting to lie to her – about where she was going – who she was meeting. Crossing the hallway, that ocean of white tiles that gleamed towards the front door, daring a dirty boot or sweaty sock to soil their polished surface. Josie tiptoed, like a naughty child, over the tiles, to the heavy front door. It swung wide, cool air sweeping into the house, a door slammed upstairs, Josie paused, a statue, straining to hear, not daring to move. Still silence, no voice calling her back, no mother coming to investigate. Josie slid from the house.

Her car was where she had parked it earlier, and she climbed inside and started the engine. It was warmer in the car, and comforting somehow, as if she was safe now, hidden. She started the engine, and drove steadily down the driveway, then turned away from Netherley Farm – even though that would be the most direct route – towards the meeting place.

The lane was dirty, mud from the fields carried on tractor tyres and smudged over the lanes. Smoke from several bonfires filled the air, entering the car through the air vents, the smell acrid and bitter. Josie swallowed and concentrated on not skidding across the mud as she turned a corner, slowed behind a horse and rider until there was space to pass, continued on her way.

He was already there, waiting for her next to the gate, leaning on it, looking away from her, across the field. He turned as the car drew onto the verge, and grinned, and her heart leapt and suddenly she didn't feel sick anymore, only excited. His fair hair was blowing in the wind, snatched upwards and outwards, and back across his eyes so he put up his hand and swept it away from his face in the gesture she knew and adored.

"Hello you!" he said, as she climbed from the car. "I wasn't sure if you would come."

"No," said Josie, her words torn by the wind and carried down the lane, "no, nor was I. I'm not sure if it's. . . sensible to be here. . . ."

Josie closed the car door and leant against it, not wanting to go to him, unsure now of what to say. She had thought last night, when trapped by tangled bedding and turbulent thoughts, that meeting him – away from other people, just the two of them – might bring some clarity. Her tortured mind had decided that if they were alone, if she could properly test her feelings, then all the worries would evaporate, the choice would be certain. But now? Now she worried that she was wrong – that even being here was wrong.

He pushed himself away from the gate, and walked towards her, his mouth grinning, his eyes serious. Josie noticed lines of tension on his face, drawing his mouth tight, so that although he was smiling there was something grim, something forbidding in that smile.

Josie looked up at him. He was taller than her, and was standing close now, peering into her eyes.

"How're you doing?" he asked, his voice low.

Josie was suddenly reminded of a sitcom, where the main character drawled those same words, and she had a sudden desire to giggle, to laugh at him. Her mouth twitched, and the suppressed laughter gave her confidence.

"I'm fine, thanks," she said. "But we need to talk. Well, *I* need to talk."

Edward stepped nearer, almost touching her, and when he spoke his voice sounded harsh, the words sarcastic.

"I'm not sure meeting like this, on our own, is a very good idea," he said. "But I thought there were things that. . .need to be said. So, I'm here, you can say what you need to say *in person,*" His voice rose, imitating the tone of her message. "I'm assuming this is to do with Jack? With *your wedding* tomorrow?"

Josie swallowed. Last night she had sent the message, asking him to meet her. But now, now that he was here, standing before her, so close that she could smell the wine on his breath, the strength of his aftershave; now she wasn't so sure.

"I have to be sure," she said. "Before I marry Jack, I have to be sure, don't I? That he's *the one,* I mean. Marriage is forever – or at least, it should be, that's what I'll be promising. And forever is a very long time, so I need to be sure, really sure. . . that there's no one else. . ."

Edward was looking at her, his head tilted to one side so that he resembled one of the dogs trying to discern what was being said.

"Don't marry him."

Josie stared up at him.

"Why?"

"Don't marry him," Edward repeated. "In the long run, you'll hurt him."

Josie lowered her gaze, staring at the ground between them. Was Edward going to tell her that he loved her, that all along, after all this time, he had realised that she was the woman for him? And did she want to hear him say those words?

Part of her did, the teenaged Josie who had waited year after year for Edward to notice her, who had watched him be with girl after girl, always returning to Josie in the interim, because she was there, waiting, available. That teenaged Josie still lurked inside, under the thin veneer of the sensible woman she had become. Even now, on the eve of her wedding to a different brother, Josie could feel the stirrings of attraction when she looked up at Edward, her eyes hungry for the power of his gaze, waiting to be lit up by the beam of his smile.

But Edward wasn't smiling, his face was very grim, almost angry.

"Don't marry him," Edward repeated. He turned from her and walked back to the fence, stood very still, with his back to her. Josie looked beyond him, to the empty fields. Crows were wheeling above the ploughed earth, dipping down to investigate the soil. There was something sinister about crows, and Josie shivered, pulled her coat tighter.

"I don't think you're right for Jack," continued Edward, "I never have. If you marry him it won't last – you don't love him enough."

Josie snorted. "So, you just want to protect Jack? You're looking out for your brother? I'm not good enough for him?"

Her voice was harsh, as bitter as the words forced from her mouth. She was shaking her head, her body quivering with anger and disbelief, and she pressed harder into the car behind her, wanting support.

"No! No, not that," said Edward, and Josie saw his face tighten, and something sad entered his eyes, something almost desperate.

"It's not meant to be *you and Jack*. If you marry him, well, that's different, isn't it? That makes it final. But you're not right for each other, I know you both, and I can tell. It's a mistake, the whole thing. Even this, you meeting me here today, shows that it isn't right. You shouldn't marry him if you have doubts, better to end it now than later.

"It's not too late, you know that right? You could go away, run away from all this. Tomorrow, when everyone's at the registry office, well, it would be a shock for Jack, but easier too, in a way, don't you see? If you just didn't turn up, then everyone would know, all at once. Jack wouldn't have to go round telling everyone. . . I think that would be the worst, everyone having to be told by Jack that he'd got it wrong. But he wouldn't have to, if you just don't show up. They'd all know, all at once, and they'd be there, to comfort him and stuff. . ."

"I can see you've thought this through," said Josie.

"Yes, well. . ." he paused, then said again, as if she might not have understood: "I just don't think you should marry him." He turned away, as if he no longer wanted to look at her.

Josie swallowed, staring at his back, at the fields beyond him, at the sky, trying to assimilate what she was hearing. Edward was not saying that *he* wanted her, and Josie knew that he had no feelings for her. In a sudden moment of clarity, Josie realised that although Edward did not want her – would never want her – nor did he want anyone else to have her. Josie had been his reserve for years, always waiting for him to return. Josie knew that he didn't love her. She also knew that despite everything, part of her still loved Edward. She always had. But did that matter? Was it possible to harbour the seeds of love for one person and yet to allow the love for another person to develop alongside, until finally the second love flowered and grew strong and obliterated the first?

She thought of Jack, his image filling her mind, and she knew that his love for her was as real and strong as hers was weak. No, not *weak,* she corrected herself, just the *wrong kind* of love. "I love Jack like a brother, he's my dearest friend," she thought. Could his love be enough? If Jack knew, if he could see into her heart, could ride the waves of indecision with her, would he still love her? Or would he turn away, angered by her betrayal, needing his feelings to be reciprocated in order for them to remain. Was love dependent on love being returned? And what if it was not returned? Does love curl and die, a neglected plant that withers; or does it persist, endure, wait with patience until at last the loved one turns and cannot help but respond? Does, she wondered, such a love even exist? Not her own love. She knew that now, with a clarity that shook her. Not her own love for Edward. That would die soon enough, it was not deep or strong, it thrived on his attention, it stood tall under the light of his flirtations. But with neither, over time, it would be as transient as a snowflake, barely even remembered.

Edward looked as if he would speak again.

"No," she said, raising a hand to ward him off. "No! I need to think about this. I need to go home."

She turned, opened the car door, climbed into the seat.

Edward stood next to her, watching, not speaking.

"Your timing is terrible – you know that, right?" she said, wishing her voice sounded lighter, that it didn't catch as she spoke, betraying her shaken emotions.

Edward shrugged, his shoulders loose. "You messaged me," he said, absolving himself from all responsibility. "I wanted to say it anyway, but didn't think there would be an opportunity. Now there is. But I'm right, if you think about it, you'll know that I am. I expect you've been rushed into all this, feel like you can't back out now – but you can Josie, it's not too late. People will get over it. . . Jack will recover, in time.

"He's too young to be getting married anyway, don't you think?"

Josie closed the door and started the engine. As she drove away, she could see Edward in her rear-view mirror. He was standing by the gate, watching her, growing ever smaller as she continued along the lane.

Chapter Twenty-Four

The following day, Tom stepped into the February morning. It was misty, snowdrops and crocus were already in flower, daffodils pushing their straight leaves towards the sky. It was a warm day and as Tom left the house he could hear birdsong, a cacophony of noise, as if they were trying to out-sing each other. He heard a couple of pheasants, with their 'sore-throat' call. Two pink-tinged grey doves, with their white collars, were flapping in the tree as they mated, the sound of their wings like a steady beat as they fought to balance, accompanied by the machine-like drill of a woodpecker, unseen but heard in the quiet of the morning.

Tom spent the morning moving truckloads of muck from the barns, the cows watching him with their interested eyes, lowing every so often as if to encourage him, sounding excited when the fresh straw was strewn across their enclosure. Then he drove it, trailer load after trailer load, down the lane and into the field, dumping it in a corner near the gate, until it formed a small steaming mountain, waiting to be spread across the earth as fertiliser. He liked the circular simplicity of using cow muck to fertilise the fields that would, in a few months, be harvested to provide food for them.

"That's how farms work best," he thought, driving the trailer back for the final stinky load, "using the waste to encourage new growth." It smelt though, and by the end of the morning, he smelt too, as if his very skin had absorbed the sweet strong aroma. He went home, for a shower.

In the house, Susan too had showered, and was sitting in front of the mirror in her underwear. She wrinkled her nose.

"Make sure you give your hair a good wash," she said, then glancing out of the window she added: "It's lucky everyone *isn't* coming back here afterwards, the whole farm stinks now."

Tom grinned at her and went into the bathroom.

"I still think you should have bought a new suit," he heard Susan shout to him through the door. "We might only be going to the registry office, but it's still a wedding. There'll be photographs..."

Tom turned on the shower, and stepped under the flow, the sound drowning Susan's voice, which was still talking – but not, he thought, about anything important.

***

They drove to an old manor house, which was also what the registry office was called. There was a little fuss about where to park, and in the end Tom left the Land Rover on a busy road alongside a park, with a lot of shopper's cars, and they walked – quickly because they were slightly late now – past the station and up the road and back to the manor house.

The rest of the family – or at least, those members who Jack and Josie had finally conceded should be allowed to attend – were waiting, and because it was beginning to rain, they hurried into the building, which smelt like a library full of damp coats and old books. Josie and her mother had not yet arrived, and Jack went to stand by the doorway. Susan watched his back as he stared down the driveway. People were huddled together, speaking in whispers, uncomfortable in their clothes. Someone knocked into Susan, and she turned to see a man who she didn't recognise.

"Hello," he said, his voice full of forced jollity, "I'm Bruce, here with Claire. . . not that Claire's actually here. Hope they're not stuck in traffic."

Susan smiled, wondering if Bruce was a relative or possible boyfriend. She felt there wasn't a way to ask, and he offered no further explanation.

"I expect they'll be here soon," she said.

"I hope so," said Jack, coming to join them and shaking Bruce's proffered hand absently. "We have a set time, we'll miss it if she's not here soon. I'd better go and find someone."

"Have you phoned her?" said Susan as he disappeared towards a door which Susan assumed must be an office. She delved into her bag and found her own phone, checking for messages. But the screen was blank.

"I wonder if there's been a holdup somewhere," said Tom. "Edward's not here yet either."

Susan looked around. Tom was right, Edward was missing.

Jack reappeared with a woman, who directed them up some stairs, and asked them to wait outside a door. He was holding his phone, repeatedly redialling, his face white with tension. Susan went to him.

"Edward's not here yet either," she said. "Perhaps there's been an accident or something, and the road's been blocked."

"I don't know why they wouldn't phone and tell us," muttered Jack, turning back to his mobile.

"Brides are always late," said Tom. "She'll get here in a little while, you'll see."

Susan moved closer to Tom, and they both watched as Jack paced away from them.

"He's worried, poor thing," said Tom, shaking his head. "I don't suppose anything's happened though, brides are always late. Perhaps we should have warned him. . ."

There was the sound of a car, skidding as it stopped too quickly on the gravel driveway. A door slammed. Footsteps crunching on the gravel, then hurrying across the tiled floor below, more footsteps following.

Jack left his parents and went to the stairs.

Susan saw his shoulders relax, heard him call a greeting, and Josie and Claire appeared on the stairs.

"Sorry we're late," hissed Josie, her face red. "Mum was fussing."

Claire was smiling, whispering hello to everyone, making her way along the corridor.

Susan watched Jack take Josie's hand, gripping it tightly, as if he was worried she might disappear again. He leant towards Josie and whispered something, and Susan saw the young woman shake her head, and smile, and lean to kiss his cheek, before they both moved, past her, towards the front of the line of waiting people.

The landing they were waiting on was not really big enough, and Susan wondered why they were not being permitted into the room where the wedding would take place. Perhaps, she thought, another couple were in there, making their vows, and they're running behind schedule, like a dentist or doctor. The thought struck her as sad, not so much because they had to wait, but that a wedding could be conducted as a routine service, like on a conveyer belt, and the venue and day were not reserved as special for one couple, or even for two couples, but perhaps a whole efficient line of couples would enter the room as single and leave as married. She couldn't think why this mattered, or why it seemed sad, so she plastered a cheery smile on her face and turned to Claire, who was hovering by her side.

"Hello Susan," said Claire, smiling through her bright red lipstick. "I didn't think we'd ever get here! Though as I said to Josie, it's not as if they could start without her!" She glanced along the line of family, her eyes stopping to rest on Ben. "All your lovely young men are here..." she said, her voice distant. "I haven't seen them for ages, years it must be, other than Jack of course. They're all grown up now...I barely recognise them. That's Ben, isn't it? The gay one?"

Susan felt herself bristle. "That's Ben at the end, yes."

Her voice was sharp, and Claire looked at her, her face colouring.

"Well, of course, there's nothing wrong with being gay," Claire said, her tone apologetic. "I have some clients who are gay, and they are the loveliest people, often very talented..."

Susan frowned. She had heard people say similar things before, and wasn't quite sure if Claire was saying that her clients were "the loveliest people" or if gay people, in general, having been lumped together into one easily labelled group, were lovely. But this was not the time to ask for clarification, so she merely smiled, and asked Claire how her interior design business was going, and was she very busy?

They were speaking quietly, worried they might disturb whoever was in the room behind the closed door. Tom was taking photographs on his phone, and Jack was looking annoyed and telling him to stop.

"But we want photographs," thought Susan, "it's part of what makes a wedding seem real. We want a reminder of the day. But at least we're here, perhaps I should be grateful for that and not keep wishing for more." She now looked across to where Jack was standing.

Behind Jack, almost as if she was trying to hide, was Josie. Susan saw Kylie go to speak to her, and the two women laughed in a nervous, self-aware way. Tom attempted another photograph, and Jack snarled at him, so Susan excused herself from Claire and went to rescue him.

"Tom, come and stand with me," she suggested. "Jack and Josie want to be left quietly while they wait."

A short brown-haired woman in sensible heels and a suit came up the stairs. She obviously recognised Jack and Josie, as she went straight to them, and began to arrange things on her clipboard. Then she looked up, and said, loud enough for everyone to hear: "If you want to take some photographs, now is the best time to take them, because there will be another wedding following your one." She looked at Tom, and smiled. "Lots of people like to use the stairs," she said, gesturing towards the sweeping staircase. "It looks nice in photographs. You can use the garden, of course, but it looks as if it will still be raining when you leave." The woman glanced at the clock above the door. "We should be able to go inside in a few minutes…"

"All right then Dad," said Jack, his voice resigned, "why don't you take a couple of photos now."

Jack and Josie stood on the staircase, a few steps from the bottom. Josie was wearing the silver-grey dress which reflected the grey of her eyes and made them look very large; her hair had been wound into a cable-plait and threaded with flowers. It was neat, but Susan, watching her, thought that Josie looked prettier when her hair was wild around her face. Her face was alternating between very red and extremely pale, so that Susan wondered briefly if Josie was ill rather than nervous.

Claire was fussing with flowers, and making Josie hold her small bouquet at an angle, and to turn slightly, so she was facing Jack. Susan could see that Josie was embarrassed, and clearly did not want to be in any photographs, and was doing her best not to scowl.

"But Claire wants it to be a proper wedding," thought Susan, her heart aching for the other woman. "This is all a bit too foreign for us; we're used to churches and flowers and photographers, and without them, it hardly feels like a wedding at all."

The door opened, and they squashed against the walls of the corridor while the other wedding party filed past them. Susan glimpsed smiling faces, and a woman in a small pink hat, and an old lady leaning on a stick. The woman with the clipboard led the way, and they entered the room.

It was, thought Susan, a pretty room. There was a large window framed by long curtains and a pleated valence. Opposite the door was a fireplace with flowers either side of an ornate mirror, and rows of chairs arranged in a semi-circle facing a small table and two chairs. They walked in, all of a muddle, with Claire leading the way with Neil, and Susan and Tom following them, and Jack and Josie somewhere in the middle. Tom was whispering that Edward still hadn't arrived, only to be told that he was just coming up the stairs. Susan turned and smiled a greeting as Edward sidled into the room and took a chair at the back. The family sat, with Claire at one end of the front line of chairs, next to the man, Bruce.

Jack and Josie sat on the chairs at the front. Josie's face was very pink.

The registrar spoke clearly, thanking everyone for attending, and explaining that this was a legal proceeding, and therefore no religious music or readings were permitted. She then asked Jack and Josie to stand, and asked the witnesses to step forwards. Susan knew that Jack had asked Tom to be a witness, and he went and stood at the front next to Claire. Susan watched them. She noted that Claire's shoes and bag exactly matched the colour of her lips, and that she had worn a hat, even though Jack had told Susan to just dress smartly, not like she was going to a wedding, because they "didn't want any fuss." Tom had taken this advice to heart, and was wearing the same suit he had worn last year to Uncle George's funeral. Susan noticed the seat of the trousers was rather shiny where the fabric had worn thin, and she hoped they wouldn't split.

Jack had not discussed the marriage with his parents again, but he had clearly absorbed Susan's feelings and sought to compromise with Josie's wish for absolute anonymity. They had, after a few weeks of what Susan imagined were fraught discussions, invited all the immediate family to the legal ceremony. Dot and Elsie were still excluded, which Susan had felt was wrong, but Jack explained that they couldn't invite Dot without inviting Aunty Elsie, and if Aunty Elsie was invited, then how could they stop Claire and Susan inviting all the other aunts and uncles, which would then extend to Josie's cousins, and before they knew it, there would be a whole circus of people watching what was meant to be a very private ceremony.

"People come in chains," Jack had explained, "and we don't want a whole bunch of people there, Josie would hate it. We've decided to compromise, we'll invite our parents, and siblings, but no one else."

He had looked at her, daring Susan to complain, to suggest that this compromise wasn't sufficient. But she hadn't, she had managed to keep her thoughts hidden, and had thanked Jack for allowing her and Tom to be present. She even managed to say the words without sounding sarcastic. She now forced herself to listen, to not be absorbed by where people were sitting or the room or clothes. This was a wedding. Jack's wedding.

Jack was saying his vows, promising to take Josie as his wife. Susan felt suddenly emotional, but whether it was because her son was committing to be married, or whether it was because this wedding was so very far removed from what *felt* like a wedding, she couldn't say. After the vows, they exchanged rings, which Tom had kept in his pocket because Jack said it was daft to choose one of his brothers to be best man when they weren't having bridesmaids or a best man, and all it would do was disappoint the other two.

Then, all of a sudden, it was over. The registrar announced they were legally married, and everyone clapped, and Claire sniffed into a tissue, and the four main people signed the register, and then it was finished. The registrar suggested they had time for a couple of photographs, and then please could they vacate the room as people were waiting.

It was raining properly when they came to leave. Tom told Susan to wait and he would go to get the car. Susan stood, in the shelter of the doorway, and watched the rain falling, listening to the hiss of it on the driveway. Bruce, the man with Claire, produced two large golfing umbrellas, gave one to Josie, and he and Claire huddled under the other and rushed out into the rain. Jack was shaking his brothers' hands, and laughing, and then he and Josie left too, his arm around his bride, the umbrella lifted high. As Susan watched them, she felt the emotion rise inside again, and she realised that she was watching two young people who were very much in love, who had promised to support each other for the rest of their lives.

Tom arrived with the car, and Susan sprinted across the driveway, almost twisting her ankles in the heels. She pulled open the heavy door and climbed up into her seat.

"That was quick and efficient," said Tom as he drove down the long driveway.

Susan was unsure whether he meant her sprint or the wedding.

"I wonder what Claire's arranged for us," he said as they drove towards Broom Hill Farm and the small reception that Claire had insisted on.

***

The hall was filled with flowers. There were topiary trees dripping ribbons, and huge arrangements on stands, and tiny posies tied with bows on the bannisters. The air was heavy with the scent of lilies, and everything was white, contrasting with the dark red wall behind them.

Josie walked with Jack, her husband, past the flowers and into the long sitting-room. More flowers greeted them, white and blue, with tall irises, and ribbons that matched Josie's dress. Jack pulled her to him.

"You'll crumple me," she protested, laughing as he kissed her.

"You feel very structured," he frowned, holding her close.

"I'm wearing scaffolding," she grinned. "My mother's idea, to hold in the fat!"

"My *wife*," said Jack, beaming at her, "is not fat. Nor does she need scaffolding. I like her lumpy bits."

Josie was saved from responding as the door opened and Claire walked in.

"Everyone will be here in a minute," Claire said, her eyes sweeping the flowers and food, assessing. "I'll tell the staff to start pouring the champagne."

"Staff?" mouthed Jack.

"Don't ask," whispered Josie. "Mum threatened to hold this reception whether we attended or not, and she's agreed to no speeches – nothing that Dad should have. . ." Her voice trailed away and Jack tugged her close again. Josie looked at him, knowing that he understood. She took a breath. "So, I sort of let her have a free rein with everything else. The food looks good anyway." She gestured towards where the dining room table had been pushed against the wall. It was laden with canapés and sandwiches and tiny pies.

A girl dressed in black and white appeared in the doorway, a tray of drinks in her hands, Claire next to her, telling her where to stand, that she should offer everyone a glass as they arrived, and then walk around, topping up glasses as necessary. Jack and Josie were told to stand by the front door, so they could greet people as they arrived.

Jack took Josie's hand and led her back to the door. Claire joined them, and the three of them made a welcoming line. They stood there, waiting as cars arrived at the farm, parked in the yard, doors slammed, voices drifted towards them. Josie looked up at Jack, at her husband.

"There wasn't really a choice," she thought, looking at his face, seeing the lines of tiredness and tension that joined his nose and mouth, knowing that he was disliking all the fuss as much as she was. "I still don't know if I love him like a husband or a friend, but I do know that I love him, and surely that will be enough. He makes me feel safe, and that has to be better, in the long run, than exciting."

The front door was opened, and Susan and Tom walked in, staring at the flowers, smiling at Claire, walking towards Josie, looking uncertain, as if they felt awkward in this beautiful house and didn't want to make a mistake. Jack was laughing, shaking his father's hand, kissing his mother before they moved to greet Josie. She felt herself blush as they kissed her cheek, pressed her hand, went to Claire, who ushered them towards the room with the drinks.

Josie watched them, saw the stoop in Tom's back, noted the bald head and the wrinkled face. "When couples get old," she thought, "they still love each other. Perhaps they love each other more. I don't expect it's very exciting, I don't suppose each other's saggy bodies or lined faces are invisible to them. But the bit of love that cares and protects and comforts – that will still be there."

The door opened again, and Kevin appeared, with Elsie leaning heavily on his arm, followed by Dot.

"Dot loves Elsie," thought Josie, watching them as they approached Jack, saw Dot slow her pace to fit the laborious steps of her sister. "She loves Elsie in a forever way, even though she's just a sister. It's a different love, but it's still real, it still matters." She turned up her face to be kissed, felt the butterfly touch of Elsie's kiss, the firm pressing of Dot's lips on her cheek. Kevin grabbed at her, pulled her into a tight embrace, and Josie laughed, suddenly happy, as she heard Jack protesting, telling the other man to "unhand my wife!"

Ben appeared in the doorway, looking very young in a suit that didn't fit him properly. He went across to Kevin, who directed him back to where Jack and Josie were standing. Josie watched as Ben touched Kevin's arm in a gesture of thanks and affection.

"They love each other too," thought Josie, "even though people disapprove, and some people probably stare at them and whisper things and even shout abuse sometimes. Ben and Kevin care for each other, despite all that seems against them sometimes, and that can't be exciting all the time. That goes beyond the physical attraction, deeper than just flirting. They want to be together, even when others disapprove. That's another form of love, proper love."

Ben was still shaking Jack's hand, turning to kiss Josie's cheek, when she was aware of Edward entering the hall. She felt a moment of panic, knew the blood had rushed to her face, wondered if she might faint and whether she could blame it on the stupidly tight underwear; and then he was with them. Edward shook Jack's hand, and congratulated him, and Josie wondered if everyone present could hear the bitter irony of his tone. Then he turned to her, and saying nothing he leant forward, and kissed the air next to her cheek and in half a second was moving away, looking for a drink, leaving her behind.

"Which is what I want," Josie reminded herself. "I chose Jack," she thought, the voice in her head stern, not allowing any silly regret, not allowing any pretence that she had made anything other than a sensible decision. "There are all kinds of love," Josie thought again. "I might not know, for *sure*, if I want to be with Jack forever, but I *do* know that I cannot bear the thought of a future without him. I want him to be part of my life, he feels like part of me – not exciting perhaps, but part of me. And that's enough."

She sidled closer to him, to her husband, and he looked at her, and squeezed her arm, and told her not to worry, it would soon be over, and he was as keen to escape as she was. More people arrived, a smattering of school friends, a gush of cousins and seldom seen aunts and uncles, and Kylie holding Noah, who reached out and tried to grab one of the ribbons in Josie's hair, Jack's aunt Cassie, Josie's great-uncle and aunt who she hadn't seen since the funeral and probably wouldn't see again until someone else died. The last to arrive was William, and he reminded Josie of

Edward all over again, so she blushed and stammered when he congratulated her, but she didn't think anyone else noticed. And then, finally, all the guests were holding drinks, and balancing plates of food, and Claire was calling everyone to silence so she could make a toast:

"Not a speech, because I've been forbidden from saying anything too long," said Claire, her thin voice raised. "But I would like you all to raise your glasses to my beautiful, brave, wonderful daughter, and her new husband. . . To Josie and Jack."

"*Josie and Jack*," repeated the crowd, a low rumble of acknowledgement.

"*Josie and Jack*," repeated Josie in her mind, feeling the heat in her face, knowing that everyone was watching her.

"I might be unsure about love, and what's real love and how you know. But I do know that it exists, and sometimes, you have to take a risk, and trust that what you have will be enough. I know that I love Jack." She looked at him, and saw his own love for her in the caress of his eyes. "I know that we love each other, and the promises we made today will give that love the chance it needs to flourish. I'm sure love fluctuates, gets stronger and weaker as time goes on, but by promising to stay together, even when it gets tough, we're giving it every chance."

Jack took her hand, and Josie stopped thinking, and took a gulp of the champagne that was pressed into her hand, before following him across the room, to mingle with their guests.

Acknowledgements

Thank you for reading my latest novel. The accuracy of any farming details are due entirely to the local farmers, who answered endless questions, and especially to Sarah, John and Nicola, who allowed me to explore their farms. Any mistakes are entirely my own.

Thanks too to the medical staff who answered my questions about the treatment and recuperation following a stroke.

As always, I send a special thank you to my family, who support and help me, and cheer me on when I feel like giving up. They have given me good advice, and suggestions, and I could not write without their support.

This story is about sisters – Susan and Cassie, Dot and Elsie. I think there is something special about the bond between sisters. Thank you Ruth, I love you.

I should also thank my God, who has enabled me to write every book, but who features a little more explicitly in this one. Like Susan, I know what it is to be loved, despite all the mistakes I have made in the past, and all the mistakes I will make in the future. A love like that changes you.

Thank you for reading, I am so very grateful for your time.

Anne

Also by Anne E. Thompson:

Hidden Faces

Counting Stars

Invisible Jane

Joanna - The Story of a Psychopath

Clara - A Good psychopath?

Ploughing Through Rainbows

Non-Fiction

How to Have a Brain Tumour

The Sarcastic Mother's Holiday Diary

Thank you for reading.

You can follow Anne's blog at:

anneethompson.com

Printed in Poland
by Amazon Fulfillment
Poland Sp. z o.o., Wrocław